THE ASCENSION
VOLUME I

A. M. D'ADDABBO

iUniverse, Inc.
Bloomington

The Pale One
The Ascension, Volume I

iUniverse books may be ordered through booksellers or by contacting:

iUniverse
1663 Liberty Drive
Bloomington, IN 47403
www.iuniverse.com
1-800-Authors (1-800-288-4677)

ISBN: 978-1-4620-0487-4 (sc)
ISBN: 978-1-4620-0488-1 (hc)
ISBN: 978-1-4620-0489-8 (e)

Library of Congress Control Number: 2011907689

Printed in the United States of America

iUniverse rev. date: 06/14/2011

To Aunt Becky
With much love

Reun

Zer

Beul

Nessin

Zef

Pezak
Lake

Coast of Huraan

Huraan

Huraan
Sea

Raum

Anzzow

Ashten
Vále

Gïe

Aran
Lake

Trynal Sea

Quwe

Trevak

Wrenal

Trym

Uam

The Sands of Chaos

Yejhet

Prologue

A high-pitched scream pierced the air. It was one that spoke of the purest pain. The shriek ended in a vicious gurgle as the limp body of a dead woman fell forward, her throat torn out. Another woman kicked the corpse off of the tall cliff, resulting in a disgusting crunch as the body landed on the rocks below.

A hideous cackle erupted from the top of the drop-off. The silhouette of the second woman shadowed the ledge. Sithel was barely five feet tall, with long, black wavy hair. Her ice-blue eyes lingered on the broken corpse far below for a long moment.

The shin-high grass waved gently as a gust of wind howled, whipping the woman's hair into her beautiful face. Something strong mingling in the breeze beset her nostrils. She turned completely around to see large red and yellow flames devouring the little village before her. Smoke billowed into the night sky, mixing well with the fall storm clouds. The sight brought an evil smirk to Sithel's face.

She began to walk toward the just-audible, terrified screams and wailing that came from the burning village. Her nimble body moved gracefully and swiftly. Without thinking, Sithel wiped the murdered woman's blood from her hand onto her travel-stained cloak. Her long-sleeved, white cotton shirt opened at her neck, the folds meeting at a point, showcasing her ample breasts. The shirt was tucked into tight, brown leather pants. Her person was quite enthralling.

The village was in complete chaos—just how she liked it—when she strode past the first flaming houses. Men, women, and children ran about, screaming as a band of orcs chased them with swords and torches. Her grin grew wider every second as she walked about, watching the orcs sadistically murder villagers. No one seemed to notice her walking calmly into the village.

Nearing the center of the hamlet, one of the brainless orcs mistakenly took Sithel for a defenseless villager and charged her. The humanoid creature was barely taller than her; its stretched skin was gray under mismatched pieces of armor, and its head featured coarse, black hair and a wild beard. It grunted through piglike nostrils, shooting phlegm down into its beard.

A look of disgust replaced the grin on Sithel's face as she watched the orc charge, brandishing a rusty old curved sword. A high arc from the sword had the woman sidestepping to her left, easily dodging the poorly performed attack. She ducked low to avoid the orc's horizontal backswing. As she did so, she grabbed a hidden dagger from her right boot, and as Sithel stood up, she buried the blade hilt deep into the monster's skull. Sithel brutally ripped the dagger out, orc brains covering the entire blade. She wore a revolted look as she bent over and wiped the brains and blood on the dead orc's hairy arms.

Seeing one of their comrades slain, several more of the gray-skinned humanoids rushed toward the seductively dressed woman, hungry canines jutting from their lower lips. Their beady, red eyes glared at her beneath brows knotted in everlasting scowls.

A frustrated sigh escaped Sithel's mouth. Lazily, she stretched forth her hand, and waves of pure red energy flew toward the orcs. Startled and not knowing what else to do, the monsters just paused and watched as the waves hit them and their bodies absorbed the energy. Then, without warning, each of the orcs exploded, sending chunks of gore in every direction.

Sithel angrily stomped to the edge of what was left of the burning village. Most of the log buildings had been consumed already, and all the residents had already fled or been horribly murdered. Now only the band of orcs rambled about, looting what they could from the dead.

With unnatural power in her voice, she shrieked, "Oram!"

The name resounded throughout the village, sending complete fear into the humanoid beasts. Hurriedly, a massive, ugly creature came lumbering toward her. The ogre was at least ten feet tall, weighing in excess of three hundred pounds. Its brown skin was stretched tightly over bulging muscles in its arms and torso. Clothing of thick furs hid most of the thing's grotesque, wart-covered body, and a leather cap concealed its oily, mane-like hair.

"Yes, Master?" the ogre grumbled arrogantly, speaking in the common tongue. The thing's thick accent made it difficult to understand. Its massive underbite, which displayed all of its lower fangs, pointing upward, did not help any.

"Hold your tongue, or I will rip it out!" Sithel snapped. She lashed out, punching the ogre's rock-hard stomach. Surprisingly, the beast doubled over in terrible pain. The woman had channeled a great amount of energy into the strike, making it much more powerful than was humanly possible. Oram cautiously stood back up.

"Your imbecile little orcs attacked me," Sithel said with so much fury that the ogre winced, anticipating more pain. Sure enough, another smack sent the monster to its knees. The orcs nearby had stopped looting, and now they whimpered in fear and skittered about, looking for cover. Once they thought they were a safe distance away from the woman and their ogre leader, they stopped to watch.

"Now I want to be clear, Oram," Sithel spat through gritted teeth. "Your large army of various monsters will aid my cause, but I will only tell you this once: all of you are expendable. I will not hesitate to kill any of you. Is that understood?"

Without pause the ogre nodded vigorously. Oram detested working for Sithel, but the fear of her unnatural powers kept the monster as her indentured slave.

"Good. Now stand up, ugly."

Oram did so, but the ogre kept its eyes low.

"Do you remember what we talked about earlier? About you and your army finding that man for me?"

"Yes, Master," Oram's deep voice rang.

"Do you remember his description?"

Again the large ogre nodded.

"My spies say he left the city of Quwe a few weeks ago heading north to Anzzow. Once you have located him, you will send little bands of your army to harass him. Then, once you have him cornered, I want you to kill him."

"Yes, Master! We will shed his blood for you," Oram said enthusiastically, a stupid-looking grin spreading across the ogre's ugly face.

"Yes," the woman whispered. "Now go."

Oram turned around and bellowed a command in a language of grunts. The orcs reacted instantly, for fear of being beaten—or worse—by the large ogre. Oram and the orcs left, making their way to regroup with the rest of the monstrous army.

Sithel stood still, watching the creatures disappear. She shook her head with a scowl on her face. She loathed those creatures, hated even using them for her campaign. Yet she would not involve her own army this early in the game … before her opponent even knew he was playing.

Chapter One

As the sun filtered downward, the sky shone bright pink. Sunsets never ceased to amaze Sedarus Perim. The monk stood on top of a knoll overlooking a valley, but his ice-blue eyes were not on the small town, unlike his four companions'. The monk's wisdom-filled eyes were mesmerized at the beautiful colors sprayed throughout the fading light.

Sedarus gazed, imprinting the beautiful image into his mind. He stood there, on top of the grassy hill, for many minutes in silence. The wind blew, and his mud-stained, sky-blue robes flapped mildly. Finally he felt a soft touch on his arm, and he turned to one of his companions.

"We are ready. Are you?" Haet Estin asked.

Haet stood six feet tall, three inches taller than Sedarus. His soft, brown hair was cut short enough for his scalp to be visible. His nose was slightly crooked, having been broken once before, but his brown eyes were warm. They gave great comfort to Sedarus.

"Yes, brother, I am," Sedarus quietly spoke.

Haet was not Sedarus's brother, not biologically speaking, but they were both monks who were raised from childhood in the Order of Valor, an order that worshipped the god of valor and courage, Tinen. The two met their three other companions through Tinen, also. Although Aunddara, Rhamor, and Rishkiin were not monks, they all lived in the Temple of Valor and worshiped the god as well. Each of them were brought to the temple at a young age and had worked together nearly every day since. That was how they became close friends.

1

"Sedarus, Haet! You're slowing us down!" Rishkiin yelled from the bottom of the knoll.

Sedarus moved his eyes from his fellow monk to the young fighter who had spoken. Rishkiin was the youngest of the group, a score and two years old, just six years younger than Rhamor, the oldest. Rishkiin was the most brash and impatient. He stood barely taller than Haet, but in his full-plate armor, with its intricate designs of ancient runes blessed by the Goodly God Tinen, he looked much taller. He wasn't weighed down, either, as the marks made the heavy armor unnaturally light.

With his thumb and forefinger, Rishkiin nervously traced his mustache, following it down to his goatee. His thick, dark-brown hair shined in the fading sunlight.

"Be silent, Rish," Aunddara said quietly.

"Aun, I'm hungry, and there is bound to be an inn in that bloody town. I mean, by the Abyss!" Rishkiin's voice was exasperated. He impatiently fumbled for the reins of his horse.

"No one holds you back, Rish," Rhamor said, his baritone voice rumbling deeply. The bear of a man stood in his full plate armor, similarly blessed like Rishkiin's. Rhamor mounted his war steed with ease as Sedarus walked down the hill.

"I can't go ahead by myself ..." Rishkiin trailed off.

"Why? Is it because you're frightened of those scary rogues hanging about?" Aunddara laughed.

Rhamor's deep laughter joined in as Rishkiin's face flushed deep scarlet, his goatee quivering in ire. The young fighter hurriedly placed his helmet on his head, covering most of his face.

Sedarus shook his head, ignoring the joke at the cost of his friend's ego. "Let us be gone," Sedarus said, breaking up the laughter.

Rishkiin silently mounted his horse, as did Aunddara mount hers. Sedarus and Haet had no horses, but they could move their sandal-covered feet fast enough.

The journey continued, filled with silence. Often, Sedarus's gaze returned to the diminishing sunlight to the west. He wished he could have had more time watching the fiery orb descend, but he did not complain out loud. He was grateful for his friends, even the hotheaded Rishkiin.

Sedarus could not help but feel gratitude that they were near him ... that they would even speak to him. He had no control over *it*, and so he could not be certain if he would be able to stop *it* if he should lose control.

No! Do not think of that, Sedarus said silently to himself. Forcefully he switched his gaze and thoughts back to the departing sun.

"Sedarus," Haet said quietly beside him so that only Sedarus could hear, "are you okay?" Concern was plastered on the monk's face.

"No." Sedarus could not lie to Haet. It was against the code of honor by which the monks lived. Even had he lived by no such code, Sedarus would not be able to lie to Haet, who was the closest thing to a brother he'd ever had.

Haet swallowed deeply, unintentionally. "Is *it* still—"

"Yes," Sedarus cut across the monk, "I can still feel *it*. The sun eases *it*, you know."

"Yeah, I know."

Of course he knows! Sedarus thought, but he felt better when he confided in someone.

"All the more reason for us to hasten," Haet said, smiling.

Sedarus smiled back, which satisfied Haet. Yet it was not a smile of comfort, but one of knowing. Sure Haet loved and cared for Sedarus like a brother, but like Rishkiin, he was also ready for the comforts of the inn ahead.

Sedarus watched as his fellow companions quickened their pace, each wanting the reprieve of the inn. He had no choice but to keep up.

At the edge of the village, the five companions were met with a feeble guard patrol. Three men in unison shouted, "Halt!" They held up spears threateningly but did not advance.

Slowly the companions stopped.

"What business do you have here?" asked a grizzled old man. *He's seen too many winters*, Rishkiin thought as he studied the guard. He was obviously the leader of the trio, although he seemed about to collapse with exhaustion. All three of the guards had on poorly made leather armor with leather caps. Besides their spears, they had short swords for their weapons, but this was hardly a group that would rattle the five companions.

"We have come to stay at your lovely inn," Rhamor said, removing his helmet to reveal long, curly, black hair and a full, black beard. Rhamor's demeanor seemed friendly enough, but his hazel eyes were stern and authoritative.

"Lovely?" the grizzled old man asked between coughs. Then he muttered, "You obviously haven't seen it yet."

"Still, we wish to rest there," Rhamor said, his voice deep and soft, though bringing out in him an aura of command.

"As you wish, but we require that all men and women leave their weapons with us."

Rishkiin spurred his horse forward in a rush, heading straight for the old man. He stopped his steed right before it flattened the grizzled guard. Before he or his two companions could react, Rishkiin's long sword was resting at the man's exposed throat.

"The only way you will ever get my blade is through your throat!" Rishkiin growled through gritted teeth, his neatly combed goatee bristling. Then his whole demeanor changed as he shrugged and said with a lighter, calmer voice, "Of course, if you would like, I would only be too happy to oblige. But I would strongly suggest against that, as it would leave these two witless wonders without a leader. Their lovely little hearts would be broken and shattered." The young fighter feigned tears as he finished. With that Rishkiin started his horse on by the guards at a calm trot, ignoring the threatening glares from the two younger guards.

"Fine, go with your weapons! But your woman stays with me!" The grizzled old man grinned. "Come on, girl. I'll keep you entertained all night."

Rhamor, Rishkiin, Haet, and Sedarus's eyes all widened. They each started for the old man, meaning to teach him about respecting women, but Aunddara had it under control.

"Or I could hit you with my mace and send your soul to the Abyss," she said. Then, her beautiful green eyes never leaving the obviously shaken man, she spurred her mount to follow her friend by the patrol men. The remaining three companions followed in suit, each of them glaring at the old guard.

"Nice bluff, Aun," Rishkiin grinned.

"Who said I was bluffing?" Fury dripped in her voice.

That answer had all four human men on their heels. Aunddara was one of the most coolheaded humans, man or woman, they had ever met. She was hardly ever violent.

"Well then," Rishkiin spoke haltingly, as if unsure what to think. "Shall we?"

"Yes, we shall," said Aunddara.

They entered the town proper soon after. It was a small hamlet without a city wall, though evidently populated enough to have that meager town's guard. The houses littering the single road were shanties and hardly even living grounds.

The inn was just as bad—quite a hovel, what with its broken windows and ripped-out shingles. The sign that read "Inn of Good Fortune" had been torn down and was now resting against the building.

"That old guard was right," Rishkiin stated, turning up his nose in disgust. "I hardly count this as an inn."

Rhamor countered, "Yes, but this is the only settlement in the next five leagues. And while the monks don't mind sleeping in the dirt"—Haet scowled at that, but Rhamor didn't notice—"I do. So learn a lesson from the monks: be humble and silence your complaints."

That had everyone but Rishkiin laughing again. He started muttering about Rhamor's mother being an ogre as he dismounted and started to lead his horse to the stables around the back.

"Hey, Rish," Aunddara said softly.

"What, Aun?" Rishkiin asked as he turned to face the woman.

She fluttered her long eyelashes, which darkened her dazzling green eyes. "Lead my horse back there as well? Please?"

"Sure! Why bloody not?" Rishkiin replied as he stomped to take her reins. "And you?" he roared at Rhamor.

"Why thank you for offering; I knew I always liked you!" Once more four of the five companions were laughing. Rishkiin took all the horses to the stable while the rest went inside the inn. They could hear him cursing through the flimsy walls.

The inside of the inn was worse than its outside. It was completely dark except for a sole candle at the bar. The floors creaked as the party walked to the first table they saw, for the inn was vacant except for the bartender and the serving wench. Dirt and mice littered the wooden floor.

The travelers sat anxiously on the wooden chairs, wondering if they would crash to the creaking floorboards. Each, in turn, sighed in relief as they realized that the chairs would hold their weight.

"Barkeep, get a round of ale for my friends and me!" Rishkiin yelled as he entered the dirty room. "And some light."

Haet was already lighting one of his homemade candles and placing it in the center of their table, shedding light about them.

As the serving girl came with her tray of ale, Rishkiin said, "We'll have bread, cheese, and your soup of the evening."

She nodded, put the mugs of ale on the table, and turned to leave.

Rishkiin took a long draught of ale and then spewed it on the table. "I didn't order orc piss! Now give me real ale, or I'm not paying for it!"

"That's all we have," the barkeep said ungraciously.

Rishkiin was angered, but he tempered his rage.

"What's the plan?" Aunddara quickly asked everyone at the table.

"Well, I'm going to eat, avoid their orc piss, and then find a nice cot to sleep on."

"No, Rish! I mean what's next for our quest?" Aunddara ended her question with a look to Sedarus, who pointedly stared at the beer-soaked table.

"We will travel to Anzzow, several weeks away, and beseech the librarians of Feldoor to help us," Rhamor responded instead. He had always been the leader of the group.

"Oh! The monks are such a bore! They have no lives!" Rishkiin bellowed.

Sedarus and Haet's faces betrayed no reaction, but Haet said dryly, "I'm sorry I am a bore because I learned to read and write while you were getting punched in the face and having a *great* life."

"Aw come on, Haet, I didn't mean you and Sed. You know that! I'm just saying that those monks who worship Feldoor the god of love are—"

"God of knowledge, Rish," Haet muttered.

"Right, thanks," Rishkiin started again. "Those monks who worship that god of nature—"

"Knowledge, Rish!" Sedarus said, exasperated. He knew that Rishkiin was just playing around, but it wasn't funny when it involved divine beings.

"Well, whatever! Those monks who worship whatever god they do are just plain boring. They don't even have good wine!"

"You'll just have to be wine-deprived until they can give us answers. Rish, you know none of us are making you come. So if you're going to whine and complain like a child, then go back to the temple," Rhamor said.

"I'm sorry, Rish, that our—my quest isn't to your liking." Sedarus's voice was somber, full of sorrow and ... fear? Not knowing what the future would bring, he did not wish to accrue ill feelings from any of his companions.

"Nah, Sed!" Rishkiin ran his gauntleted hand through his wavy, shoulder-length hair. "It's not you, nor is it the bloody knowledge monks. It's just we've been on the road, what, three weeks? And we haven't encountered anything! No orcs, goblins! Not even ogres! I mean, what is the world coming to?" He let out a long, overexaggerated sigh.

"So what you are saying is, since you haven't killed anything lately, you're irate?" Aunddara asked, her voice dripping with sarcasm.

"Yeah, that is exactly what I am saying," Rishkiin returned without missing a beat.

Silence encompassed the five as the serving wench brought their food. She placed the whole tray on the table and went back to the bar to continue her conversation with her master, who was also her lover.

"What in the Abyss is this?" Rishkiin roared as he examined the moldy loaf of bread. He lifted the blue-green-spotted hunk to his nose and sniffed. "Whew!"

"The cheese is spoiled also," Haet said nonchalantly. He examined the soup next, which consisted of creamy white globs of goo and chunks of raw meat. "I don't even want to know what kind of soup that is," he muttered.

"It's pig entrails with a special ingredient of mine," the barkeep said from across the empty room, smirking.

"I'm not hungry anymore!" Aunddara piped in, her voice raising an octave.

"Me either," Haet said through a disgusted face.

"Nor me," the deep voice of Rhamor sounded.

Sedarus said nothing, keeping to himself.

"I am, but I want golden mead with rabbit stew. Not orc piss and a pig's crapper!" Rishkiin stated rather loudly.

"We'll have three rooms for the night, barkeep," Rhamor said soothingly, getting out of his chair and crossing the room to the bar.

"That'll be four gold pieces ... for each," the bartender said with a toothless grin.

"What?" Rishkiin shouted. "What kind of establishment are you running here?"

"One that's running out of business!" the barkeep curtly returned.

"I can see why!" Rishkiin muttered.

"In that case, make it only two rooms—" Rhamor started, but he was interrupted.

"Make it one," Aunddara stated.

"Are you sure, Aun? We will pay for an extra room," Rhamor stated.

"It's okay. The monks will just have to close their eyes," she said, smiling at the two blushing, robed figures, who were not meeting her gaze.

"All right then. Barkeep, we will have one room for the night." Rhamor handed over four gold pieces, leaving his extended hand open waiting for the key to the room. It never came. A look of curiosity crossed over Rhamor's face.

"Pay him for the food and ale, Rhamor," Sedarus said quietly.

The leader sighed. "What do I owe you for that?"

"One gold piece." Another grin spread across the inn owner's face.

"What? One gold for moldy cheese, pig crap, and orc piss! By the gods, we won't pay for it!" Rishkiin yelled, his face quivering with rage. His eyes popped wide when Rhamor handed another gold coin to the portly bartender.

The man smiled stupidly as he handed the old, rusty key over to Rhamor. "First one on the left," the portly man said.

Rishkiin sneered at the conniving innkeeper before following his friends. They walked down a hallway lit only by Haet's own candle. Rhamor put the key into the specified door and twisted. Instead of the lock clicking open, the key broke off in the keyhole.

Rhamor looked at his companions, his eyes asking, *Are you kidding me?*

"What should we do?" Haet asked after a long moment of silence, during which they all had just stared at the door.

"Let us go and speak with the innkeeper again," Aunddara said quietly.

"There is no way in the Abyss! He'll charge *us* to fix his rotten old inn." Rishkiin's face was red with anger as he pushed passed his friends and, open palmed, pushed on the door. The termite-infested door swung open haltingly. "It wasn't even locked, and that old goblin fart knew it!" Rishkiin turned angrily, as if he was about to march down the hallway to the bar and punch the innkeeper square in the jaw.

"Just forget it, Rish," Sedarus said soothingly. He always had a way of calming the irate young man.

Sedarus softly walked into the room, which was hardly accommodating for one person, let alone five. There was one cot made out of straw, but it was covered with creepy crawlers. Rishkiin curled his lip.

"I think that it is only right that the lady should have the privilege of sleeping on the bed," Rishkiin said with a slightly mocking bow.

"Only if I also get the privilege of smacking you on the head with my mace," Aunddara lightly said without missing a beat. Everyone, including Rishkiin, laughed.

The rest of the party slowly entered the decrepit room, the rotting floorboards croaking in protest. Rishkiin dropped his backpack on the floor next to the straw mattress, and rats skittered from beneath. The young man jumped onto the bed, a terrified mask plastered to his face, screaming, "By the gods! Get them! Kill 'em!"

"Rish, calm down! They're just mice," Rhamor said.

"No! They are *rats*! Not mice," Rishkiin kept on shaking his head.

"By Tinen, Rish! You will fight orcs and ogres, but you are frightened of mice?" Aunddara asked with a slight touch of humor to her voice.

"They are rats!" Rishkiin replied through gritted teeth. "And yes, I would rather face an army of orcs than one of rats."

"Will you get off the bed?" Rhamor asked, rather annoyed by his young friend.

"Once you kill the rats or run them out of here," he insisted.

"You are impossible," Aunddara said, chortling.

"I love you, too," said Rishkiin without looking from the rats that still skittered about the room.

To Rishkiin's relief, Sedarus and Haet shooed the creatures toward the broken door. Once the rodents had all vacated the premises, Rishkiin stepped down, sighing in relief.

"Well, at least none of us panicked," Rhamor said, grinning devilishly at Rishkiin.

"Go to the Abyss."

Aunddara and Rhamor burst into laughter, turning to their monk companions. But Sedarus and Haet were kneeling on their bedrolls, already spread out, and praying.

Aunddara and Rhamor's faces suddenly became serious. They dropped their packs, rolling out their own bedrolls, crowding close to their praying friends. As soon as they were ready, they likewise knelt in communion with their god.

Rishkiin, although a follower of Tinen, almost never prayed to the god. He always thought that the god of valor and courage didn't want his followers on their knees for any reason. As Rishkiin started to roll out his own bedroll, a rat raced over his plated feet. With a yelp, he jumped once more onto the bed. "Bloody rats," he muttered to himself, trying to be as quiet as he could for his praying friends' sake. "This is nothing but blind robbery. Plain, simple robbery. But do we stop this crime? No! We enable it."

On the bed, still looking for rats, Rishkiin did not see Rhamor, a holy knight of Tinen, open one eye and suppress a laugh.

Chapter Two

Aunddara's captivating, green eyes were filled with worry. Heavy bags began to form under them due to lack of sleep and a concerned heart. The cleric's gaze was locked on Sedarus's fidgeting form.

Her four companions had long ago fallen asleep, but she, as usual, lay awake, frowning with apprehension while she watched her monk friend toss and turn. He grunted and spoke quietly, lamenting some unforgotten memory. Aunddara could well guess which one. She could not help wincing as Sedarus suddenly lurched as if in pain. She thought him awake, but he soon settled back to his bedroll. He continued to fidget unconsciously.

The woman slowly reached out her arm, laying it gently on Sedarus's shoulder. She could feel his tightly clenched shoulder muscles, unrelenting as they refused to let him rest. At her touch, instantly the man's agitated sleep calmed. Aunddara slowly raised her caress to the monk's head. She stroked his scalp lovingly, her hand gliding through his silk-like, inch-long black hair. She smiled as she looked into his face, the lines on his forehead smoothing out in comfort.

Aunddara's heart started to race as she subtly moved closer to Sedarus. Her ears pounded with the rush of blood flooding through her veins. Her hot breath came in short gasps. She tilted her head slightly as she neared Sedarus's lips. As she moved closer still, she closed her eyes. Aunddara's face eased up to the monk's, her lips parting slightly.

Then Rhamor's voice rang out, the deep rumble in his chest filled with concern and subtly reproachful. "Aun."

Instantly, faster than she had ever moved, Aunddara retracted her face, her hands coming to her chest. Blood rushed to her cheeks, and the cleric did not need her steel mirror to tell her that she was stark scarlet.

"Aun," Rhamor said, his voice barely above a whisper.

Slowly Aunddara rolled to her side to look into Rhamor's ocean-deep blue eyes. She could not hold his penetrating gaze. The cleric mentally berated herself for her stupidity and wishful thinking. She could not believe that she had almost slipped into temptation. She knew they could never be together.

"Get some sleep," Rhamor said in a knowing voice, yet he remained calm. Aunddara recognized the warning in Rhamor's deep voice. "I'll watch over him."

She didn't even trust her voice enough to reply. She noticed, as sleep swept over her, that Rhamor had said, "I'll watch over *him*," not, "I'll watch over *us*," as was the norm. Aunddara was indeed grateful that sleep was upon her, for she knew that she was still crimson in the cheeks and the ears.

Sedarus stood in the cobblestone courtyard, still and tranquil, not twenty feet from his opponent. The man was barely taller than him, and their builds were close. The opponent's face was stern, his brow creased into a scowl.

An old man walked between the two monks. His gait was light, concealing his age, but his gray mane and beard told that he was older than he appeared and acted. His light-brown eyes pierced the hearts and souls of those who looked upon him. In unison, Sedarus and Edgar, Sedarus's opponent, bowed with grave serenity to the elderly man. Sedarus knew that to underestimate Grandmaster Taulyen was dangerous. Without a doubt, Grandmaster Taulyen was the wisest of the men and women in the Temple of Valor, holy house of Tinen.

The old man spoke, his voice crackly and weak. "Edgar," Grandmaster Taulyen moved his gaze from Edgar to Sedarus, "and Sedarus, you now face off in the Shelke dow nou drakean," the grandmaster started, as was the routine speech about the competition at the beginning of a match.

"The Valor of the Dragon will be obtained this day by one of you two. Using our martial practices, the Claw, Tooth, and Tail of the Dragon, you will face off in a battle that will lead you to valor and courage. Now, bow and begin."

Sedarus breathed deeply, steadily. He had, over the past week, participated in thirteen matches. Sedarus had conquered his opponents with little trouble, but so had Edgar. They were by far the two best unarmed fighters in the Order of Valor. Now they faced in the end trial, the championship match, to discover who would wear the title of Dragon Heart.

As Sedarus bowed to Edgar, he was keenly aware of his four friends on the edge of the gathering crowd, which enveloped the courtyard. He saw their eager expressions, each silently wishing him luck.

As he and Edgar came out of their bows, Edgar rushed forward in a flurry of movements. Sedarus was caught slightly off guard and had no time to contemplate his sidelined friends. He repeatedly slapped his open-palm hands against the vicious, perfectly performed blows coming from Edgar. Sedarus knew that he had given his opponent an advantage early in the match and that he would soon be finished if he did not correct the mistake and focus.

With a surprising roundhouse kick, Sedarus bought the moment he needed. Edgar hadn't expected the kick since it was an unwise counter, leaving Sedarus slightly exposed. It worked perfectly for Sedarus. Edgar did the only thing he could do: he launched backward, shooting his head back and away from the powerful kick.

Sedarus didn't stop moving but melded the kick into a backflip in one solid motion. That gave the monk enough room to square off against his opponent. Edgar rushed in with perfect balance. He balled his fists and slammed blows at Sedarus in rapid succession. Sedarus dodged, ducked, and deflected the powerful punches with relative ease now that they were on equal ground.

Edgar's face scrunched into a feral scowl, his teeth gnashing. He lurched suddenly at Sedarus, his right fist leading. Sedarus used his open left palm to push the incoming fist just to the right of his head. He could feel the wind blow past his ears.

Sedarus wasn't finished. His right hand flashed up, smacking the underside of Edgar's chin, forcing it skyward. Then with the middle and ring finger of his right hand, Sedarus poked Edgar in the eyes. As he was doing that, his left hand chopped Edgar in the throat. Edgar fell backward, his feet kicked out from underneath him.

Sedarus thought that he had Edgar beaten as he watched the man fall to the ground, but he was mistaken. Although momentarily blinded, Edgar grasped at Sedarus's outstretched arms, pulling him down to the ground with him.

Tumbling in a heap, Sedarus and Edgar grunted in pain as solid blows erupted from each of them. Then, with a sudden and rather vicious head butt from Edgar, Sedarus reeled, his nose freely spurting crimson blood.

Instead of trying to fight the head butt's force, he accepted it, executing a backward somersault and landing on his feet. His stance was momentarily staggered, though, his head swimming in pain and dizziness. He quickly conquered that. It was a good thing, too, for Edgar was back on his feet. The man rushed forward and jump-kicked. Sedarus Perim sidestepped the kick and let his opponent land and face him once more.

They glared into each other's eyes, slowly circling each other. Sedarus spat on the cobblestone, a glob of blood flying with the saliva. His mouth was full of blood, filling from his broken nose. He seemed oblivious to it.

Sedarus finally leapt at Edgar, his right hand rushing forward in a strike, clenched into a fist. Sedarus's aim was for Edgar's throat, and the blow would have ended the fight. But Edgar, having witnessed Sedarus pull this move before, was ready. He stepped to his left, grasped Sedarus's hand with both of his, and twisted brutally.

This maneuver would have snapped Sedarus's radius and ulna bones had he not seen Edgar's intention in his mind. Instead he performed a sideways flip, using Edgar's violent twist as a momentum boost. Just as he landed on his feet, Sedarus brought his left forearm across Edgar's hands, breaking free of the man's grip.

Edgar wasted no time lamenting the loss of his arm lock and kicked at his opponent. Sedarus had no time to block or move away, so he accepted the brutal kick in the ribs. He even used it to set up his counter, as he caught Edgar's ankle right under his armpit. Sedarus clamped down, locking Edgar's ankle to the side of his chest. He could not immediately perform the rest of his counter, for the kick to his side had cracked his ribs, making it difficult to breathe.

Sedarus quickly recovered his wind, knowing if he wasted time he would lose what advantage he had garnished from accepting the damage in the first place. He held Edgar's leg, extended to its full length, forcing the man to balance and hop about on his one free leg. With a sudden, vicious downward elbow to the knee, Sedarus made Edgar roar in pain. Both knew instantly that the right leg was now useless. Sedarus released the leg from his iron-tight grip.

Edgar's right leg was unable to support him, and he crashed unceremoniously to the ground. To the fallen competitor's gleeful surprise, Sedarus walked up to him. Just as Sedarus seemed about to speak, Edgar wailed and struck out, his right fist fully connecting with Sedarus's groin. Moaning loudly, Sedarus tumbled next to his opponent, who took up his regained advantage. He grabbed Sedarus in a front chokehold.

Already gasping for air in ferocious pain, Sedarus began to panic. He knew in the next ten seconds that if he did not muster the strength to break free, he would pass out.

But the pain! How was he supposed to deal with the welling stomach ache of the groin punch when he could not take the deep breaths needed?

Terror started to fill his mind as his eyes started to glimpse white dots. Then a foreign feeling pushed its way into his body. It was a sensation of the purest power, a deep feeling of control, fighting for self-preservation. The sensation started to swell, reaching the boiling point within milliseconds.

Sedarus tried with all his might but could no longer contain the power—even though from somewhere within, he knew that if it escaped his body, it would bode ill for all in the close vicinity.

Past all self-control, Sedarus was forced to release that which swelled within him. He saw a light-blue flash as pure energy rushed from him to Edgar. The blue energy entered the center of the man, who was still choking him. Then a blast erupted from Edgar, who instantaneously became nothing more than chunks of body parts and bloody gore.

"No!" Sedarus shouted as he bolted upright on his bedroll. He was sweating terribly and trembling with convulsive shivers. His four friends were instantly awake and huddling at his side.

Aunddara reached out her hand, and Sedarus grasped at her, needing to hold on to something pure and good. The cleric tightened her grip on him as he started to sob. Tears fled from his ice-blue orbs unabashed.

Despite his irises being filled with weepy tears, Sedarus knew that his friends were all sharing the same look of frightened worry. He also knew that they were all looking back upon that fateful day in the cobblestone courtyard. A day that was etched into their memories. A day that, try as they might, they could never erase.

Sedarus heard the fear in Aunddara's voice as she quietly told him that it would be okay and that their god, Tinen, was with him. But still, long minutes passed before Sedarus could even cease to weep. He relinquished his grip on Aunddara and moved away; he was suddenly hesitant to look at his companions. He was terrified that if he looked at them, they would fear him and flee. Above all else in the world, he did not want to be alone.

"Are you okay?"

It was the voice of Aunddara, who was right next to him again—rather close, actually, now that he thought of it, but he'd hardly heard her. He just nodded silently, still looking down at his own road-weary robes.

"Well then," Rhamor started, befuddled, as if he did not know what to do next. "Let us get some sleep, shall we?"

No one answered aloud, but they all moved back to their bedrolls. As the minutes passed, Sedarus was aware that none of them had fallen asleep, that they were thinking of him and of the deceased Edgar.

More tears battered at him, but he held them back. The minutes slipped by, becoming hours, and finally Sedarus was aware that one of his companions had fallen into a deep sleep. Judging by the wild snores, it was Rishkiin. Then soon Haet's breathing became smooth and steady, and Sedarus knew that his fellow monk had slipped into unconsciousness.

Sedarus knew he would not be able to find sleep but dearly hoped that his friends would be able to find peace and rest. He was kidding himself. Aunddara was always overly concerned, causing no end to her worry and sleepless nights. And Rhamor, although he put on a good facade, was disturbed by what happened. He rarely slept when Sedarus was overwhelmed by the revolting flashbacks.

Sedarus could not blame Rhamor, because he himself was disturbed. He could not believe what had happened that day, but he could not blame anyone but himself. He hated himself for having done it. Worse, he could feel the power within him awaiting a time to be released and cause havoc among those who surrounded him. It was always present, always waiting around the corner, lurking in the dark.

Sedarus had dreaded every day since the incident two months ago. He could not help but think of accidentally destroying his closest friends. Grandmaster Taulyen had implored Sedarus to search out answers, and it didn't take much to convince him. He was impatient to reach Anzzow and speak with the monks of Feldoor residing there. He wanted answers, and he wanted them now.

Fear trembled through his chest so that he could hardly breathe. He could not go on living like this!

He nearly jumped out of his skin when he felt Aunddara's soft touch on his arm.

"It'll be all okay, Sed," she comforted. "We will figure it out. I promise."

Chapter Three

Rishkiin stood on the front porch of the Inn of Good Fortune. He took in a deep breath and slowly let it out in a sigh of relief, fog billowing from his chilly lips. The crisp air made his lungs ache, but the young fighter did not mind. Rishkiin was glad to be out of the horrid establishment.

The sun was yet to rise, the sky still dark. A light breeze assailed the fighter's shoulder-length hair, causing it to wave gently

"A bloody good day," he said. A grin spread across his face, showing white teeth from beneath his brown, neatly combed goatee. "Eh, Sed?" he asked, nudging the monk, who was stationary next to him.

Sedarus slowly rotated his head so he could look into his friend's eyes. A rare, yet genuine smile creased his face. "Yeah, Rish," he said. "It's a good day."

The silence resumed as the two waited on the constantly creaking porch for their friends to join them. It lasted a long time; the sun had started to peek above the eastern mountains by the time all the companions were reunited, its orange flare erupting golden rays upon their faces.

"I'll get the horses," Rishkiin quietly said, tearing his gaze from the wonderful view. He left, and soon after, Rhamor, Aunddara, and Haet began to converse about their traveling plans for the next couple of days. Sedarus ignored them, staring straight at the sun while praying for the strength to control his shaking hands and racing mind. Heavy, purple-black bags rested beneath his eyes. He was used to them, as they were a constant feature of his complexion.

"Sedarus," Rishkiin whispered reverently.

"Yes?" the monk asked, turning to face the three who were now mounted, as well as Haet, all staring at him. Aunddara's alluring, green eyes caught his gaze. He could see the worry that was constantly on her face now. He had to look away.

"Ready?" Rhamor's deep voice fluttered.

A rueful smile took over Sedarus's face. He almost laughed in despair, but he controlled the crushing emotion. He slowly nodded and followed as they began to stalk the nearly abandoned dirt street. The street started to fill with awakening merchants and marching guards.

The friends passed a person so dirt-covered Sedarus couldn't be sure if it was a male or a female. He found out just a few seconds later. "Money for the poor?" a feminine though scratchy voice croaked.

Sedarus's eyes narrowed; the voice was forced. The croak was faked. After a better inspection, he saw that the dirt was not caked on but probably newly, artificially applied. Then Sedarus noticed her teeth— fairly well taken care of, not discolored from years of decay. Her hair was recently washed, not matted and greasy. *This is not someone who has been digging in garbage for food,* Sedarus thought.

To his surprise, Rishkiin answered the scamming hag. "Of course, milady!" He even bowed a little, something Sedarus had rarely seen him do before to anyone. Rishkiin fished a few pieces of silver from his money pouch and tossed them to the woman's feet. She thanked him and groveled to the ground.

"Rish," Sedarus said as they moved along, "that was no beggar."

"I know," the fighter said in a low tone. "It was probably the innkeeper's ogre-spawn wife."

That stopped Sedarus in his tracks. His face was filled with confusion, and he was completely and utterly stunned. "Then why did you give her the money?"

"Well, maybe they'll be able to improve that bloody disgrace of an inn!"

"A few pieces of silver?" Sedarus was baffled. Rishkiin grinned and shrugged without care as they continued down the road.

"You are a complete idiot, Rish," Aunddara said, laughing.

Sedarus stopped again suddenly. He didn't know why, but he had an eerie feeling. The hair on the back of his neck rose in goose bumps. By the look of him, Rhamor felt it, too, for his face turned into a scowl as he glanced about, his hand going to the hilt of his sword.

Sedarus heard a slight click and saw a sudden movement in the corner of his eye. With reflexes faster than lightning, he lurched forward, tackling the oblivious Aunddara from her horse. The crossbow bolt whizzed past and struck a passing guard in the side of the head. He died before his body slumped to the ground.

Screams erupted throughout the air as monsters swarmed from the forest just outside town. The town guardsmen were caught flatfooted; it didn't matter that there weren't more than a dozen of the murderous creatures.

Sedarus rolled off of the thankful Aunddara. He came to his feet quickly, facing an orc with a giant axe raised above his head. The creature's muscular frame pulled its skin tight. Thick, coarse hair covered most of its body. Its lower canines protruded from its lips, slobber running freely between the teeth. The thing's pig-like eyes squinted with bloodlust, ready for the kill.

Sedarus was the faster, by far. With balled fists, he grunted as his knuckles collided with the un-helmeted head of the orc. The head jerked back, but the axe was already in motion. It was a vicious, purely feral swing. The force behind it would have cleaved Sedarus's head in two, had it come close.

Click!

Sedarus twisted to the side to avoid another crossbow bolt. As he did so, he clasped his orc's Adam's apple. Blood gushed between his fingers, and he dropped the dead orc's trachea.

The monk glanced quickly around to see his friends reacting to the monsters, but then his gaze went to the crossbow archer. The creature was small, its leathery skin a dull yellow color. Its nose was flat with wide nostrils; it looked almost identical to the orc, just with a different skin color. This was an example of the orc's smaller, less intelligent cousin.

Goblin, Sedarus thought with disgust. Goblins weren't too much of a threat alone, but rarely were they alone. They only fought when they had favorable odds. They were cowards, one and all.

The creature was fumbling for another bolt, trying to ready the crossbow for a third shot. Sedarus leapt, closing the ten-foot span in one amazing leap. A quick knee to the goblin's midsection sent the creature flying back, landing hard on the dirt.

With idiotic luck, the goblin kept a hold of the crossbow. When the creature stopped skidding in the dirt, it fired at Sedarus. The bolt hit the monk in the gut, taking him completely by surprise, for he'd thought the goblin incapacitated.

A grunt passed through his white teeth as he quickly closed the ground between them again. He raised his foot and stomped unceremoniously on the cowering goblin's head, collapsing its skull.

The attack had caught Rishkiin by surprise, but still he hesitated none. His long sword was in his hand before the orc charging him could attack, and Rishkiin was ready to make the killing blow. At that moment, his horse neighed and reared up, jostling the fighter from his saddle.

Rishkiin kept his cool, landing on his heels and falling to his backside. As he rolled and the orc advanced, he struggled to free his steel shield from his back.

Pig eyes glared at the fighter as the orc swung its cracked and horribly made sword. As quickly as his armor would allow him, Rishkiin rolled away from the strike, which connected with the ground. He slid his arm through the straps of his shield and struggled to his feet. Then he turned, sword leading quicker than his full plate armor should allow. His deadly weapon severed arteries, muscle, and bone. The orc's head hit the dirt before the body.

The young fighter grinned. He was grateful for the enchanted armor, which had been a gift from Grandmaster Taulyen.

Haet moved as soon as Sedarus did, catching a glimpse of a dull, yellow-skinned goblin to the left of him. He dove, flying far and closing the gap between them, ending in a tuck and roll to come face-to-face with the small, smelly creature. Its red eyes were glassed over. Haet wasted no time; he grasped the back of the goblin's head and pulled down with such force that the goblin was stunned. The goblin's head met the ascending knee, and the goblin fell to the ground, its whole face smashed into its rather small brain.

Aunddara was still on the ground from Sedarus's saving tackle when a goblin smashed its crude morning star down. The cleric rolled to the side, barely avoiding the weapon.

Having no time to pull out her heavy mace to fend off the creature, she prayed to her god for help. Tinen, never one to abandon one of his followers, answered. He opened a gate to the celestial plane and sent a dog through.

The terrier had a silver coat of short, thin fur. It was majestic, filled with breathtaking beauty. The celestial dog was small, yet its hackles were raised, ready to shield Aunddara.

Guttural curses flew from the goblin's wide mouth as it swung at the dog and missed. The celestial godsend, answering a telepathic message from Aunddara, snapped its fangs as it flew through the air, lurching forward, its jaws clamping down hard on the goblin's throat. The vile creature viciously tore at the heavenly beast, fighting death, but the dog clamped even harder. Finally the goblin fell to its knees, still weakly clawing at the dog's eyes. Finally it lay still and gasped its last breath.

An orc leapt onto Rhamor's horse behind him. It sliced with its dagger, aiming for Rhamor's throat, but all it got was the holy knight's spiked gauntlets.

Rhamor snapped his head back ferociously, smashing his plated helmet right into the orc's face. The orc fell backward off the horse, and the knight slid off after.

He pulled free his sword and faced off with a second orc, which wielded a huge axe as it came rushing at the knight. Rhamor slung his shield on his left arm just in time to block the great axe's swing. The large steel shield held magnificently against the axe, but the force set Rhamor back on his heels, his arm tingling.

Rhamor leapt back as the first orc, now recovered from the tumble off the horse, lunged at him once more. The orc was too slow and went past, allowing Rhamor a quick sword slash to its back, severing its spine.

The maneuver left an opening for the second orc to swing once more. Rhamor was ready for it; he ducked, avoiding the great blow. As he came up, his sword slid through the orc's meager armor. Lungs pierced and bleeding severely, the orc slid to the ground and died.

The holy knight wiped his blade clean on the monster's filthy, worn cloak and sheathed it. He looked up just in time to see Aunddara pat her celestial terrier on the haunches and then dismiss it back to its own heavenly plane. He cast his gaze around the small town. Bodies now littered the road, most of them of the unskilled guardsmen. The corpses of the monsters mostly surrounded his friends. He then saw Sedarus, blood on his road-weary robes. Concern flooded him. He rushed to his monk friend, yelling for Aunddara.

The cleric of Tinen got to Sedarus at the same time as Rhamor. They just stood beside him, silently, for the monk was deep in concentration, his eyes closed tightly.

Then suddenly his eyes flared open, and Sedarus pulled the bolt from his gut. A pain-filled grunt escaped his throat. He took deep breaths.

"Here, let me," Aunddara said. She held her delicate hands above the torn robes and Sedarus's deep belly wound. She prayed to Tinen for divine healing. A flash of bright, white light erupted from beneath her hands. She suddenly felt fatigued, like she'd been running for miles. Recovering quickly, she looked back over Sedarus and sighed in relief.

"Thank you, Aun," Sedarus said, examining his wound. It had scabbed over, as if weeks of healing had passed.

"Sure," Aunddara said, blushing slightly. She quickly went to each of the others, searching for wounds. She found one, but Rhamor refused healing for his injured shield arm.

She then went to the closest screaming townsperson. He had sustained a mortal wound; his chest had been punctured. Aunddara was about to ask Tinen, humbly, to heal the man, but she was cut short by a yell.

"Halt! We have clerics to do that!"

She looked up to see a portly man walking toward her and her companions. He had intensely gray hair, almost silver—at least what was left of it behind his dramatically receding hairline. Yet his eyes were still bright, showing intelligence earned with his age. They were piercing—so much so that Aunddara had to lower her gaze.

"I beg your pardon, but this man needs help," she said, looking at her would-be patient.

"And he will get it. But if you are a part of the group that killed these monsters, then I would like to speak with you," the man said, his voice sharp.

"Who in the Abyss are you?" Rishkiin said, walking up. His blade was still in hand. "And why in that bloody hell would we come with you?"

"I apologize for my impatience and rudeness," the man spoke. As he said this, his gaze enthralled Rishkiin. "I am Lord Mayor Fodd, and this small group of monsters was just a diversion."

Chapter Four

The five companions and Fodd stood in front of a shattered manor. It had collapsed under some sort of devastating and unrelenting power. What once might have passed for beauty now was a pile of rubbish and splintered wood.

"By Tinen! What happened here?" Rhamor asked, his face ashen.

"Like I said, the attack on the town was only a ruse," Lord Mayor Fodd said quietly, his voice wafting through the slight wind.

"What did they want?" Sedarus questioned, his demeanor distant and unattached.

"They kidnapped my wife," the old man said, his eyes lighting with an inner fire of rage.

"And they are holding her for ransom," the perceptive Sedarus finished, nodding his head.

"Yes."

"What are they after?" Aunddara wondered.

"They want someone," Lord Mayor Fodd said, slightly confused. "A monk," he added, digging out a piece of parchment and handing it to Sedarus.

Scribbled lettering creased the paper. Sedarus read it quickly.

Your wife is in my care. Give us the monk and she lives. If payment is withheld, then her head will be delivered on a platter.

Krug

Sedarus passed the note among his friends. They stared at each other in utter astonishment. Sedarus's ice-blue eyes filled with fear. He had a daunting feeling that he was the monk mentioned in the note.

"How did your house crumble to bits?" Rishkiin asked, trying to break the silent tension.

"A rather large boulder flew from afar, overhead, and smashed into my home," Lord Mayor Fodd said, choking up. A few moments passed before he could continue. "Please, get her!" he pled with the group before him.

"We know not where to start, Lord Mayor," Rhamor said. "If you have any idea, it would greatly help our search."

"I have already sent my bodyguard to prepare. He is a ranger, well practiced in the ways of tracking the beasts," the old man said to quell the party's doubting looks.

"That would be appreciated," Rhamor said, bowing slightly.

Rhamor turned to his friends, fear in his own eyes. The common thought was clear: how did they know we were here?

Within moments a man walked up, his gait one that displayed experience in the art of stalking silently. He sported leather armor with a forest-green cloak. At his hip was a long sword, and a dagger was mostly hidden in his left boot. On his back was a longbow with a quiver full of arrows.

"Lord, I am ready," the man said. He stood six feet even, his black hair pulled back in a ponytail. His chin was devoid of hair. The man's arms were taut, his chest broad.

"Good, good. This is Andrew," Lord Mayor Fodd introduced to the group. Each greeted in turn.

"I witnessed some of the monsters retreating into the forest. That is where we will start." Andrew did not wait for a reply; he turned and started for the forest.

Slightly caught off guard, the companions hesitated.

"Go on, I'll make sure your steeds are well taken care of," Lord Mayor Fodd said.

Rishkiin laughed, "Like I am just going to hand you the reins!" He choked in surprise as Rhamor and Aunddara handed over their horses. Reluctantly the young fighter followed suit. The group turned and tailed the ranger. They walked less than a mile to the edge of the pine forest from which the monsters had come and into which they had fled. Almost instantly Andrew was hot in pursuit of fresh orc tracks.

They walked through the dark forest, Andrew leading silently with Haet and Sedarus, equally quiet, performing as liaison to the louder three. Rhamor and Rishkiin were followed by Aunddara, whose position in the back was best for casting healing spells, if need be. All three of them had their shields strapped to their left arms and their weapons drawn.

The forest ground was littered with fallen pine needles, broken tree limbs, and downed trees. The early morning sun broke through the thick canopy of needles in places, spreading rays of gold across the foliage on the ground.

An hour passed in relative silence. There was the occasional twig snap or fumbling misstep of Rishkiin, which of course was followed by a loud curse.

Soon Andrew, out ahead, stopped and signaled for the others to do the same. He silently rushed back, his face grim. "I found orcs, goblins, and gnolls. I can't see Lady Fodd, but the gnolls are guarding a crypt-like entrance."

"Gnolls?" Rishkiin asked.

"They are hyena-headed monsters with fur covering their bodies. They stand on their back two feet," Haet explained.

"They are a type of humanoid," Andrew further clarified. "They are only loyal to those who give them screaming victims to feast upon. They are vicious creatures one and all."

Rishkiin smiled and asked, "Tough opponents?"

"Very."

"Good." Rishkiin's smile widened even further. "What's the plan?"

"I will quietly kill as many of the orcs and goblins as I can, one at a time. They are acting as sentries. Then I will shoot my bow, aiming for the more distant gnolls, who are by far the most dangerous."

"Save some for me!" Rishkiin said, exasperated.

"Haet and I can help with the guards," Sedarus said confidently.

"Silence is my goal," Andrew said skeptically, "and you don't even have a weapon."

"Do not underestimate the monks," Aunddara warned. "They can kill just as efficiently as any of us."

Taking the woman's word, Andrew nodded. "Fine, we take as many as we can. At my first bow shot, you three rush in and finish up. When you come in, make as much noise as possible. Frighten the cowardly creatures."

They all nodded.

The two monks and the ranger departed, silence as their companion. Andrew led them up a small hill encompassed with pine trees, their needles changing from green to brown.

"Just beyond this is a clearing," Andrew whispered to the other two. "The larger orcs and gnolls bully the small goblins, so they are on watch."

He let that sink in, the two monks understanding his meaning. Killing the goblins silently should be easier than killing the others. That was a stroke of luck.

"Good hunting," Andrew said, drawing the dagger from its boot sheath. With that he departed, heading to the left of the small knoll.

Sedarus looked Haet in the eye and nodded, both knowing that their friends' lives were in their hands; they would show no mercy.

Sedarus moved off to the right, mirroring Andrew's movements. He was the first to encounter a goblin. The small, hunched-over monster was facing the clearing, where a small group of orcs was feasting on burnt meat, drinking mead, and singing a rowdy song. Sedarus couldn't understand the slurred words of the guttural language, but he guessed that they were lewd.

The wind was louder than the slow-moving monk. He came up behind the goblin with ease. The goblin was too busy cursing the orcs in its language to notice.

Sedarus inhaled deeply but silently and then acted quickly, without compassion. His left hand cupped the goblin's head, his right hand followed suit on its chin. Sedarus twisted, suddenly finding he was nose-to-nose with the goblin. The thing's body was still facing the clearing as he lowered the twitching corpse to the ground.

Sedarus dragged the corpse and deposited it into a bush, completely obscuring it from sight. He started off again to the right, slowly and steadily, once more leaving only silence in his wake.

He came upon another grumbling goblin. The creature's flabby, yellow skin sagged out of its mismatched furs. The monk snuck right behind the foul monster. Quicker than lightning, he snaked his arm around the goblin's throat. The crook of his elbow crushed the goblin's windpipe as his forearm and bicep cut the circulation from both its carotid arteries.

Struggling and gurgling on its own spit, the goblin fought feebly for air. Drool rolled down its flat face. It tried to head butt Sedarus, but the motion only furthered the monk's goal, extending the neck and stealing the air needed for the goblin's survival. Seconds later the monster slumped to the ground, dead.

Sedarus continued around the clearing, finding no more guards that could be covertly slain. He positioned himself near a pair of goblins just out of reach of the trees and waited for Andrew's arrow to strike.

Haet watched as his two companions disappeared into the forest. Moving forward, the monk saw a goblin resting against a large pine tree. He knew that there was no way he could kill it from behind, and there was no way to kill it silently from where it was positioned.

A sudden idea flared in his mind. With a running start, Haet kicked off against the base of the goblin's tree. He soared through the air, barely catching hold of a limb twenty feet from the ground with naught but fingertips. With amazing ease, he pulled himself onto the fat limb.

Unfortunately the maneuver was not totally silent. The stupid goblin straightened up, its hand resting on its spiked wooden club. It walked around the tree, searching for the culprit who made the noise.

Haet was in perfect balance as he pulled a rope from his pack, quickly tying a makeshift noose. Just as the goblin walked beneath him, he lowered it, aiming perfectly. It snagged around the goblin's neck, and before the confused monster could yell, Haet dropped the full twenty feet with the rope in his hands.

As he went down, the goblin went up. The creature's neck did not break; the goblin wiggled viciously, fighting to undo the knot. Failing to release itself, the goblin strangled quietly, its life ending with a last gurgle.

Andrew drew near a goblin from behind, his blade in his right hand. Hidden in shrubbery, Andrew drew a deep breath. He loved the idea of there being fewer monsters in the world, but he hated doing what he was about to do.

He released his breath and started silently once more. A stride away, he almost gagged on the goblin's sordid smell. He quelled his stomach, knowing he needed to remain in control.

Suddenly he grabbed the goblin's long, matted hair and pulled back, fully exposing its neck. In the same motion he slit its throat so deeply with the dagger that after finishing the swipe, the goblin's head was only attached by flabby skin.

A shudder coursed through Andrew as he looked into the goblin's pig-like eyes as its life slipped away. The man dropped the dead creature. He wiped the hot blood from his right hand, but the act was permanently stained in his mind. The smell was just as horrid and just as enmeshed with his hand.

Andrew replaced the dagger in his boot and drew out his bow. He strung it and nocked an arrow in one swift movement.

A twig cracked behind him. He swiveled speedily, pulling back the arrow, readying it to let loose.

He never fired. The sound was Haet, letting the ranger know that he was behind him. They both nodded to each other. Andrew asked quietly, "Where is Sedarus?"

Haet shrugged, not knowing but wholly unconcerned. "He will position himself to the greatest advantage point. Do not worry for the likes of Sedarus."

"Fair enough." Andrew lowered his bow. "Where are you heading?"

"Right there," Haet said, pointing at two particularly drunk orcs that were also conveniently close to the forest's edge—close enough so that he could attack swiftly and deadly after Andrew fired his bow.

"Good. I'll fire on the count of fifty."

Haet nodded and moved off, quieter even than Andrew's stealthiest motions.

Andrew started counting as he examined one of the gnolls, the largest of the four. It was a garish creature. Reddish-brown fur covered its entire dog-like body. Sharp teeth filled its snout, and it saw with beady, black eyes. It had a scale mail type of armor, and its neck was adorned with a necklace of teeth, easily discerned as being from humans.

He is the head figure of the gnolls, Andrew thought. His suspicions were confirmed when that gnoll started to bark orders to the other three.

"You die first," Andrew said quietly but aloud, lifting his bow and aiming for the gnoll's exposed shaggy throat. He let the arrow fly with a twang!

The arrow soared through the air so fast it whistled—too fast for the gnoll to react. The point plunged deeply into the beast's upper chest, snapping its collarbone. The gnoll collapsed, releasing a piercing howl into the air, sending nearby birds fluttering away and woodland animals scampering deeper into the trees.

Another arrow, this one to the right eye, silenced the canine-like monster.

"Come on!" Rishkiin growled with irritation. It had been several minutes, and the three trailing companions had heard no signal to advance.

"Let them do their job, Rish," Aunddara advised patiently.

"They will be done soon enough." Rhamor stated.

"I know, but did you think it would take them *this* long?" the young, impatient fighter asked.

"Yes, Rish, what they do takes time—"

Aunddara was interrupted by a pained, wolf-like yowl. Then Rishkiin wasn't even there. He was rushing forward, unencumbered by his armor, his finely made sword glittering in the early morning's rays. He burst through the last of the trees and into the clearing, heading straight for an orc that was getting to its feet with an inebriated stagger.

The orc was easy pickings, and its severed head rocked back and forth on the makeshift table around which the creatures had been feasting.

Rishkiin didn't slow his charge, his gaze fixed on a gnoll right before him. The gnoll, seven feet tall, flexed its sinewy muscles, readying itself for a fight. The beast snarled, lips curling back to reveal long, sharp canines.

It swung its battle-axe hard, but Rishkiin did not underestimate the beast. He had his shield up, deflecting the blow, even as he supplied one himself. His own attack was not one to kill or even to wound. It was to test the gnoll's defenses. The blade clanked harmlessly against the gnoll's steel shield.

The gnoll roared in anger and swung at Rishkiin again. This swing was wrought of ire and skill. Rishkiin wasn't quite fast enough to block with his shield. The axe head landed squarely on his head.

The helmet halted the axe from burying itself into Rishkiin's skull, but his head ached and his ears rang from the strike. The force of the blow had the young fighter spinning. He went with the momentum, adding his own, to set up his next attack—one that would sever the head from the gnoll.

But the blow to his head had dazed him more than expected. With his aim completely off, his blade instead sheared the gnoll's right arm, its axe arm, and continued into the chest of the beast. Hitting armor and then ribs, the blade halted. The gnoll wasn't quite dead, but Rishkiin knew that death would come to it soon enough.

In a moment of mercy, the young fighter jabbed his blade into the heart of the gnoll, ceasing its suffering.

Rhamor followed after Rishkiin's wild charge. He rushed up the small hill and through the clearing, past the beheaded orc, still lying on the blood-soaked wooden table. The holy knight went to the right of Rishkiin, taking on the next gnoll in line.

The monster raised its arm in a swing, but Rhamor was not about to let the thing attack him unchecked. He slashed with his brilliantly made sword. The blade severed the furry hand of the monster. It howled, pointing its dog-like snout skyward.

Rhamor couldn't finish that creature off, for a second gnoll took a swing at him from his left. The man easily blocked the battle-axe. His retaliation stab went right through the gnoll's metal shield, perforating the monster's hand, rendering it useless.

A feral growl escaped the monster, its mustard-yellow mane bristling wildly. It dropped the shield, being too heavy for its lame hand to support.

The gnoll jabbed its axe forward, the head tipped with a small, jagged blade. Rhamor countered with his sword, completing a high arc, moving the axe tip completely out of harm's way. Then with strength from his barreled chest and back, the holy knight bashed the gnoll in the snout with his shield, tossing the beast backward.

When it was too late for him to recover, Rhamor understood his mistake. The first gnoll, the one with a bleeding stub of an arm, roared and lunged at him, its sharp teeth leading the charge.

Rhamor heard the sound that would either be his savior or exact vengeance. He could only hope that the arrow reached the raging monster quick enough to be the former.

Sure enough, the arrow pierced the hairy hide of the gnoll before it reached Rhamor, digging deeply into its heart. The vile creature slumped to the ground. Rhamor did not have a chance to thank Andrew because the second gnoll was roaring wildly and swinging its axe. The battle-axe sliced along the seam of his shoulder plate. Far better a weapon than any orc or goblin blade, the axe entered his left shoulder, severing muscle, tendon, and ligament.

A throaty roar of pain escaped Rhamor, who stabbed at the beast. Receiving a severe gash to the thigh, the gnoll fell to the ground, blood pooling from its leg. It swung feebly as Rhamor stood over its dying form. Rhamor had no way to deflect the attack, his shield arm injured severely, yet the blow never touched Rhamor. Rishkiin, having just slain his opponent, rushed quickly to his friend, battering the gnoll's axe away with his shield.

Rhamor quickly smiled thankfully to Rishkiin, and then jabbed his blade into the throat of his enemy, vanquishing the evil monster.

Sedarus patiently waited for the signal to attack in an ant-infested bush. He resisted the roaring urge to swat the bugs away and leave his hiding spot; it was perfect for an ambush. Before him were two goblins speaking in their strange language. They both were turned toward him but absolutely oblivious to their mortal peril.

The monk heard a sudden crack! Instantly, he moved deeper into the bush, but he was safe. The snapping sound was caused by a drunken orc stumbling on twigs at the clearing's edge, ahead.

The orc started to growl at the two goblins and then started laughing crazily. It swayed terribly before crashing to the ground, passed out. Its contented snores rang loudly.

One goblin, the larger of the two, stalked forward. When it was sure that the orc wasn't going to wake, it took out its morning star and started to bash the orc over the head. Blood sprayed on the goblin, but it ignored it, giving in to its wild frenzy.

Just then, Andrew's arrow whizzed through the clearing. Sedarus jumped forward, attacking the unsuspecting, murderous goblin by cupping both his hands and performing a downward blow to the back of the head. The goblin's skull caved in, and it died instantly.

The second goblin turned from the mutilated orc and nearly leapt out of its skin. It turned to flee and even got a few strides in before it felt an erupting pain in its back. Sedarus had snapped its spine. With a stomp for good measure, the monk moved on into the clearing, searching for his friends who might need his help.

The signal for attack caught Haet's ears. He lurched forward, foolishly getting his foot tangled with an exposed root of a nearby tree. Down he went, right in between two gray-skinned orcs.

Though they were drunk, they still had weapons, and Haet did not want to be on the ground. One of the orcs hastily readied his great axe and swung at Haet while he was down. The blow clipped the man on the shoulder. Blood spurted forth from the gash as the monk rolled forward, escaping the second orc's swing.

In an amazing maneuver, Haet leapt from his somersault, turned, and kicked at the first orc. His foot landed on the side of its neck with such force that it snapped the bone.

Haet's kick was costly, and he came out of it with a gash on his left hip. He landed on his feet only to collapse to the ground, not being able to hold his own weight.

The second orc rushed forward but halted when a dirt-stained, sandaled foot reached up and slammed into its nose. The blow shoved the nose bone into the orc's brain, killing it with naught but a crooked-looking nose for visible injury.

Haet grunted as he sat up. He grimaced in world-spinning pain as he tried to stand. Finally the monk collapsed and just lay in the dirt.

Aunddara had been caught flatfooted when her two companions rushed off. Now she started to run, pausing only to pull out her heavy mace. By the time she arrived at the battle scene, all the monsters were slain. She rushed straight to Rhamor, whose blood was flooding his armor, pouring from the shoulder wound.

"Let me heal you," Aunddara said, already in converse with her god.

"No, Aun." Rhamor's deep voice halted her in the middle of her prayer.

"Why not? You're hurt." She scrunched up her face in anger and agony at having to see her friend in pain. "If this is some ridiculous, prideful act, saying you don't need a woman's help, then knock it off!" she continued, absolutely enraged.

"It's not, Aunddara Firespirit." Rhamor laughed. He had long ago bestowed that name upon the quiet yet fiery-tempered woman.

Aunddara couldn't help but chuckle. Her eyes were still filled with concern and confusion.

"Aun, I'm fine, don't worry about me," Rishkiin said sardonically. The cleric glanced over him. He seemed unhurt, so she ignored him and looked back at Rhamor.

"I am a paladin, Aun," Rhamor said, "a holy knight of Tinen. I shall call upon Tinen's healing powers myself."

With that he closed his eyes in prayer. He placed his hands on his bleeding cuts, and soon his whole body flared with brilliant, yellow-white light, his wounds completely healed. He sighed with reverence as he opened his eyes, silently thanking his god.

Aunddara wasn't surprised; she had seen other holy knights perform this same miracle before.

"Aun!" Haet called out in a pain-choked voice.

Surprise arrested her, and then concern for the monk filled her astounded eyes. Aunddara ran over to the fallen monk. They were soon joined by all of their companions, including Andrew.

"Don't worry, Haet," Aunddara said, taking in a large, deep breath. She prayed to be the conduit of healing magic.

To her great relief, her prayer was answered. A burst of bright white light flooded Haet, wrapping him in waves of healing. Sinew reattached and muscle healed. As the light faded, Haet stood up, stabilizing the now-dizzy Aunddara.

He gave her a hug and said, "Thank you, Aunddara." He then thanked his god. His wounds were covered in dark scabs, his sky-blue robes tattered and ripped.

"If we are ready, we still need to move on. We still have to enter the crypt," he said, pointing across the clearing to a gaping black hole that seemed to foretell of doom.

Chapter Five

"Light," Andrew said. "We need light. Does anyone have a torch?"

"We've got it taken care of," Rhamor said. "Light your shield, Aun."

Andrew's confusion cleared as Aunddara muttered a word and her shield flared like a torch. The light was gold-white, leaving a black emblem in the middle of the glow. It was of a rearing dragon, the symbol of Tinen.

They stood in the middle of a passage, just down the stairs that led into the crypt. The obsidian corridor had been fashioned a long time ago; it's once perfectly round ceiling was now blemished and fractured. Toward the walls were elaborate statutes of winged gargoyles and majestic dragons.

"I will go first, with my bow, and see what is up there." Andrew then turned to Haet and Sedarus and said, "Come slowly, but be ready for battle. All of you," he finished, peering at each of the companions. His gaze lingered on Rishkiin for just a moment, his face showing that he was impressed with the young fighter's skill.

The ranger started, his footsteps hushed. The rest of the group began their somewhat quiet march, shadowing the ranger's movements, Haet and Sedarus once more playing the role of middlemen.

Aunddara's shield cast golden light twenty feet in every direction. Even so, after walking a short time they could no longer spot Andrew. Soon the group came to a cross tunnel. The ranger was nowhere in sight, yet Sedarus insisted that they press straight forward.

"How do you know?" Rishkiin whispered. Sedarus pointed at three stacked pebbles located in the center of the passageway directly in front of them. With their weapons at the ready, the companions continued on. Corridors and hallways often branched from their route of passage, yet at every breakaway, pebbles were stacked, indicating which way to go. They jumped at each shadow and at each noise, prepared to fight. Rishkiin had to constantly stifle a yelp of fear as mice and rats skittered at the edge of their magical light. Many agonizing minutes passed.

Then suddenly Andrew appeared, rounding a corner. "Quickly! Douse the light!"

Aunddara spoke a hushed word and the light died. Darkness assailed them, leaving them momentarily helpless. Sedarus couldn't help but think that Andrew had ordered the light to be doused so he could take advantage and slay them all. But the killing arrow never pierced his heart, and he breathed a sigh of relief.

"This way, carefully," came Andrew's whispering voice.

Haet and Sedarus shuffled forward, their sandals making no noise. Aunddara's footfalls were somewhat quiet, with her high, leather boots, but Rhamor and Rishkiin clanked loudly in their plated boots.

They turned the corner and saw a light at the end of the tunnel, no more than thirty feet away. Down the long corridor, the monsters were so engrossed with themselves that they would not have noticed the approaching light, anyway. The brutes were gathered in the room, preoccupied by something unseen to the companions.

"Lady Fodd must be in that room," Andrew whispered. The companions could clearly hear the anxiety in his voice.

"What is the plan?" Rhamor asked.

"These two," the ranger indicated the monks impatiently, "and I will sneak down silently and surprise whatever is down there. Then we will need your services."

Rishkiin grinned devilishly. He was wholly unconcerned with what was at the end of the tunnel; he was excited to start fighting again.

Without another word, the three started down the tomb hall, melding with shadows. Andrew's fear for Lady Fodd's wellbeing had been chipping away his patience, and finally seeing where she may be, he could no longer control himself. He broke into a full-on run.

As he entered the chamber, he saw the bound Lady Fodd amongst four bugbears—large versions of the goblin, although much stronger and more vicious. Their smashed snouts were swathed with foamy saliva. Sharp canines protruded from their lips. They wore nothing but loincloths. Their barrel chests shuddered with laughter as Lady Fodd quivered in terror.

With a bellow of rage, Andrew nocked an arrow and shot it on the run. The arrow zoomed through the air, penetrating the seven-foot, muscular bugbear standing closest to the tied woman. Its light-yellow-furred chest turned red as blood seeped from the arrow shaft. Its red pupils widened in terrifying pain. The bugbear's mouth opened wide in a horrifying screech.

Then there was a tumult as the three remaining bugbears came rushing into the tunnel.

Sedarus leapt forward through the air, overhead and to the right of Andrew. He faced the fastest bugbear. The monk leapt up, bringing his knee to the ribs of the tall monster. The bugbear grunted through the pain as its bones cracked.

Sedarus heard the bowstring's plunk; he knew that Andrew was hard at work. The crashing of his friends' armor told him that they were not far behind.

A massive swing from the bugbear's huge, spiked club had Sedarus diving forward, close to the considerably large creature. Coming out of the roll, Sedarus applied a shin kick to the beast's groin. It grunted loudly and dropped to its knees, making the monster slightly shorter than the monk.

Sedarus caught a glimpse of movement from the corner of his eye. He skipped to the side, barely dodging a colossal club made from a tree trunk. The swing struck the wounded bugbear instead, catching the bugbear's head and ripping it off.

Sedarus looked up to see what sort of monster could supply such a massive blow. He froze. Standing in front of him was a twelve-foot hill giant, and its backswing was heading right for Andrew.

Haet followed Sedarus's example, except he leapt to Andrew's left. As he landed, a bugbear's large mace connected with his left shoulder, flinging him backward. The spiked ball at the end of the mace ripped his tendons apart, rendering his whole left shoulder useless and numb.

Haet lay on the floor, gasping for breath that seemed to evade him. He was vaguely aware that the bugbear was grinning, stalking in for the easy kill.

The bugbear raised its weapon over its head, and just when its arm was about to drop, Rishkiin rushed in, swinging his sword. His blade tore through its chest, ripping a lung and severing several arteries. The bugbear fell to the floor, gasping for breath just before Rishkiin slit its throat.

The last bugbear faced off with Rhamor and Aunddara. A mighty swing came at Rhamor, only just missing the paladin.

Rhamor's blade cut through the air, but the bugbear leapt to the left … right into Aunddara's heavy mace.

Its collarbone shattered, leaving its weapon arm useless. The monster roared and kicked, its large foot skillfully aimed to smash into Aunddara's chest. She flailed backward, hitting the ground hard. She wasn't injured terribly but knew that at least one rib was cracked.

Rhamor ran and jumped, his blade tip leading. With a feral thrust, the blade entered the tough hide, piercing through Adam's apple and bone. The paladin and the corpse tumbled down just in time to duck a swing from the hill giant.

Andrew looked for an opening to shoot his bow. He found many, but he held off. He alone spotted the giant but had not wanted to draw attention to himself until his companions could rally with him.

The hill giant had been sitting in its granite throne, watching with amusement as his bodyguards and the intruders fought each other. But Andrew's attention shifted when he saw a human figure that he recognized. The old, sleazy town guard was scrambling toward Lady Fodd with a dagger in hand.

Andrew could well guess his intentions and could not let that path continue. An arrow soared through the air, piercing the old guard's back through his leather armor, sliding in between his ribs. The old man toppled over, screams coursing through the air.

The dull-witted hill giant finally stirred, realizing that the intruders were easily winning the fight against its contingent of monsters.

The thing stood up, well over twelve feet tall. Warts covered the left side of its stone-like face. Its flab was crammed into its loose-fitting clothes.

It picked up the colossal spiked club resting at the throne's side and swung its overly long arms, which were molded out of muscle. Blood splattered on the club, and the giant grinned toothlessly. It seemed not to care that the reckless warm-up swing had just slain one of its own bodyguards.

The giant's low brow crinkled in curiosity as an arrow bounced off of its rock-hard skin. With a speedy backswing, the club came at Andrew. The ranger tried to move out of its path, but it was too quick.

Then the ranger was no more.

Sedarus saw the gore of Andrew splatter against the stone wall. Rage beyond reason swelled within the monk. It built as milliseconds passed by.

Everything seemed to slow down, reaching a standstill. He was suddenly aware of the power within him that he despised. It was sitting there, waiting for his call. Going against his better judgment, Sedarus reached inside himself, harnessing the wild energy. His muscles started to bulge as he convulsed with the pure power. His skin started to glow a light blue, and his body began to tremble.

Nearing the edge of control, Sedarus pushed forth his hands; his fingers were extended, pointing upward, his palms aiming at the hill giant. With a scream of anger, pure, blue energy surged from Sedarus. It shot forward, bursting into the momentarily stunned giant. The energy was absorbed into its body.

Then an explosion unlike any Sedarus had previously witnessed shook the dimly lit crypt. The ground trembled, the ceiling cracked, and the giant's gore and blood scattered everywhere, covering everyone in the room. Sedarus looked around, seeing that he was the only one still standing on his feet. All of his friends had been cast to the ground during the blast.

Without looking at his friends, immensely worried that they would want nothing to do with him, Sedarus rushed to the barely living Lady Fodd. Bruises covered her face. One eye was swollen shut; black and blue decorated the skin surrounding her broken nose. Her lips were split horribly, leaving dry blood on her chin. Her tear-streaked cheeks were caked with dirt.

"Good lady," Sedarus said quietly, "I'll free you; do not worry." With that he untied and un-gagged the plump woman. She opened her one good eye and nodded her thanks.

"Let me, Sed," Aunddara croaked, her voice still stolen by the shock.

Sedarus could not bear to look at the cleric, so he just nodded, still staring at Lady Fodd. Stepping aside, Sedarus let Aunddara come close enough for her to heal the captive.

He moved through the room, avoiding the side wall that was covered with the chunks of Andrew. He then noticed the old man, dead with an arrow in his back.

"Hey! Come look at this!"

The others rushed to his side, except Aunddara, who was deep in spiritual union with Tinen.

"That's that old dragon turd from the town!" Rishkiin barked. All of the men covertly looked at Aunddara. They turned their backs on the deceased man, gazing at the dead bugbears and the chunks of skin and blood that were once a hill giant.

"Well now we know how the boulder ruined Fodd's manor," Rhamor said.

Rishkiin looked at him, confused, but Haet and Sedarus nodded knowingly. "Come on, Rish!" Haet said. "That giant must have thrown the boulder."

"But how did they know you were here?" Rishkiin asked, addressing Sedarus.

"We don't even know they were truly looking for Sed," Haet said feebly.

"They were," Sedarus said, dismayed. He had a sinking feeling in his stomach.

"Well, whatever the reason they wanted you, we know how they found you," Rhamor said, his eyes returning again to the old man.

"Bloody idiot!" Rishkiin muttered at the deceased old man.

Sedarus quietly turned to the large granite throne. Upon a quick inspection, the monk found a large chest obscured behind it. He called to his friends.

Rishkiin rushed forward with a grin plastered to his face. He examined the chest, realizing that it was locked. With a swipe of his sword, he exclaimed, "Bloody thieves! Who needs a lock pick when you have a sword?" The oak chest opened at the slash, revealing a bulging pouch of coins. "Loot!" Rishkiin whooped in joy as he grabbed the sack. He left Sedarus, sitting to the side as he started to count the contents of the bag.

Sedarus delved deeper into the chest, finding nothing else but the shards of a sword and a heap of tattered, rolled-up silk fabric. As he picked up the fabric, it unfolded partially in his hands, revealing a small, perfect obsidian cube. The cube's sides couldn't have been larger than an inch.

The workmanship awed him. He dropped the silk, forgotten from his mind, and held the cube in his hands.

Instantly he felt a slight tug on his senses. Somehow, Sedarus knew that this cube was filled with some sort of enchantment.

"What is that, Sed?" Aunddara asked, helping the healed Lady Fodd to her feet.

"I don't know," Sedarus explained. "It's some small cube. It is enchanted."

"How can you possibly know that?" Rishkiin scoffed, disbelieving.

"Here, let me see." Aunddara held out her hand. Sedarus gave it to her.

The cleric closed her eyes and prayed. The cube flared a bright-red color.

"It is indeed magical. I cast a spell detecting magic items," she said, quelling Rishkiin's doubting look. "How did you know, Sed?"

"I am not sure," Sedarus said sincerely.

"Well, we can figure this out later," Rhamor said, supporting the former prisoner. "We have a lady to deliver safely to her husband."

"Right! Let us be gone," Rishkiin said, and he led the way out of the crypt.

Silence encompassed them, except for Lady Fodd's intermittent disheveled sobs. They hurried back to town.

When the group finally made it back to the hamlet, they came upon Lord Mayor Fodd ordering the guards to pile the dead and make ready to bury. Lady Fodd broke free from Rhamor's supporting arms when she saw her husband and rushed to him, falling into his loving embrace.

They wept joyfully for a moment. Then Lord Mayor Fodd called five of his guards to take his wife to their safe house. The man then turned to face the companions.

"Where is Andrew?" His face crinkled in confusion. Then it sagged with comprehension as each of the friends' faces darkened with sorrow.

"How?" came the solemn question.

"A hill giant," Rishkiin replied.

"I mourn for him; he was a good bodyguard, and a better friend." Lord Mayor Fodd closed his eyes momentarily, holding back tears that seemed intent to overcome him.

"We are sorry, Lord Mayor," Rhamor's deep voice rang with true remorse. "If there is anything we can do, please just let us know."

"There is one thing."

They all looked at him.

"Take a token of my thanks."

"We couldn't," Sedarus said. His ice-blue orbs were almost distant, as if he were trying to forget some heinous act.

"It would insult me if you did not." The lord mayor's brow crumpled in a stern stare.

"If that is the case, then of course we will accept." Rhamor shot Sedarus a warning glare that plainly said not to insult the man. It was completely lost on Sedarus, who was looking more distant by the minute.

"Good." A smile erupted from the man's face. "Follow me please."

The companions did so.

Sedarus was visibly in a haze, and he knew only that he was to put one foot in front of the other. He spoke not at all through the short journey to the lord mayor's safe house.

Lady Fodd was there when they passed through the wooden portal. She sprang at Sedarus, wrapping him in a hug, muttering, "Thank you, thank you," over and over.

That shook the monk from his haze. He stood rigid.

Sedarus gazed around the cozy little abode. Comfortable-looking furniture surrounded a small table. The room was lit by candles and an eastern window, letting the sun's rays enter.

"Dear," Lord Mayor Fodd said quietly, "we need to go; these good people are in a hurry." With that the elderly lady let go of Sedarus. "I love you, dear. I'll be back up soon, and we can talk. I promise," he added as his wife's upper lip started to tremble. He lovingly patted her on the cheek and turned, the companions following suit. They descended a spiral staircase into a dark room.

Instantly Sedarus was assailed by a tugging sensation similar to the one he'd felt upon first holding the obsidian cube—but this was to a much greater scale. The room suddenly lit, shedding light on its subject. The shelves and tables were all littered with objects: rings, circlets, weapons, armor, shields, and more.

"These are all the magic items I have collected over the years. I want you each to pick one." He paused, then added, "Each of you pick any item you would like, and then each also pick a ring."

The companions were stunned. They had never seen such a collection of magically enchanted items. Not even the Order of Valor's Grandmaster Taulyen had an assortment this large. Sedarus could feel the power emanating from the room, and he knew that these weren't common items with minor enchantments. He could hardly believe that someone would so freely give away his magical possessions, especially since they were powerfully enchanted.

Sedarus and Haet opened their mouths to protest, but Lord Mayor Fodd held up his hand to silence them. "I insist."

Rishkiin wasn't about to be bashful. He went straight to the weapon rack. He saw a long sword glimmering in the light, and he just couldn't pass it. The fighter picked it up and test-swung it a couple of times. He swung, then he suddenly stopped and changed directions.

Satisfied, he said with a huge grin, "Found mine!"

"Ah! Glimmer, that one is called," the lord mayor replied with a genuine smile on his wrinkled face. "Good choice."

Rishkiin, still grinning, replaced his old sword with the magic one.

Aunddara walked through the room looking at various items. A jet-black chain shirt caught her eye. It was finely made, each chain ring intricately weaved, making penetration nearly impossible.

"I would like to have this, if that would be acceptable," Aunddara said even as she turned slightly red, embarrassed to ask for a gift.

"Of course, good lady, of course! No need to ask!" Lord Mayor Fodd chuckled.

Aunddara nodded in appreciation. She took the black chain shirt and went upstairs to change in private.

Haet passed the armor and blades. He espied a quarterstaff rod and approached it. It was four feet long. The oak wood was stained dark, and at the top of the staff was a statuette of a snake.

"That, my good monk, is the Rod of the Python. When you throw it to the ground, it turns into a huge constrictor snake, which follows only your directions. A valuable ally."

"I'll take it." Haet looked up the stairs, making sure that Aunddara was out of earshot. "Don't tell Aun that it turns into a snake."

"Why?" Lord Mayor Fodd raised his brow quizzically.

"She is absolutely terrified of snakes. She's going to pop a blood vessel when she finds out!" Rishkiin said, chortling slightly. He pictured the frightened expression that she would make. He swallowed hard with realization knowing how enraged she would become. He hoped that he wouldn't be within arm's reach when that happened. "Have you found anything, Sedarus? Rhamor?" called the young fighter, wanting to get off the subject of an angry Aunddara.

"Yeah, I like this cloak." As soon as Sedarus donned the cloak, he felt a surge of energy rush through him; once more he just knew that magic was about him. Wearing this cloak, he felt that his reflexes were quicker and his will was stronger.

Rhamor walked up and down the little aisles. Finally he stopped in front of a long sword. The holy knight was enthralled by its beauty and the detail of the crosspiece, which took the shape of a rearing dragon. He nearly jumped out of his skin when the lord mayor spoke right next to him.

"They say that the spirit of a paladin was captured and infused within that blade. They say that only a true paladin of Tinen can wield it." There was a pause, then, "Go on, my boy. Pick it up."

Rhamor slowly reached out his gauntleted hand and closed it around the gold-entwined hilt. A cool sensation ran from his palm all the way up his arm. Instantly Rhamor knew that the blade was made specifically for him.

A warm voice filtered inside his mind.

Well met, Rhamor Inthgar!

It startled the paladin, but he refrained from showing it. *Who are you?* Rhamor mentally asked.

Sir Markham, came the reply.

You were a paladin of Tinen? Like me?

Yes, and I shall help you through your trials. I have many properties about me that will come to you as aid.

With that Rhamor felt the cool sensation recede back into the sword.

"It suits you, Rhamor," Sedarus said. For it truly did: both blade and wielder looked every part of a holy knight.

"Well that just leaves the rings!" Lord Mayor Fodd said excitedly as Aunddara came back down the stairs. She was dressed in the jet-black chain shirt, along with her black leather breeches and high leather boots.

"This way." The man led them to a shelf that was littered with rings of all sorts of grandeur.

Rhamor was the first one to pick his ring. It was an unextraordinary band, but with an opal gem set in the center.

"That, my paladin friend, allows the wearer to walk on water." Lord Mayor Fodd smiled warmly as Rhamor slid off his gauntlet and put the ring on his right index finger.

Aunddara, Haet, and Sedarus picked up three separate rings, although they were of the same make. They slipped the plain gold bands onto their fingers.

"Those are rings of protection," the older man explained. "To some extent they act as invisible shields. Very good! Now your turn, young fighter."

Rishkiin curled his lip. "I don't like rings."

"May I suggest one?"

Rishkiin shrugged, not caring.

"In the old days, this ring was my favorite," the lord mayor said as he picked up a simple silver ring. He handed it to Rishkiin. "It lets the bearer turn invisible. Being invisible could be a great asset to a fighter of your repertoire."

A large grin spread across the young fighter's face as he remembered that he liked *some* rings. He hastily took it and placed in on his left forefinger.

He closed his eyes and disappeared.

Sedarus couldn't see his friend, but he could hear the clanking of his heavy plate boots. It would indeed be an asset in battle, Sedarus thought.

After a few moments of experimental fun, Rishkiin reappeared.

"Where were you all heading, if I may ask?" Lord Mayor Fodd inquired politely.

"We were heading for Anzzow," Rhamor stated, fiddling with the hilt of his new sentient sword.

"May I question why?"

"We are not supposed to speak of it," Aunddara cut short.

But Rishkiin said, "The grandmaster at the Temple of Valor stumbled upon a powerful object. He sent us to find out what it does and how to control it."

"Rish!" Aunddara snapped, trying not to look at Sedarus.

"What? This old man, no offense—"

"None taken," Fodd smiled widely.

"—Might know something, Aun. Look around you! You don't collect all these magic items without knowing a thing or two. And face it, we know nothing," Rishkiin finished, looking at Sedarus, who was meeting his gaze. Then the monk shrugged in agreement.

"What does this object do?" Lord Mayor Fodd asked.

"What we know so far is that it sends a sort of energy into an enemy, and then that person or thing literally explodes," Rishkiin explained.

"And it can tell if something is magically enchanted," Sedarus added. His companions looked at him wide-eyed with befuddlement but quickly changed their looks.

"Ah! I would really like to examine this object. Is it with you?"

Above all, Sedarus did not want to answer that, but he was bound by his code of honor not to lie.

Before he could reply, Rishkiin spoke. "I'm afraid not. Our grandmaster kept it at the temple."

Sedarus was about to refute that, but Aunddara elbowed him.

The old man nodded thoughtfully with a slight frown. "Is this object intelligent?"

"Well …" Rishkiin covertly looked at Sedarus, a sly smile forming at the edges of his mouth. "That is to be debated."

"Yes, it is very intelligent," Rhamor said, scowling at Rishkiin, who just smiled and shrugged. Sedarus smiled; he knew the insult was good natured, letting him know that his friends were still with him.

"Hmm." Long moments passed in silence. "Does this object have allegiance to a god?"

"Yes."

"Which one?"

"Tinen."

"Well, when you get to Anzzow, visit the Grand Library and the monks of Feldoor. Look for references on relics of the god of valor and courage."

"Why?"

"Well, from what you describe, I'd say that this object is god blessed."

Chapter Six

A figure stood on the edge of the thousand-foot drop. He seemed unaffected by fear, or if he was, he buried it masterfully. He gazed upon five figures setting up camp below and to the west, near a slow-moving river, he saw four men and one woman, all bickering over some insignificant issue.

"Typical humans. Tehehe!" the figure's melodic voice rang. The laughter was high, yet lovely, majestic.

The man's brow was adorned with an elaborate golden circlet. It matched flawlessly with his golden hair and peculiar irises. The shapes of his irises were that of an eagle's, which was why he could see the five companions so far below.

His black leather clothing was very tight, yet unbelievably comfortable, making it look as though his light, fair skin was in reality black. He wore ridiculously high boots that reached mid thigh, his leather pants tucked into them. He had no backpack, nothing to hold his personal items except a small belt pouch.

On his left hip was a rapier, on his right a dagger. He also had a hand crossbow, positioned not at his belt, as one would expect, but on his right shoulder. He had rigged a holster so that the hand piece was precisely next to his right ear, ready to be pulled out and fired in an instant.

His black, hooded cape with silver edging flapped in the strong wind. The bright-orange sun was shedding its last rays into the sky, painting a masterpiece of colors.

"Good one, Reth," the beautiful voice said, referring to the god of the sun. He had spoken as though Reth and he were old friends. The figure giggled, almost angrily, as the last glimmering spray of light flared.

In that last flare, the golden-haired man spotted something in the corner of his eagle-like eyes. Barely discernible movement drifted quickly toward the group.

"There!" the figure's high voice spoke to the wind. He focused his gaze on the movement. "Ogres!" He spat off the ledge in disgust. Then a smile appeared on his delicate face, flashing shiny, white teeth. Tinkling laughter erupted from his mouth once more.

His watchfulness switched rapidly back and forth between the five companions and the small band of ferocious ogres. The ogres' run started to turn north away from the group. A sigh of disappointment escaped from between his teeth.

But then a sudden, loud cackle burst from the lone silhouetted man upon the cliff edge; the band of ogres had suddenly curved back west. "The brutes smelled them! Tehehe!"

With a bow to Beth, the moon goddess, the figure stepped over the ledge.

"No, Aun! I won't give up the staff!"

Haet was more out of control than he had ever been in his twenty-four years of life. He held his Rod of the Python closely to his chest, protectively.

Earlier that day he had cast the rod to the ground, enabling its magic for the first time. It had rapidly grown into a twenty-five-foot constrictor snake. The monk used the snake to kill a doe, so that even while they were not within the luxury of an inn, they could still eat as if they were. Aunddara had not appreciated the trick.

Rishkiin laughed as he turned the spit above the fire. The flames licked the meat, cooking it.

"Hold your tongue, Rish!" Aunddara roared.

"Hey! I did not even speak," the fighter said, muffling a chortle. "I'm not even in this conflict, so leave me be."

The young man remembered the day, little more than a week ago, when Haet had received the rod, recalling that this scene was one he had predicted. He was relaxed on a fallen log, dagger in hand, occasionally twisting the spit.

Rhamor and Sedarus were in between Haet and Aunddara, physically blocking the woman from charging the monk with her mace. Rage mixed with a touch of fear mingled in the cleric's dazzling eyes.

"Break it! Burn it! I don't care, just destroy it!" Aunddara was past the point of exasperation. She began to hyperventilate, making herself dizzy.

Had Rhamor not been near, she would have collapsed. "Aun, you are overreacting! Now just calm down," he said. "Haet is in total control of the snake."

"Aunddara," Haet's voice was calm, under control once more, "I would never allow it to bring you harm. You are my sister, in spirit if not blood."

The cleric nodded, looking down at her black leather pants. "I know, Haet," she said, letting one tear run for dramatic effect. She looked into the monk's eyes. "It's just that I'm so terrified of those … monsters!" she spat in disgust.

"I know, and I am sorry. But I am keeping the rod."

A silent, awkward moment passed. Everyone felt it but Rishkiin. "Dinner's ready!" he said in a laughing tone.

The group turned and faced the young fighter somberly, but no one said anything. All but Rishkiin were cheerless as they ate dinner.

The firelight was welcoming, as was its heat. The moon shone brightly, happily at the chance to shed its radiance, to show its glory.

"I'll take first watch," Aunddara said. "I won't be able to sleep anyway." Her gaze shot daggers at Haet. She stalked off into the night, her magical, jet-black chain shirt allowing her to fade away in silence.

"I fear she will not forgive me," Haet said to Sedarus as they unrolled their beddings.

"She will, in time." Sedarus's voice was confident. "Before long, she will find out that the things in life that are truly golden are your friends. Aunddara is smart and able to admit her mistakes. She will forgive you."

Haet let that soak into his mind before praying for guidance and forgiveness. Then he fell asleep.

❦

As the man fell freely from the cliff edge, he grinned excitedly. When he was within one hundred feet of squashing against the ground, the dark figure touched the feather-shaped brooch holding his cape together with both his forefingers. Instantly, his fall slowed to that of a leisurely falling feather. He hardly touched the ground before he rushed off, making less noise than an earthworm.

He raced off through the woods in a westerly direction, never losing his way. His straight line to the ogres brought him close to the perimeter of the companions' camp, their fire a beacon to all creatures for miles around.

Yet Aunddara, on watch, never caught a glimpse of him, never heard a whisper. The man scrutinized her for many moments before continuing on his way.

The ogres were not that difficult to find. They were large, lumbering creatures with no skill in the art of shadow. They were gathering near a crowd of trees. Most of the nine-foot-tall monsters were silent, but a few were arguing in the giants' tongue. Luckily, the figure spoke giant.

"We go and smash!" one growled.

"Then we eat!" another put in with a toothy grin.

"No! They be powerful!" the largest of the ogres said. It was the only one that had jet-black teeth and claws, its pupils stark white. Two curved horns protruded from its brow.

An ogre mage, the hidden figure mentally lamented. It was a very dangerous monster. He would have to change his tactics. An intelligent ogre with magic was something few survived.

The thought brought a silent laugh. Of course he was still going to kill some, if not all of the ogres. It would be just too much fun to pass up. There were only eight of the brutes, counting the mage. Besides, he thought, three of the brutes were acting as guards! Easy killing!

He drew his thin rapier from his hip, the sword quietly crackling in the air—not due to intense heat, but extreme cold. The blade was coated with magical frost. Picturing himself right behind one of the three ogre sentinels, he instantly appeared there, at the back of a particularly fat ogre, thanks to the magical properties of the ring on his left middle finger.

The brute heaved a great breath, oblivious to the dark figure behind it. It scratched its head, moving the wild mane it sported.

The dark figure gave a silent, "Tehehe!" Then he leapt, slashing left to right.

A yell became a grunt as the frost blade entered the side of the ogre's neck and reappeared on the other side, the flat of the blade blocking the brute's windpipe. The two tumbled to the ground with nary a sound but a slap of the huge body hitting the earth.

The figure was already running again moments later, his next victim in sight. His booted feet barely touched the ground with each stride. The dull ogre never saw him coming; it only heard its own grunt of pain. A freezing cold blade had punctured the back of its neck.

"Tehehe!" the man laughed quietly again as he pictured himself behind the third and last of the ogre guards. He opened his eyes, not surprised that the ogre stood before him. His boots slapped against the dirt, not even leaving a footprint. Yet luck was with the ogre. It turned and saw the running man.

That was where the ogre's luck ran out. A frozen, blue flame erupted from the blade. The ogre's throat was cut, frost burn covering its neck. It fell to its knees, both hands clutching at its slit windpipe. The brute fell over, dead.

"Tehehe!" the tall, thin man laughed uproariously now. He proceeded to sheath his magical sword. He turned almost completely around in some sort of wild dance as he made his way to the gathering of ogres. Silently, boldly, he walked into the middle of the still-arguing brutes.

Silence enveloped the stunned monsters. They knew not what to think or what to do.

The lithe man said one word in perfect giant tongue, a wide grin spread on his delicate features.

"Greetings."

Chapter Seven

"I see that your band is heading west," the dark figure said, unperturbed by the fact that he was surrounded by ogres. He ignored the gaping, drooling brutes and stared straight at the ogre mage, the leader.

"It wouldn't happen to be because of that flaring campfire, would it?" he continued with perfect inflection of the grunting language. No answer. "Of course it is, tehehe! But of course, that is a problem, my very large friend," he said, his friendly visage suddenly changing into an uncharacteristic scowl. "Leave them be! They are mine and my ... master's."

He winced slightly as he said that final word. He believed he had no master, but on occasion he found himself being ordered around.

Sense of what the figure was saying finally hit the monster leader. The ogre mage roared two words: "Kill him!"

The minion ogres started the charge, and a smile replaced the scowl on the dark figure's angular face. He stood still, not looking from the ogre mage as he began to giggle maniacally. At the last possible moment, he quickly drew out his hand crossbow and fired. His aim was true, the bolt flaring in the night sky as it hit the ogre mage square in the left cheek. The magical crossbow had infused the small dart with fiery power.

The ogre mage roared in pain, its huge hands coming up to cover its seared face. Within seconds it started to convulse as electricity coursed through its veins.

One of the wart-covered brutes swung its great club, but the man was gone in a flash. He backpedaled, eying the attacking ogres the whole time. With amazing skill, the man loaded another bolt and cranked back on his hand crossbow. Perfect aim guided the bolt to one of the monsters, hitting it in the fat neck. It dropped its javelin and clutched at its searing throat. The fur-covered ogre died and then convulsed with electricity even after.

The man placed the crossbow back in the holster and drew his rapier and dagger just in time to deflect a thrown spear. Now the first ogre to charge was coming in fast; the figure swung his frosted rapier, though he missed the brute completely. He stabbed with his dagger, which was glowing ocean green. The slightly curved blade entered the ogre's gut.

The retraction was quicker than the actual attack. The dark figure was hard-pressed, with two ogres on him and another one coming. Deflecting a jab from a spear, he had no time to dodge a great club. It clipped him in the hip and flung him backward.

With amazing agility, the dark figure stayed on his feet, limping slightly. He blocked the pain from his mind and stood his ground as the three ogres charged. The two ogres in front reached him at the same time.

He leapt up. He slashed with his frosted sword, cutting a thin line across the throat of the ogre he had stabbed earlier. So thin was the cut that he feared for a second that he'd missed. Then the brute fell to the ground, gurgling in its life's blood.

With his glowing, ocean-green dagger, he stabbed deeply into the second ogre's armpit, severing a nerve. That arm became limp, useless at its side. A confused look covered the ogre's face as its arm stayed stationary, despite its exerting every ounce of energy. "Tehehe!" was the last thing the brute heard before the dark figure punctured its windpipe.

The smiling man turned and faced the last ogre. It had its javelin raised as if it were going to throw it. Yet the stupid, scared look on its face told the man that the spear would not fly. Instead the ogre dropped the wooden spear, turned tail, and ran.

"Tehehe!" went the lithe man's laughter again. With a ferocious throw of the still-glowing dagger, the figure watched as the blade twirled through the air then entered the ogre's spine. The brute yelped in pain as it fell to its knees, arching its back.

"Perfect!" the grinning figure said to himself, cackling still more. He then pictured himself right in front of the arching ogre and was there, in close range to the exposed throat.

The ogre's expression was one of sheer surprise, bringing out another cackle as the dark figure's frosted blade stabbed into the stunned ogre's heart. He pulled his sword free; it was unblemished, not a drop of blood on it.

Or maybe there is blood, he thought. It just freezes. That notion brought one more mad giggle.

With a grunt, the figure was able to roll the dead brute over and retrieve his dagger. His face crumpled in disgust when he saw the gooey, black blood that sullied his glowing blade. He wiped the blade clean on the ogre's russet brown skin and then returned both his blades to their sheaths in one quick motion.

A moan from behind caused the man to turn about. The ogre mage was trying to crawl away, its eyes scorched shut. A loud burst of laughter emanated from the figure. He stalked over, his limp barely slowing his light gait. He gazed down at his wounded hip and said, "Oh! I need to fix you."

Surprisingly, he then started to sing. Wisps of blue began to intricately weave around his body. He felt his hip mend, pain fading instantly. When the blue wisps had done their job, the dark figure ceased to sing. The wisps had even mended his torn leather pants.

With that business concluded, he looked back at the defeated ogre mage. It had given up on crawling away. The brute lay there helplessly, accepting its fate. The dark figure kicked it in its ribs.

The ogre mage rolled to its back and started to cast a spell, one that would turn it into a gaseous form and allow it to escape, but it was hindered by a blade pushing up against its throat.

"Should I push my blade further? Or are you going to stop?" the man asked, pushing the glowing dagger a little deeper to the brute's throat.

The ogre mage had already stopped casting. "Now, I can't help but blame *you* for all this blood and destruction," the figure said in giant tongue.

"Me? How?"

"Well, I did say, 'Leave them be!' but you didn't listen. *You* insisted on trying to kill *me*! Tehehe!" Then the figure's face became a scowl. "As I told you before, my master has plans for these humans." A smile quickly replaced the scowl again. "But you won't be able to see any of that! Tehehe! Of course, you *can't* see."

"You black demon!"

"Black demon?" The dark figure's mouth curled in a frown. Then, as always, it lit up once more. "Yes, I am the Black Demon!" the figure laughed exultantly.

"Leave me be!" the ogre mage growled almost incoherently.

"It is such a vicious world out here in the wild. How long would you last, I wonder? A week? A month? Nay! Not even a day. It'd be so much more merciful if I slew you here and now!"

The figure didn't even wait for the ogre mage to register the threat. He slit the creature's throat ear to ear with one swift swipe.

He stood up, saying with a sigh, "Ugh! This is such a dirty business." Then the smile that could never be away from his face for too long reappeared. "And it is too much fun! *Tehehe*!"

"Rhamor!" Aunddara shook the holy knight.

He woke up instantly, his hand going for his blade. He stood up, his sentient blade welcoming his touch. "What is it, Aun?"

"I hear fighting."

"Where?"

"To the east," Aunddara said, pointing.

"Well," Rhamor said, thinking quickly. "Rish and I will go check it out. Rish!"

"Wha'? Go away!" the young fighter said, moaning. He rolled over on his bedroll.

"Fight!" the paladin bellowed in the fighter's ear.

Instantly Rishkiin was fumbling for his helmet, jamming it on his head and fishing his sword, Glimmer, free from its sheath.

The two monks were already on their feet and ready for battle. They exchanged quizzical looks and then stepped up beside Aunddara.

"Where is it?" Rishkiin asked excitedly.

"We are going to find it," Rhamor replied.

"Rhamor," Rishkiin said, smiling, "I never knew you had it in you!"

"We are going to *find out* what's going on, not *start* a fight."

"Oh." Rishkiin shrugged.

"What's happening?" Sedarus questioned.

"Aun's heard some fighting; Rish and I are going to check it out," Rhamor explained.

"We're coming, too," Haet said, grabbing his Rod of the Python.

"Well I'm not staying here all by myself," Aunddara said. "Plus, if there *is* a fight, you'll need me."

"Fine. Let's pack up camp quickly. Douse the fire, Sed."

The makeshift campground quickly reverted to nature. They were on the move within five minutes. The group went directly east, straight for the battle clamor, using only the bright moon as light. Then all of a sudden, the noise ceased. That unnerved them, enough so that Rishkiin pulled Glimmer from its sheath. They were all startled to see that Glimmer had begun to glow a fiery orange.

"Douse it, Rish!" Rhamor said quietly but urgently.

"I don't know how!" the alarmed young fighter barked.

"Command it to dim the light!" Sedarus hissed from the front of the line.

Rishkiin closed his eyes as he asked Glimmer to dim the glow. From his friends' sighs of relief, he could tell that it worked. Opening his brown orbs, he saw that Glimmer's thin edge was now the only thing glowing. It was perfect, shedding enough light so he wouldn't trip over exposed roots, but not enough light for enemies to be able to see him from afar.

"Okay, let's go," Sedarus said as he turned to lead the way again.

The Black Demon saw the flare of light through the trees. He smiled as it dimmed, a snicker coming from his teeth. He knew what to do. They were coming for him. Well, not for him, but to investigate. They would find the copse filled with dead ogres.

He clicked the heels of his outrageously high boots together and then started to feel lighter with each passing second. When he couldn't get any lighter, he started to levitate. Up he went, forty feet to the tallest branch of a nearby pine tree. He reached out his arm and anchored himself to that branch. When his levitation effect wore off, he landed on the branch.

It was just then that the group entered the area of carnage. The Black Demon had to cover his mouth lest a loud chortle of delight give him away.

"What happened here?" Aunddara asked to no one in particular, stating what they all were thinking. "What force lays down eight ogres, including an ogre mage, in that short time span?" the cleric continued.

"I don't know," Rhamor stated. "Whatever did this is formidable."

"Whoever, you mean," Sedarus corrected.

"What?"

"These are sword slashes, not claw tears," the monk explained, pointing out a perfect cut mark on one body.

As the rest of his companions examined the cut, Sedarus stood up straight. Something assailed him, a feeling that he was being watched. He quickly snapped his gaze to the tall tree branches. He saw nothing, but he was positive that whoever had killed the monsters was still there, watching them.

Sedarus was about to suggest moving on when Haet called out, "This one lives!"

Sedarus rushed over to his fellow monk.

"It's saying something that I can't understand," Haet said, looking pointedly at Sedarus as their companions joined them.

Being able to speak some the giant tongue, Sedarus leaned close, listening carefully, intensely.

"What is it saying, Sed?" Rishkiin asked impatiently. He wanted to find something to kill with his new sword.

There was a pause, then Sedarus's face blanched.

"The Black Demon."

Chapter Eight

"The Black Demon?" Rishkiin asked, composed.

"Yes," Sedarus said as the ogre gasped its last breath. "That is what it said."

"I don't like the sound of that," Aunddara said, looking over her shoulder as if a bat-winged demon would attack her right then and there.

"Oh, it's just a demon," Rishkiin said, smiling and cocky.

"You've never seen a demon!" Aunddara exclaimed as she shuddered in memory. "You can't know the pure evil that rules their very existence."

"Bah!" The impudent young fighter stomped off.

Still feeling like someone was watching them, Sedarus spoke. "We should move on, and now."

"I agree," Rhamor said. "We are only a day from the next town. Aun, your shield. Rish, light Glimmer brightly. If we run into a monster of the dark, let's face it on our terms."

The cleric instantly lit her shield, the mark of Tinen flaring brightly. Rishkiin willed Glimmer to shine with all its brilliance. His sword lit like a torch. The fighter grinned.

Yet Rhamor and his blade put them to shame. His sentient blade began to shine with the purest white light. It nearly blinded the paladin when it first illuminated.

"Looks like your sword has some tricks also," Rishkiin said, slightly angered that Rhamor's blade shone brighter than his.

He has no idea! His is a little twig compared to me, came the telepathic snort.

61

Rhamor laughed. Everyone looked at him, confused at why he would laugh at Rishkiin's comment. He just shrugged and led them north.

Sedarus quietly thought back upon the day when Rhamor had received the sword. He remembered that the lord mayor had said the soul of a holy knight was infused into the blade. The monk suspected it was a genuine conclusion.

The Black Demon watched as Sedarus snapped his gaze upward. His eyes caught the monk's momentarily, and he feared that he had been seen. Then Sedarus's stare filtered to all of the tall branches in the surrounding vicinity.

He didn't see me, The Black Demon thought. *Or did he, and looking at the other trees is just a ruse?* He laughed in his mind. He did not know, nor did he care. As long as the monk made no move against him, he would play along as if he had not been seen. At that moment, he overheard that there was one ogre still alive.

Anger at himself that he had let one live suddenly changed to joy and a big smile when he overheard the name "The Black Demon." Fear shone in all but Rishkiin's eyes.

"I like him, tehehe! He's got a fighter's spirit," the Black Demon whispered to himself. He was almost constantly muttering to himself aloud. Spending so much time alone, he had no one else to speak to. He preferred it that way.

The group started to move on, and he followed slowly, going from tree to tree. He soon was left behind. Then he pictured himself behind Rishkiin, who was the group's rearguard.

The Black Demon was within a foot of the man. Instantly, he clicked his heels, and his ludicrous boots lifted him into the sky. It was a good thing, too, for right then Sedarus whipped about.

The others threw curious glances at the monk, but none as curious as the Black Demon's. Could the monk feel when he initiated his magic items? The answer was one that he feared.

He had to know, whichever the answer may be. The Black Demon fetched an item from his belt—a diamond in the shape of a sphere attached to a string. The dark figure aimed it at Sedarus and lightly blew on it, sending it spinning wildly.

Instantly the Black Demon knew that Sedarus had three magic items of his own on his person. None of them, this diamond told him, would bestow him with knowledge of a magic item being used. Yet just then, the monk turned and faced him again. After a moment, Sedarus turned back, not being able to see the magnificently hidden man.

For only the third time in his entire life, the Black Demon did not feel like smiling.

"What is it, Sed?" Rhamor quietly asked.

"We are being followed," Sedarus concluded from his inklings. He started forward once more.

"By the Black Demon?" the paladin asked so that only Sedarus could hear.

"I would say so, but whatever it is, it's not a demon. It's using magic items," the monk whispered.

"How can you know that?" Rhamor did not want to doubt his friend, yet he found it difficult to believe that Sedarus could know that whatever was tailing them was using magical objects.

"I can feel it tug on my soul when he or she uses them. I feel it when you speak with your sword, when Rishkiin lights Glimmer, when Aunddara lights her shield." Sedarus added with hint of annoyance, "They all tug at me. The more powerful the item is, the greater the pull. I've been feeling this ever since we left the lord mayor's house."

Rhamor didn't speak; he just stared at his friend. He knew Sedarus was becoming something powerful, yet so far that power had proven uncontrollable.

"So now you can blow things up—" Sedarus's brow scrunched into a scowl, but Rhamor continued, "—and you can sense when there is a magic item around, and you can sense when it is being used?"

"That sums it up," Sedarus curtly stated.

Silence encompassed them. Then the holy knight spoke once more. "You need to control your power."

"I don't want to control it! I want it gone; I want it the way it used to be," Sedarus barked.

Rhamor didn't back down. "It will never be the same, Sed! You have to deal with that." A sigh came from his bearded lips. "I apologize, but *we* need you to control it."

Sedarus nodded. "I'm sorry I snapped at you."

"I know, Sed."

"I'm frightened of it, though," Sedarus admitted.

"I am too."

That caused Sedarus to turn around. The whole group stopped, although the three following behind still did not know what was going on.

"I am too," Rhamor said again. "But let us cast that fear into a harness, be in command of it!" His fervent voice rang through Sedarus's soul, and the monk knew that what his friend said was true.

"Okay, Rhamor," Sedarus said with trembling sigh.

"What's going on?" Aunddara asked, her voice coated in worry.

"Nothing," Rhamor said, not looking from Sedarus. "Let's get going again."

Hours passed in silence, and the sun began to rise, its yellow-orange beams shooting forth, happy to be cherished once more. When the sun was fully in the sky, Rhamor called for a halt for breakfast.

Rishkiin grumbled in his hunger as he rummaged through his pack for the smoked meat that they had prepared the night before. The fighter handed out the food.

"Here, Sed," Rishkiin said as he came close to the monk, but Sedarus was deep in contemplation. He was sitting with his legs crossed and his hands resting on his knees, palms up. His eyes were shut tight.

He could feel the power deep within his core. Yet he did not immediately grasp at it. He hesitated; calling forth the energy and controlling it was a must, he knew. Yet actually doing so was difficult.

Finally, holding his breath, he grasped the destructive energy and brought it to his hands. They started to convulse as he tried to control the wild power.

"Sed!" Rishkiin yelped, jumping backward, dropping the meat.

The yell made all his companions aware of Sedarus, even though the monk was not conscious of them. He was flickering with an intense blue color.

Suddenly, triumphantly, Sedarus stood and forced the energy from him into a fallen log nearby. The blue energy wove its way into the log, and then the log exploded. The shattered log sent shards of wood in every direction.

Sedarus shook himself back to the present and found, like the last time he'd used the power, that he was the only one remaining on his feet. He quickly raced to pick up his friends. They all accepted his help—all but Rishkiin.

"You ... monk of ..." Rishkiin trembled with rage, stuttering to find the right word, not wanting to insult someone who could destroy things with but a thought.

"... You destroyed my log! I was going to sit on that!" Rishkiin gave up on name calling, settling on laying blame.

"I'm sorry," Sedarus said, but he had a hard time not laughing.

"Sorry?" the fighter's now-wild goatee quivered with utmost rage. "Sorry you destroyed my food and my seat? Or that you sent about a thousand slivers up my bum?"

"The former," Sedarus said with a childish grin, the first grin from him in a long time.

"Well, why in the Abyss did you do it?" Rishkiin asked, his anger fading with each second Sedarus grinned at him.

"Well, I thought that you would like to walk your horse," the monk stated, his face straight once more.

"No, I wouldn't! I'm not a bloody monk who likes to have my feet ache," Rishkiin snarled.

"Nor are you a monk who can kill a giant with a thought," Rhamor said. "So be silent and sit down so we can eat."

Rishkiin's face turned stark red. He muttered under his breath, "Easy for you to say, you rotten ogre fart. *You* don't have a thousand slivers in *your* butt!"

Only Sedarus could hear that, and he held a chuckle as he started to eat a piece of venison.

The Black Demon's breath had been completely knocked out of him. He was honestly surprised that he hadn't fallen from his perch high in the tree. He had witnessed Sedarus sit in meditation. Then the monk had started to glow blue, and his already-corded muscles seemed to bulge. When Sedarus released the energy, the Black Demon was physically blown back.

No laughter was forthcoming.

He did not know what to think, except that he had been mistaken in taking this job. Although, he thought, even this job was better than the alternative, which happened to end with his painful death.

"You controlled it!" Rhamor whooped in delight after they had eaten breakfast and were examining the destroyed log.

Sedarus went slightly red. "Not completely. I was aiming for the tree over there," he said, pointing to a fat pine.

"You have to aim this power? A power that comes from your head?"

"Not from my head," Sedarus corrected the paladin. "From the center of my body. And I aim with my hands when I force the energy away."

"Wait, wait," Rishkiin said, startled. "You mean you almost killed me?"

Sedarus went redder, yet his gaze never wavered from that of his friend's. "I would have never let harm come to you."

Rishkiin felt like arguing but decided it wise to let it drop. He sat down, wincing with pain. The fighter leaned slightly to the left and rubbed his buttocks. "We need to work on your aiming, then," he muttered heatedly.

"Should he practice on you?" Aunddara raged toward the young fighter.

"No, I was just saying that he needs practice," Rishkiin retorted. "Let him use trees or logs that are not near us!"

"Or maybe he could force some energy into your thick head!"

"Then my head would be gone!"

"At least you wouldn't have so much air in it!" the cleric badgered further.

"Oi!" Sedarus berated Aunddara and Rishkiin. "I will find a way to practice away from you."

"You don't have to," Rishkiin said, grinning. "I actually want to watch. But I want to know when you are going to make things explode. That way I can stand *behind* you."

"Then what was with all your yelling at him?" Rhamor's deep voice was filled with irritation.

The fighter shrugged.

"Well, will you hold your tongue then?" Rhamor said, exasperated. "I mean, by the Abyss!"

Silence fell over the group until Haet broke it a minute later. "Sed, come stand near me. Everyone else, get out of the way," the monk advised.

The others did.

"Aim at those three trees." Haet pointed toward three small saplings set in a row. "Just go down the line."

"Okay, I'll try."

Sedarus closed his eyes. He felt the flow of power within him. He reached in and grabbed at it. It came to his bidding. Then, with an outstretched hand, Sedarus pushed the force out. The blue energy flew from him, but it did not hit the first sapling—or any of the others. The power was absorbed into a larger tree behind the saplings, having a similar effect as with the log.

"That wasn't even close," Rishkiin mumbled from the ground.

Aunddara's eyes shot daggers at the fighter.

As he picked himself up from the ground, and the others did the same,

Rishkiin stated, "I'll stand back about … forty feet." So he left, closely followed by Aunddara and Rhamor.

"Don't think of your power as a weapon," Haet advised. "As Grandmaster Taulyen says regarding the martial arts, they are a defense, not an attack. This power is a defensive maneuver for you and your friends. Now, harness it!"

With that, Haet stepped backward a pace, allowing Sedarus the space needed to concentrate. Once more, Sedarus delved deeply, but this time he had a different attitude toward the energy. Now it didn't seem as wild or uncontrollable.

Once more he started to glow blue, and then he pressed the power from his core into the heart of the first sapling. It exploded, and when the explosion was complete, there were not even pine needles left.

Sedarus heard the distant cheer of congratulations, and he was already at the flow of power, in the core of his body and soul, ready for the second shot. The next tree disappeared in an explosion.

"Well done, Sed!" Haet shouted with elation from the ground. He hadn't even picked himself up from the last blast. "Now try and contain the explosion to only a certain limb."

Sedarus did just that, focusing. While he couldn't contain the explosion to one limb, this time only half of the sapling vanished.

After half an hour of rest, the group started out once more. Sedarus was immensely more confident in his mysterious abilities, even though their practice had left him extremely exhausted.

Chapter Nine

Supported by Rhamor and Aunddara, Sedarus stumbled through the wooden door. His eyes were half closed, and large bags of weariness had formed beneath his ice-blue orbs. They had stopped to practice again just a few miles outside of the town. He had used all of his energy.

The establishment they entered was well kept. It had clean tables— well, somewhat clean, now that half the night was gone and patrons had been eating and drinking. A fire roared inside an ornate stone fireplace. The circular common room was well lit, packed with laughing patrons, and filled with delicious-smelling food. Feelings of welcome instantly overcame the companions. All but Sedarus, who wasn't feeling anything but fatigue.

"Not stricken with the plague, is he?" the innkeeper asked over the jovial clamor. Rhamor shook his head. "Bring him over here then, near the fire."

The innkeeper motioned for the companions to follow him to a recently cleared table. The man was quite young for a tavern owner. He was tall and exceptionally well built for a man who took food orders all day.

"Thank you, sir," Rhamor said to the man as soon as he and Aunddara deposited the exhausted monk.

"Of course, first round of ale is on the house for followers of Tinen," the innkeeper said, looking at Aunddara's shield, featuring the roaring dragon of Tinen. He then showed them his signet ring. It was of that same symbol of the god of valor and courage.

Rishkiin whooped with joy, instantly the innkeeper's new best friend. The young fighter pulled up a chair next to the muddled Sedarus.

The innkeeper motioned for the serving girl, who came over with a tray of mugs foaming with frothy ale. Rishkiin licked his lips in anticipation. As the serving girl left, she gave the young fighter a wink. He didn't notice, though, and she left with a glower. Rishkiin's gaze was only for the golden mead. After a hearty draught that left froth on his goatee, Rishkiin patted the innkeeper on the back, who smiled. The innkeeper talked pleasantries with the group for a little while, and then he left, promising hot potato soup with venison.

The inn noise quieted somewhat when a lute player started to strum a melody and sing. None of the companions paid attention to the bard, each impatiently waiting for food.

Within minutes the innkeeper returned with the food and another round of ale. He let them eat in peace. Sedarus took a few bites and one swig of the potent drink before he fell asleep. His head slumped to the side, resting on Aunddara's shoulder. She seemed not to mind.

"What is wrong with him?" the innkeeper asked when he came back a bit later. "He's not a wizard, is he?" The question was wrought with suspicion.

"No, good sir," Rhamor said.

The innkeeper nodded, grabbed Sedarus's unfinished mug of ale, and started swigging it. "Where are you coming from?" he then asked as if they were all old friends.

"From the Temple of Valor, down south," Rishkiin said, taking another draught of ale.

The innkeeper nodded knowingly. "Velin or Quwe?" he asked, referring to two very large cities, each sporting a Temple of Valor. Both of the cities had many thousands of people residing within the gates, and were renowned for being hubs of commerce.

"Quwe, several weeks south of here," Rhamor said, yawning.

It was late in the evening; darkness had already taken over the sky. The companions would have made good time had Sedarus not stopped every hour or so to practice controlling the power within him. Each time he used his powers, he had been left fatigued, yet he always recovered quickly. But this last time had taken more out of him, leaving him overly weary.

He had become fairly adept. He could now force energy into a sapling's core, making it explode with destructive power, destroying all but a single pine needle. Or he would push energy into one pine needle and force that single needle to explode. The strength of the blast would still knock over the sapling, but the tree would remain intact.

But the power had taken his physical liveliness. It left him wasted and worn out, with barely enough strength to breathe. The last two miles of the journey had consisted of Rhamor and Aunddara half carrying, half dragging the monk.

Now he was sleeping peacefully and soundly. His breathing wasn't labored or disturbed by revolting memories. If a dragon attacked the inn, he would sleep through it.

"I've been there on occasion. Good city," the innkeeper added, keeping up the conversation.

The companions nodded in agreement.

"He looks just as drained as a wizard after they cast spells. I once knew a mage who had summoned a demon, which then escaped his control. The wizard had to destroy the demon. Afterward the wizard looked like your friend." The innkeeper continued. He had the serving girl bring over more mead.

The patrons of the inn started to filter out, most of them stumbling and laughing in inebriation. By the time the tray of ale mugs reached the companions' table, only a handful of other people were still sitting at the inn's tables. Most of them were passed out in their chairs. One of the men, a shadowy figure with golden hair, was smiling and staring at the companions. Yet they failed to notice, as none of them were looking too terribly hard.

"Do you know anything of someone who calls himself the Black Demon?" Aunddara asked suddenly, soft tunes from the lute player floating in the air.

A drunken man who overheard the question raced to the door, shouting wildly, "The Black Demon! He's coming! Flee, fly, get out of here—"

Then the man passed out cold, lying at the inn's threshold. Someone opened the door and left in a hurry, the door swinging shut on the drunk's head. He did not notice. Shortly after, the companions heard screams and shouts, all about the Black Demon's coming, ringing through the tranquil air.

The innkeeper sighed and said, "No, but I'm sure I will tomorrow. Rumors will be flying wildly. People will be swearing that they have had sightings of this Black Demon by the morning."

"Sorry," Aunddara said, flustered and flushed.

"Meh," the innkeeper said, shrugging. "All in a day's work," he continued, smiling.

A long moment of silence followed, accompanied only by the crackling of the fire, the snoring of passed-out men, and occasional sips of ale. Rhamor broke it by saying, "We would like three rooms for the night, sir."

"Of course." The innkeeper motioned for the serving girl to prepare the rooms. "Breakfast also?"

Rishkiin nodded, intoxicated with many glasses of ale. He fought to get to his feet, and only with help from Rhamor could he make it up the stairs to their room.

"Sedarus," Aunddara said quietly. "Wake up! We need to get you to your room." She stretched out her hand to shake Sedarus awake, but Haet stopped her.

"You better let me," the monk said. "You will want to back up."

As he was speaking, he rested his Rod of the Python against the wall. Aunddara did as the monk suggested. The curious innkeeper stood up and moved next to Aunddara.

Haet shook Sedarus, who leapt into motion, his fists swinging in powerful jabs. Haet had expected this, knowing that Sedarus would start to defend himself as if under a surprise attack, as Haet would do himself. He swatted away the blows, which were meant to stun. The fierce attack went on for many seconds before Sedarus realized that he was fighting with one of his own order.

Sedarus halted, embarrassed. "I apologize," he said, exhaustion once more taking hold of his body.

"I was unharmed. I thought you would react in that way," Haet said.

"That was amazing!" the innkeeper roared. "The best hand-to-hand fighting I've seen in years!"

Now both monks looked embarrassed. Haet had not meant to put on a show, but it seemed that was exactly what he had done. The remaining patrons who were still somewhat sober were drooling, wide-eyed.

Sedarus, Haet, and Aunddara marched up the stairs. The cleric's room was the first on the right, and the monks' room was four down.

The two monks entered the cozy room. It sported two straw beds with hand-sewn sheets. Sedarus collapsed on his bed, instantly asleep. Haet went about his normal rituals before he began his slumber.

Sedarus suddenly awoke. The room was silent, tranquil. He looked over to where Haet should have been, but his friend was missing. Worry instantly took him over, his chest tightening in fear.

"Concern yourself not with Haet, my son."

The voice was strong, yet warm. Sedarus trembled in reverence of the voice he would know anywhere. The monk instantly fell to his knees, bowing his head deeply, his chin to his chest.

"Please, stand up and face me," Tinen said.

Sedarus was not about to deny his god. The monk rose to his feet. He raised his gaze, and his heart was pierced by awe.

The form of a magnificent man stood before him. The figure was Rhamor's height, with the same bear-like build. Yet this being was mightier, far greater than any mortal could ever be. He was adorned with brilliantly shining silver armor. His strength was courage; his power was valor.

"Sedarus, my son, I have been waiting a long time for this."

Sedarus remained silent, unconsciously lowering his gaze. His body shook with the glory emanating from Tinen.

"Look at me, my son." Tinen's voice was calm, filled with love.

Sedarus did so.

"You have done well so far on your journey," Tinen spoke, "but you will need help for what is to come."

"What will I be facing, my lord?" Sedarus could barely muster a whisper.

"Do not address me as such. Rather, call me Father."

"What am I to face, Father?" Sedarus had composed his voice, though he felt as if his insides had been obliterated.

"Your greatest challenge, my son, which is why I am sending you the guardian," Tinen said. The deity turned to leave, fading slightly with each passing second.

"How will I know who this guardian is, Father?" Sedarus called to his god.

"You will know," was the simple reply as he faded away.

Chapter Ten

The Black Demon saw the companions enter the inn and gritted his teeth. He knew that he would never be able to follow there without being seen.

Then he smiled. "Tehehe! You don't know what I look like, do you?" he asked them rhetorically and from a distance. With a cheerful gait, the dark figure stepped out of the shadowed trees and onto the well-used dirt road. His golden hair, with a thin braid on each side of his head, clasped at his crown, was down, covering his ears and falling to mid shoulder.

He paused before continuing and reached into his pouch of holding. It was small in outward appearance—just the size of his fist—but it magically contained all of his personal items. He pulled out a large lute, its wooden face stained a rusty red color. Its strings were pulled tight and were tuned masterfully to produce perfect sounds.

The Black Demon started to pluck at the strings, playing a wonderful-sounding melody. He started to walk as he played, never missing a step. Then he began to sing also as he played, his beautiful, melodic voice harmonizing with the song flawlessly.

"Your mother's an ogre, and really not fine. I thought I was drinking ale, but it was wine. I never had the chance to digest my food, and when she started stripping, I just spewed!"

Passersby gave many different reactions to his song. Most of the men grinned, while the women curled their lips in disgust. One admiring man even flipped him a silver coin. With amazing dexterity, the Black Demon caught the coin with his still plucking fingers, never missing a beat. He grinned at the passing man, offering a little bow, and then continued on with the song.

As he reached the inn's door, he opened it and began strumming a different song, one that was smooth and would inspire tears. The Black Demon started to sing tenderly. Instantly the girls turned, their faces brightened by the song.

He made his way to a seat on the opposite side of the inn, swallowed by shadows, where he sat down, still playing and singing. The Black Demon smiled at the women, old and young. The charismatic figure received the fluttering of eyes and the blushing of cheeks in return.

His song told of two lovers. The young woman was betrothed to someone else. The two made plans to run away and live with naught but their love. Yet the girl's father tracked them down and took her back home. Her lover came to rescue her but was slain by her father.

Near the conclusion, the girls in the tavern were weeping, almost violently so, holding onto their lovers with affection renewed. The men, who had been frowning at the beginning, were now grinning at the shadowy figure playing before them.

The Black Demon returned the grins and ended the song. He was offered ale, food, and invitations to join several tables. He accepted the first two but graciously declined the latter. The Black Demon had business to attend to.

People paid him less attention as he started to strum on the lute once more. It was as if he magically slid back into the shadows. He sang not at all, but he watched his marks intensely. His gaze never left the companions, who were drinking and eating with the innkeeper.

"Interesting," the shadowy figure said quietly to himself. He watched as Aunddara stared at the monk resting on her shoulder. She patted his arm, but Sedarus could not notice, as he was deep in slumber. The playing figure saw the intensity in her eyes as the cleric watched the monk. He saw the love, love beyond that of just friends.

The dark figure laughed his trademark laugh, but lightly. Things had just gotten a lot more interesting.

"Ah, love!" he said to his lute. "But is it one-way or two? Tehehe! Of course it's one-way, or this monk is no longer a monk!"

He laughed again.

He could easily tell what each of the companions wanted by watching them—all but Sedarus. Rishkiin was the easiest. He wanted to slay monsters, to attain martial prowess, and to drink good ale. He was doing a good job of the latter, as of then.

Aunddara was the second easiest. The cleric of Tinen wanted above all else to be with Sedarus, to have his love and adoration. The Black Demon also saw the sadness in her eyes.

She knows they can never be together, the man thought with an internal cackle. Knew Sedarus could never love her the same way she loved him.

Rhamor the holy knight wanted to perfect his blade skills. Even more than that, he wanted evil throughout the world to end. He was accomplishing that by killing one monster at a time.

Haet wanted to perfect his body, making his body and spirit become one, and he wanted to have absolute control over himself.

"Sedarus," the Black Demon said aloud. "The monk who has the power to destroy most anything, yet he wants nothing to do with it." The figure sighed. He couldn't discover the desires of one who has no desire. "What do you live for?" the Black Demon asked Sedarus quietly. Of course, Sedarus never heard him, never even stirred.

Long moments passed, the Black Demon mindlessly playing his lute. Then he perked up, another question on his tongue.

"Why are you here?" he asked aimlessly. He could guess why Sedarus was on this journey, but why were the rest? What were their reasons for remaining with the highly dangerous monk?

He thought silently to himself for a very long time. The Black Demon could surmise that Aunddara accompanied Sedarus because of her hopeless love. Haet followed him for the same reason, love for his brother. But Rishkiin and Rhamor ... the Black Demon could not understand why they followed the monk.

People started to leave the inn, so not to draw the attention of the companions the Black Demon opened his pouch of holding and started to place his lute inside. However, he paused when he overheard Aunddara ask the innkeeper, "Do you know anything of someone who calls himself the Black Demon?"

Wanting to put a grandiose face on that of the Black Demon, he played a quick, quiet, and fast melody. He hummed an upbeat tune alongside his playing. Magical waves shot into a drunken man. The man instantly did as a telepathic suggestion whispered.

"The Black Demon! He's coming! Flee, fly, get out of here—" The man slumped to the floor at the door and passed out.

The Black Demon giggled maniacally as he finished his melody and finally placed his lute inside his pouch. He was one of the few people littering the tables now, and the only one who was still sober.

The man watched with a smile as Rhamor helped the stumbling Rishkiin up the stairs. Moments later he observed the spectacle of the two fighting monks, one half asleep. He was very interested in their style of combat. Soon after he was the only patron in the common room. The serving girl began to clear the tables, and the innkeeper made his way over to him.

"Good sir," the innkeeper started to speak, "there is a man who asked for you."

"Who is it?" the Black Demon asked in return.

"He would not say, but he asked me to tell you, 'Velvenbrox is near.'"

Instantly the dark figure was on his feet. "Where is this man?"

"At the front door," the innkeeper started to say, but the dark figure was suddenly gone.

The Black Demon appeared in front of the inn using the magical properties of his ring. It was almost pitch black outside, but his eagle eyes made out another shadowy figure. He could not see specific details of the man, but he knew what the man looked like. He would never forget, could never forget.

"Master," he said with a slight bow.

"Do not call me that," the serene voice said, "after all that we've been through. No, you'll never have a master, least of all me."

The Black Demon dipped into another bow.

"You've been keeping an eye on him?"

"Of course. I was not going to deny you," the Black Demon said, shuffling his boots nervously.

"You could have."

"And been killed?"

The person shrugged as if it did not matter. "You've been busy. The Black Demon?"

"Tehehe!" The Black Demon tittered as he ran a hand through his gold hair, his old luster coming back. "A name given to me by a dying ogre mage," he said with another bow.

"It suits you," the shadowed man said. Then, "Watch him carefully, but under no circumstances are you to confront him … yet. The time comes soon to act."

"And what of the message you left with the innkeeper?" the Black Demon asked.

"Ah, I thought that would get your attention. Yes, Feldoor and I have been working furiously to find Velvenbrox, and we believe we have him cornered. I may need your assistance for that little problem as well. But for now, tail the group."

The Black Demon quirked a thin eyebrow and asked, "Is Feldoor here?"

The Black Demon's master scoffed, answering, "He wouldn't even consider leaving the library."

With another bow to the man, the Black Demon pictured himself on top of the inn. He was there the next moment. He silently went over the conversation in his head. Over and over again.

Chapter Eleven

Rishkiin sat at a table, his head in his hands. The word *headache* did not even come close to describing what the man had. He had woken up early and come down to the common room. Now he was alone, except for a single figure playing a lute. Surprisingly the music did not bother the young fighter. Rather, it soothed his hangover.

Rishkiin never thought to glance at the instrument's player. If he had, he would have seen a smiling, shadowy, slender man with gold hair.

Rhamor was the first to join the young fighter. He ordered breakfast: eggs with bread that was toasted. He and Rishkiin hardly spoke, each preferring the quiet scraping of fork against plate.

Aunddara and Haet walked downstairs next. They ordered their breakfast and Sedarus's, who would join them shortly. As Sedarus came down the stairs, Aunddara knew instantly that there was something unusual about her friend. His gait was lighter, as if some of his life's load had been stripped from him.

"You seem lively today. Have a good night?" the cleric asked.

"Yes, I had a visitor."

All the others' faces crumpled with confusion. Aunddara's brow darkened into a scowl. Sedarus looked around, checking that no one was eavesdropping. The monk saw no one but the smiling lute player. He thought nothing of it.

"Tinen came to me in person."

His friends' mouths gaped open. Food even fell from Rishkiin's mouth into his goatee. They could not have been more stunned had a dragon suddenly appeared at the next table.

"What did he say?" Haet had the sense to ask.

"He told me that he was sending a guardian to aid us." Sedarus's face brightened. "He is sending help."

"That is good news. Maybe this guardian will know what we need to find at the Great Library," Rhamor said, a grin finally spreading across his bearded face.

"But *who* is this guardian?" Haet asked.

"I do not know. Tinen said I would know when the time came to meet this person." Sedarus sat down at the table and began on his eggs. Silence encompassed the companions. They finally got the strength to begin eating once more.

As soon as they were done, they called to the innkeeper. He walked over, a genuine smile spread on his lips. "Morning, masters and mistress," he spoke with a slight bow.

"We wish to pay the bill now," Rhamor stated, fishing out coins from his money pouch.

"That is unnecessary."

"It is, my friend," Rhamor argued. "We will not accept your hospitality free of coin."

"I do not presume you would, Lord Paladin." The innkeeper pointed at the slim figure, who continued to play the lute and sing quietly, and said, "That gentleman paid your tab."

As if on cue, the shadowy form looked their way, and with a smile, he nodded slightly. Sedarus and Haet instantly got to their feet. Rhamor, Aunddara, and Rishkiin were right on their heels, ready to thank the man.

At that moment, a clamor erupted from the kitchen, causing the five companions to twist quickly. The cook embarrassingly apologized and with a red face turned away. When the companions twisted back to face the playing figure, he was gone.

Befuddlement crossed all of their faces, but there was nothing that they could do. Thanking the innkeeper for his hospitality once more, the companions went on their way.

A suppressed chuckle escaped from the dark figure's mouth after he had paid the companions' bill. He turned from the curious look that plastered on the innkeeper's face. The Black Demon walked calmly to his normal seat, one that was enveloped in shadows. Once more he brought forth his lute and began to softly play, his fingers strumming the notes flawlessly, unopposed.

Then the first of the group that he was tailing walked—stumbled—down the stairs. Rishkiin had his gear on his back, his helmet in his hand. His free hand was rubbing his temple, trying to ease a roaring migraine.

With another laugh to himself and a huge grin, the Black Demon started to play a soothing, soft song. Instantly the young fighter, who was setting his gear below the table, felt relief in his pressure-bound head.

Rishkiin was soon joined by his companions. They ate with very little chatter. The Black Demon didn't listen to what was said. He was preoccupied with the conversation he had the previous night. When the friends were done, they loudly called the innkeeper to their table, shaking the lute player from his thoughts.

"Tehehe!" the Black Demon laughed as the innkeeper pointed at him. Another laugh shook his slender body. The irony of him paying their bill and instantly gaining appreciative feelings from them, and yet soon being the one to bring chaos to their lives, was too much to contain to just one mad giggle. His grin widened, and he sent a slight bow the companions' way. They arose, intending to walk over and speak. As amusing as it might be, the Black Demon had orders not to make contact yet.

Looking for an escape route, the Black Demon played to the cook's clumsiness. With a blink of an eye, he was on top of the inn, above the front door. Grinning and laughing quietly, the Black Demon watched as moments later, the group walked up to a caravan master waiting close to the inn near the back of his train. The caravan master smiled widely as Rhamor stated they were heading north. The portly man, who sported an unkempt beard and mane, jovially said they were welcome to ride along if they were willing to be hired as guards. The companions quickly agreed, and departed to gather their three horses and then joined the cavalcade in the front.

A devilish grin appeared on the Black Demon's face as he walked up to the same caravan master. "I would like a job as a guard," he said, his melodic voice ringing with the purest gold.

The portly man turned, and his eyes popped wide. He had never seen someone as exotic as the Black Demon, or one with eyes like his.

"Uh … sure," the caravan master said, his brown eyes still wide. "Why don't you go to the front of the caravan? I've just sent some guards up there; you can join them."

"Ah! But if we are all in the front, who will protect the rear?" the Black Demon asked, smiling all the while.

Without knowing why, the caravan owner was suddenly grinning as well. One of his front teeth was missing, and the rest of them were rotting. "Okay, you are the rear guard. I'll send some of the others to you."

"That would be inadvisable," the slender figure said. "I will be fine all alone." He let out a laugh. "It is how I work best."

The fat owner was dazzled by the figure before him. "Oh! Of course!" he agreed.

"Perfect!"

With that, the Black Demon started off. His steps were hindered when his new employer called to him, "Be on the watch for the Black Demon!"

Another giggle quietly erupted from the darkly dressed man. His huge grin turned into a feigned face full of terror as he twisted toward the caravan master. "A black demon? What does it look like?"

"No! *The* Black Demon! It stands twelve feet tall, has huge, black bat wings."

"Oh, of course. Does it have fangs and claws?"

"Yes, so be careful, and watch the shadows."

"I will!" The dark figure turned once more, a grin spread on his face. It was absurd how quickly rumors could be generated. "Tehehe!"

"The Black Demon is near," Sedarus said quietly to Rhamor. The two were sitting with Rishkiin on the bench of the front wagon, Sedarus directing the horses.

The paladin's face filled with concern as he placed his hand on his sentient sword. Sedarus felt a tug on his senses, and he knew instantly that Rhamor was conversing with the magically enchanted sword.

"How do you know this?" Rhamor then asked quietly as he scanned every shadow.

"He is using magic items. Items that are familiar to me," the monk replied. "Be on your guard."

The paladin nodded and whispered the word to Rishkiin, whose headache had completely cleared.

A scowl appeared on the fighter's face. He stood up and was about to leap from the rolling wagon when Sedarus's hand halted him. "What are you doing?" Sedarus asked distantly.

"Warning the other guards," Rishkiin replied.

"I'll warn Haet; you warn the others."

With that Sedarus handed the reins to Rhamor and stood up. He turned and looked at Haet. Sedarus made a subtle movement with his hands, and his fellow monk nodded seriously.

Rishkiin jumped from the wagon and raced to the other guards.

"Maybe this Black Demon is no threat to us," Rhamor stated.

Inspiration from his sword, Sedarus thought as he felt a tug from the telepathic message. "What do you mean?" he asked with all seriousness.

"Well, all we know is that this 'Black Demon' has killed a bunch of ogres. If anything, we owe him thanks right now."

Sedarus's face crumpled in thought. "I've never even considered that." His visage became racked with disturbance. He was troubled that he had not thought out everything.

"Maybe we need to make contact with this Black Demon," Rhamor stated.

Rishkiin walked down the wagon line, which consisted of ten wagons. The front and back two wagons each had guards. The young fighter had a private word with each of the guards, telling them only that they were being trailed by something.

None of the guards refuted him; they just clasped their hilts tighter. Their eyes were housed with scowls. The guards handed the reins to the merchants, whose eyes were wide with fear mixed with excitement.

When Rishkiin got to the last wagon, he found that it had only one guard. He was confused that there should be only one rear guard, reasoning that there should be just as many there as at the front. Yet it was not his caravan, so he did not voice his opinion.

The young fighter jumped onto the moving wagon and settled himself next to the guard. Even though the man had his cowl pulled low over his eyes, Rishkiin thought that the person looked familiar. He could not place the shadowy man, though, so he let it drop.

"There is something out there," Rishkiin said, nodding toward the forestry.

"Really?" a melodic voice questioned, intrigued. "What is it?"

"My friend believes it is the Black Demon," Rishkiin stated before it registered in his brain that the words might cause panic and chaos. But when he looked at the figure, he saw a smile plastered on the shadowy figure's angular face.

"How in the Abyss would he know?"

"He has this ability that lets him know if there is a magic item around and when it is being used. The Black Demon uses magic items." As Rishkiin finished, he cringed in regret and anger. He hadn't meant to reveal Sedarus's powers, yet for some reason he was compelled to speak freely. Rishkiin couldn't help but feel this guard was more than he seemed.

"Really?" The Black Demon was not truly surprised, of course.

"No," Rishkiin recovered.

"Really?"

"Yes."

"Yes he has a strange ability, or yes he does not?"

"Uh ..."

"Tehehe!" the mysterious guard chuckled. He advised, "If I were you, kid, I would not go around telling people about your curious monk companion. For your friend's safety, and yours."

"Er ... thanks!"

Rishkiin jumped down and ran to his place at the front of the caravan. It wasn't until he sat down that he realized he had never mentioned that it was one of his monk friends who had the gift. Curiosity beyond measure filled him. But fear sunk in deeper, down to the core, numbing him. Had he just put himself and his friends in danger?

Chapter Twelve

The days rolled on slowly and without incident. The Black Demon had decided that it would be best if he refrained from using his magical items. He watched the companions from his station as rearguard. Now the third day of travel was ending, and the sun god, Reth, was receding. The caravan was heading to the town known as Ashten Vale and was still two days of fast riding away. Soon the caravan master called for a halt. The caravan pulled off the road. They nestled against a hillside to the west. Pine trees blanketed their immediate surroundings.

The Black Demon performed his daily routine, which consisted of sitting leisurely against a tree, surreptitiously watching the five companions while the caravan workers unloaded the tents and put them up.

A sudden smell assailed his unnaturally superior senses. The Black Demon gazed up the hill, trying to penetrate the thick forestry with his eagle eyes. He did not know what it was, and curiosity got the better of him. He walked toward the tree-covered hill slope, muttering to the others about relieving himself.

Within fifty yards, he was out of sight and into the woods. He clicked the heels of his exceedingly tall boots. His weight started to leave, and gravity's hold on him began to slip. His weightlessness allowed him to float to the top of a tree.

The Black Demon knew that Sedarus would recognize his magic item use and would be along in a little while. He didn't care. He knew he would finally be able to reveal himself soon enough, much to the regret of the companions. Now, he did not have the time or the patience to see if Sedarus came searching for him.

With running leaps, he jumped from limb to limb, each time getting a little higher in the trees. Soon he was eye level with what he had seen near the camp. A group of raiders waited up in the rolling mountain hills.

He knew instantly that the time for his secrecy was over. A mad laugh came, and his face protruded in a grin of anticipation.

"What is it, Sed?" Aunddara asked the monk as his gaze snapped to the forest.

He ignored her, trying to pinpoint the tugging he was feeling. He started walking toward the hills but halted when he felt the cleric's soft touch on his arm.

"What is it?" the woman questioned again.

"The Black Demon. I feel him close by." Sedarus never took his gaze from the forest, as if losing eye contact would make him lose the direction from which the magic item was used. "I am going to speak with him," the monk continued.

"I will come with you." Haet walked up with the Rod of the Python ready in his hands. Sedarus nodded his agreement.

"As we all will," Rhamor stated.

Sedarus was shaking his head while the paladin spoke. "No."

"But Sed, you will need us," Rishkiin stated, hurt that his friend would take all of the fun from him.

"They are right," Haet whispered to his fellow monk.

"Fine. Rishkiin, you will come with us. Rhamor and Aun, you stay here, just in case he gets past us."

Rhamor nodded. Aunddara just looked at Sedarus closely, as if trying to see into his very soul. "How do you know the Black Demon is a he, and not a she?" she asked.

Sedarus paused. He did not want to answer. He did so anyway. "I can feel *his* soul surrounding the magic that is imbued within the items he possesses."

All of his companions rocked back on their heels, their eyes opened wide. It took a second for even Haet to compose himself.

"We should get moving. I feel him moving farther as we speak." With that Sedarus started into the hilly forest, Haet and Rishkiin close behind.

Only silence accompanied Rhamor and Aunddara as they watched their friends disappear. Just as Rishkiin's back vanished into the mountainous terrain, Aunddara spoke. "He just keeps on getting more and more powers." Her voice was almost shocked. "What does it all mean?" Tears flooded her bedazzling, green eyes. She sank to her knees and began to sob. She felt Rhamor's powerful arms surround her in a protecting hug—a hug of an older brother to his younger, precious sister.

"We will figure it all out in Anzzow," he soothed. "We are only two days from Ashten Vale. It's only a few more days' travel after that. We are so close to getting the knowledge that we so desperately need!"

"I know, but it is difficult watching him go through all this pain. He carries it without complaining, but he also hides it within himself!"

"I know, Aun."

Rhamor did know. He was just as worried about his monk friend as Aunddara was. He also knew that Aunddara was scared. Not for herself, but for Sedarus.

"What can we do for him?" the cleric asked, wiping her hand across her red, puffy eyes.

"We have to be there for him—on those rare occasions when he *does* open up to us."

Sedarus led his two friends up the side of the mount. He stopped underneath a tall pine and looked up.

"What is it?" Rishkiin asked, sliding Glimmer halfway out of its sheath.

"He was up there," the monk said, pointing to a limb.

"How do we get up there?" Haet asked. He was an adept climber, but he did not particularly like the idea of climbing trees that the Black Demon might be waiting in.

"How do we fight when we *are* up there?" Rishkiin wondered aloud to no one in particular.

"He is not up there anymore," Sedarus whispered.

When his friends looked at him, they saw that his eyes were tightly shut in deep concentration. He came out of the trance seconds later, pointing farther up the mountain, into the thicker woods. "He went that way."

They started off once more, at a slow, yet steady pace. A quarter of an hour later, they came across something that disturbed them: fresh footprints, and none of them human.

"What do you think made these?" Rishkiin asked, looking at the largest of the assortment of prints.

"I don't know," Sedarus replied honestly. His brow was crinkled in befuddlement. The large prints' tips were rutted deeper, as if the maker had clawed feet.

Sedarus snapped his head up, scowling. His blue eyes furrowed as his eyebrows scrunched, almost touching.

The Black Demon, he thought.

The Black Demon watched as the raiders huddled in a war meeting, sketching out their battle plan. After a long wait, he caught the band leader's eye and smiled. The leader gave a signal—one that the Black Demon knew.

"Tehehe!" he chuckled. With a blink of his eyes, the dark figure was on his way to the camp, to Sedarus.

As he went, he found his way was blocked by none other than the monk. The monk and two of his friends were looking over footprints. Then Sedarus snapped his head up, looking right into his eagle eyes.

"Those particular prints are that of a girallon," the Black Demon's melodic voice chimed. "It's a nasty creature, really."

He stood in front of the small group and then bowed slightly to Sedarus, who took no notice of the gesture.

"He is the Black Demon," the monk calmly informed his friends.

"Correct you are!" the man congratulated with his trademark maniacal laugh. "I knew you'd figure me out sooner or later."

"He doesn't look so tough," Rishkiin scoffed.

"Ah! But see here!" With amazing speed, the Black Demon drew out his hand crossbow and pointed it directly at the young, impudent fighter. "I could kill you with this little crossbow here and now."

Rishkiin would have laughed had it not been for the tone in which the figure spoke. His deceptively musical voice carried tones of death and destruction.

"That is, if you could pull the trigger fast enough," Sedarus said calmly, locking his gaze with the figure's.

The crossbow switched to aim at the monk's head.

"Tehehe! I know what you can do, my monk! And let me tell you—" then, with just as quick reflexes, the figure replaced his crossbow, "—I wish no confrontation with you or your friends."

"Why have you come?" Rishkiin asked, fully confident now that Sedarus had his back.

"Well, to warn you and our charge, of course! We are, after all, guards to a caravan." The figure threw his head back and cackled at some unknown notion. "Or have you forgotten?"

"What have you come to warn us about?" Haet asked.

"Of what you stand on! A girallon leads its raiding band toward the caravan. They are beastly creatures one and all!"

"Why did you not just destroy them as you did with the ogres?" Sedarus asked. "You certainly seem powerful enough."

Rishkiin snorted at that. "Do not underestimate him, Rish!" Sedarus whispered underneath his breath.

"Yes, do not underestimate me!" The man laughed once more at the look on the companions' surprised faces. "And to your question," he stated, as serious as he could be, "I could best each of the creatures one on one, certainly. Even three to one. But seventeen monsters are past even my prowess," the figure lied.

Sedarus did not even finish listening; he sprinted as fast as he could. Would he make it? he wondered. There were many men on the caravan, but they were not fighters. The guards totaled ten, counting him, his friends, and the Black Demon. If he did not make it before the monsters, he would find his friends lying scattered in bits and pieces. Rage welled within him. *That* he could not allow! Then without knowing how it was possible, he was instantly back at the caravan line.

What's going on? Did I just teleport? Sedarus asked himself. He did not have time to wonder about it. He ran, shouting for Rhamor and Aunddara.

"What happened?" Rhamor's deep voice bellowed.

"Raiding monsters are coming! We need to prepare."

He felt a tug at his senses, and he knew instantly that the Black Demon was behind him. Gasps of surprise came from Rhamor and Aunddara.

Sedarus turned to face the angular figure, whose fair skin was almost completely hidden. "How did you do that?" the singsong voice asked. "Just appear here?"

"It is none of your business!" Aunddara yelled, immediately on the defensive for Sedarus. Her own eyes were just as filled with surprise, yet she masked it quickly.

"Mistress, I am politely asking Sedarus how he did it," the Black Demon said calmly to Aunddara.

"It is still none of your busi—"

"Knock it off!" Sedarus roared. "There is a band of raiding monsters rushing to kill us, and here you are arguing like little children." The monk sighed and then faced Rhamor. "Get to the caravan master; tell him we are being targeted. Have him send the women and children on toward Ashten Vale. Beg him to send the rest of the guard with them."

Rhamor nodded and rushed off.

"How many are there?" Aunddara asked.

"*He* says there are seventeen." Sedarus nodded to the Black Demon.

"Ha! Only seventeen!" Aunddara scoffed.

"Minotaurs, owlbears, trolls, worgs, and a girallon," the man said. "Have you ever faced the half-bull, half-human creatures or the gigantic owls that stand on their hind legs as they maul you to death? Or have you cut the limb off of a troll, only to watch it grow back another?"

The descriptions gave Aunddara pause, and she gulped slightly. She had heard of trolls and their regeneration ability and had read in a scroll of the ferocity of minotaurs. She knew then that her friends were going to be hard-pressed.

"Let us start making preparations!" Sedarus called as Rishkiin and Haet came clamoring down the mountain, out of breath.

Chapter Thirteen

Rhamor joined the group just as they began emptying the wagons of their contents. Complaints and mutters of anger sifted through the crowd of merchants.

It took the intimidating Rishkiin to give them sense. "Would you rather run and tell the tale that you survived?" he yelled. "Or would you protect your material possessions like a greedy thief and die clasping a few trinkets worth no more than a handful of silver pieces?"

Less muttering came forth then. The merchants assisted in the emptying of the remaining wagons. The men tipped a few of the wagons over to create a defensive position.

"I suggest that you take what you need," Sedarus began, "and catch up with your families. If we cannot stop these raiders, you will at least have a chance to get a solid head start."

"No way in the Abyss!" one young merchant shouted, brandishing a short sword. He held it awkwardly; he obviously had never been trained how to use it. His sweaty brow creased above terror-stricken eyes.

"You would die to protect a few wagons, horses, and items?" Rishkiin's voice was so serene that the man had to close his eyes and swallow to rebuild his resolve.

"Yes," was his answer, though in a shaky voice.

"You've never shed blood, have you?" Rishkiin asked, stalking up to the man, eying him with his stone-hard gaze. "Your sword has never tasted the likes of blood? Still a virgin blade?"

"Silence! I don't care about my bloody trinkets! My wife—I want to give my wife a long head start! No bloody monster, nor demon, nor dragon shall ever touch her!" The young man's face contorted with painful rage as horrible images forced themselves into his mind.

Rishkiin paused. He smiled a little and said, "Good." He stretched out his hand, offering it in the brothers-at-arms embrace. They gripped each other's forearms, and for a second no one moved, no one drew breath.

"But you would only hinder us," Rishkiin said, looking into all the eyes of the remaining merchantmen. "I mean not to dismiss your courage or your resolve, but if we die today, it will lay upon you to protect your families! Your job will be the hardest, but I ask of you! Will you leave your precious wives and children to the wilderness, to die of thirst and hunger?"

Murmuring erupted from worried men. Some immediately started off after their families. Some growled with increased enthusiasm, anger, and defiance.

"Please, I beg of you! Do not let the deaths of your families lay on your shoulders!" Rishkiin yelled, his voice choking. So emotion-filled was the air that Aunddara walked into the middle of the circle of men to her friend and placed a comforting hand on his shoulder.

Finally the last of the men followed after the others. "Please! Promise me you'll cut down the mongrels!" the young merchant gasped, still with a white-knuckled clutch on the hilt of his sword.

Rishkiin's brown eyes locked with the man's. In that silent instant, Rishkiin's orbs said it all. "I promise, my friend. I will cut them into ribbons until they all pass into the next world—or until I gasp my last breath!"

Satisfied at the answer, the young man took off, his inner fire lifting his already quick pace. Long moments passed silently. Then Rishkiin let an overexaggerated sigh pass from between his teeth. "I thought they would never leave!"

Stunned looks from all but the shadowy figure with foolishly high boots greeted the fighter as he turned. "What?" Rishkiin asked, his face portraying his confusion.

"That whole … speech was a … fake?" Aunddara asked, wide-eyed.

"No. It was real, just not as heartfelt as you would have thought."

A grin erupted from the Black Demon, and a dark chuckle slipped through his teeth. Rishkiin and the other four stared at the figure, their expressions mixed with confusion, anger, and curiosity.

"So why did you go through with that heart-wrenching speech if it was a facade?" Aunddara asked angrily, returning the attention back to Rishkiin.

"Well, when I put a facade on, I like it to be good."

That brought another chortle from the dark figure.

"Plus, with them out of the way, Sed does not need to worry about, let's say, distractions while he calls his power."

"Rish!" Aunddara yelled, her face flushing a bit. "We have company!"

"Oh, relax, Aun. This guy knows!" Rishkiin replied.

"Knows? How?" Aunddara asked, turning to the peculiar man, immediately suspicious and immensely angry.

The Black Demon was not listening, wasn't even looking at the five friends. "They are here! Ready your weapons! *Tehehe!*"

"That is really annoying, and I've known you for about twenty seconds!" Rishkiin growled.

"*Tehehe!*" was the man's only answer.

Rishkiin thought about sliding Glimmer into the Black Demon's gut and wondered if he would still make that laugh then.

Before he could finish contemplating it, a wave of howls emanated from the woodsy hill. Within seconds, a pack of worgs rushed through the fringes of the trees.

"These wolf-like beasts are just the first wave. The creatures with two legs will wait until their pets tear at our defenses," the Black Demon stated, wholly unconcerned.

The large beasts could easily be confused with very large black wolves, racing forward, their yellow teeth snapping, eager for blood to spill upon them. Their coarse, midnight-black coats stood straight up on their necks and shoulders. Their intelligent red eyes almost glowed with bloodlust.

The companions huddled among the tipped wagons, weapons drawn. Aunddara was farthest back, ready to call upon Tinen for magical healing. The Black Demon covered a space between two wagons, as were Rishkiin and Sedarus. Rhamor and Haet calmly paced between the three, ready to assist any who was over pressed.

The Black Demon knew that he was able to hit one of the worgs with his hand crossbow at any time, but he purposefully held out, waiting to strike until one of the overeager, intelligent creatures leapt over a wagon. An insane laugh blew from him as he quickly pulled out his magically frosted rapier. The worg's hard skin would not, could not, resist the tip of the amazingly made and magically enhanced sword tip. The Black Demon's blade slid up through the throat, severing the spinal cord, and protruded from the other side. Not a sound came from the beast, not even a half-effort whimper. Using the dead worg's falling momentum, the figure twisted and shoved the limp body so it landed on the dirt with no more than a thud.

The Black Demon's sword came out unscathed, unblemished by blood. He recalled thinking, as he had when he slew the ogres, how it was possible that the sword was bloodied but he couldn't tell because the blood had already frozen.

"Tehehe!" he laughed loudly, drawing the attention of a second worg.

This second wolf-like beast slid underneath the wagon, snapping its powerful jaws at his legs. Yet with amazing agility and quicker feet, the Black Demon jumped back, avoiding the strike. The beast lunged again but drew back with a yelp as the figure's rapier sliced the tip of its snout. With another snap of its jowls, the worg leapt again at the Black Demon.

He was ready. He stabbed down with his ocean-green-glowing dagger, perfectly timed. The blade pierced the inside of the worg's mouth, delving through tongue and bone before hitting the ground, digging into the dirt, and holding the thrashing worg stationary.

With his magical sword, he hewed off the worg's head. Blood gushed onto his dagger hand. He then realized that when he'd punctured the beast's mouth, its sharp teeth had done some damage.

"Not too bad," he declared as he removed his hand from the salivations of the dead worg. "It's nothing that can't be fixed. Tehehe!"

At a howl to the right of them, Rhamor and Haet rushed away to defend their companions' flanks.

"Do not call upon your power unless in dire need!" Rishkiin said to Sedarus.

"I know, Rish." Sedarus was calm, his body taut and ready for the fight.

"The first one's coming to you, I'll see to that." Rishkiin grinned devilishly as he winked at his monk friend.

Sedarus had no idea what was about to happen, but knew that he had to be ready for anything. Two worgs came rushing at them, one right after the other.

The faster one leapt at Rishkiin, ready to tear his face off. The young fighter had other ideas. With a smile, he bashed the worg to the left with all of his might. His steel shield clanged with protest, yet it was sturdy and unyielding. The worg fell right into Sedarus's hands and was no longer Rishkiin's concern.

The second wolf-like beast came in fast, though not quick enough. Rishkiin smashed his shield into the oncoming assault, stopping the charge cold, yet the creature's force knocked Rishkiin backward. An attempted blow with Glimmer resulted in a gash on the worg's shoulders, not the slash across the beast's throat that the fighter had hoped.

Still, the yipping worg jumped back, dodging Rishkiin's backswing. Rishkiin quickly squared off with the beast, stalking in a circle. The worg snarled a primal growl as its haunches rose in anger. It suddenly lurched at the young fighter, catching him by surprise.

The snapping jaws clamped onto the young fighter's left bicep. Blood started to ooze from within Rishkiin's punctured armor. Unwanted tears leapt to his brown eyes, but he willed them away. He brought Glimmer up, quickly positioning the blade between his face and the worg. With a slash, Rishkiin caught the worg in the eyes. It yelped loudly, fiercely, yet did not release its iron grip.

In a high arc, Glimmer cut the worg's spinal cord, instantly releasing the creature's jaws. The worg slumped to the ground, quietly whimpering, yet also snarling at Rishkiin all the same. With a swipe, the young fighter ended the malicious life of the worg forever.

Sedarus had seen Rishkiin's intentions a split second before the worg was flung at him from the fighter's shield. The monk grasped the coarse, black fur as it flew at him and, with a directional tug, sent the worg flapping down, its throat meeting directly with Sedarus's powerful knee strike.

The beast coughed, trying to supply itself with air. Sedarus took his opportunity to sling his arm around the beast's neck. With a tight lock and a quick twist, the worg's neck snapped. It flopped to the earth, dead.

Haet whacked the final worg with the Rod of the Python as it raced toward Rhamor. The beast ignored the blow completely, lunging fully at the holy knight, but the flying beast's aim was thrown off by the blow.

Rhamor slashed, barely nicking the creature's shoulder. Haet smoothly jabbed the butt end of his rod into the eye of the wolf-like beast, which yelped and drew back, but not before the monk got in another whack.

Rhamor rushed forward and chopped the worg's head clean from its neck. The paladin wiped his blade clear of blood on the beast's fur coat. He held the sword aloft and roared at the woods in defiance.

"That is the spirit!" the Black Demon called with a mad peal of laughter, applauding the holy knight. The man walked over to converse directly in front of Rhamor, pointedly stepping over the pooling blood of the headless worg. "But the main attack is yet to come. We must be ready." He paused before continuing, "Of course, with how quickly we dispatched the nuisance the raiders count as pets, I doubt that we will have trouble. Tehehe! *Too* much trouble, that is!"

"Man, does anyone else feel like stabbing this fairy?" Rishkiin asked under his breath.

The Black Demon gave his favorite laugh before adding, "I assure you, my young fighting friend, I am no fairy."

"Look sharp," Sedarus growled. "Here comes the second wave!"

Chapter Fourteen

The front line consisted of three hulking minotaurs. The monsters ran on their hind hooves. The creatures' bull-like heads and razor-tipped horns had most mortal men running in terror. Their shaggy, russet-brown fur flapped in their wild race toward the companions. Growls and roars filled the air.

The second line was alike to the first, another three massive minotaurs, but they held back for reasons unclear to the companions. They waited, impatiently fiddling with their gigantic weapons.

"Steady," Rishkiin said, playing the part of military leader well. Even so, it was unnecessary. All of his friends were battle hardened, not wavering in the least. The Black Demon just chortled his customary laugh.

The first line of minotaurs had massive weapons strapped to their backs with no other visible weapons—other than their dangerous horns, that is. Just as they reached the wagon line, they lowered their heads, leading with their rock-solid skulls.

The Black Demon laughed as he charged maniacally at the minotaurs, brandishing his two blades. The lead minotaur shouldered a wagon, sending the cart flying directly at the Black Demon, ready to smash the laughing man to death.

But then he was gone, disappeared.

Using his momentum plus his magical ring, the mysterious man was in the air, vertically equal to a seven-foot minotaur in the second line. His frosted rapier was leading, and it entered the unsuspecting creature's throat right above where the two collar bones connect, sliding in without determent from the tough hide. The gasping beast dropped its huge axe, using its hand to stem the bleeding. The gesture did nothing to stop the visiting specter of death.

The minotaur in the front line had barely caught on when it turned and charged just in time to see the Black Demon retracting his blade from his fellow, close behind. In one fluid motion, the blade came out of the dead minotaur and slashed along the front one's thighs, hamstringing it. Then, with two quick jabs of his glowing dagger, the Black Demon left two holes in the beast's ribcage.

The ferocious monster reared in a roar and shot its head forward, intending to smash the slender figure's head with its own massive skull. The dark figure let forth a hysterical chuckle and watched as the bull-like humanoid crashed its head into the unyielding, slender rapier instead. The minotaur's brain matter began to ooze from the puncture even as the Black Demon pulled his sword out.

"I love this job! *Tehehe*!" the figure laughed loudly, jovially. He turned to the forest, not worrying about the five companions, to see three trolls rushing at him. Trolls. *One of the three monsters in the world that I detest battling,* he thought. "I hate this job!"

Then a sudden thought popped into his mind. With one more mad laugh, he disappeared.

Sedarus instinctively knew that the first minotaur would crash through the wooden wagon, leaving the path clear for the second. He spoke quietly to Rishkiin, "Be ready for the second mongrel; I'll take the first."

Rishkiin looked at his friend and nodded.

Sedarus let the minotaur play out its plan, but right when the beast slammed into the cart, Sedarus was on the move—airborne and ready to deliver a mighty blow. What he had not counted on were the sharp shards of wood exploding everywhere. One particularly nasty shaving flew straight at the monk, causing him to call upon his magnificently honed muscles to switch his momentum. His kick landed at the creature's furry abdomen, not to its unprotected throat. The blow was entirely ineffective.

The minotaur grunted as it quickly pulled the huge axe off of its back and swung. The axe blade bit deeply into Sedarus's left shoulder.

The monk nearly swooned as he twisted in flight from the gigantic blow. Scarlet blood fell freely from the axe wound. Lying on the ground, he looked at his shoulder to see a ghastly gash showing bone, tendon, and ligament.

A scream pierced the air, forced from the monk by the severe pain as his adrenaline pumped, allowing him to live ... momentarily. His eyes started to roll back into his sockets. Blackness swarmed around him, calling his name.

The last thing he saw before the darkness overtook him was a minotaur stalking in, grinning, ready for the kill.

Rishkiin's gaze was only for the second minotaur, one brandishing a massive sword that could easily slice him in half. The blade was more than half his height, but the worst thing about it was that the minotaur wielded it easily with one hand.

Yet Rishkiin was unperturbed. He smiled slightly, eager for the challenge of arms. His smile turned into a devilish grin as an idea entered his mind.

The first minotaur blew through the wagon, the second not far behind. At that instant, Glimmer suddenly shone blindingly bright as the second minotaur closed in. The beast roared in protest, covering its beady, red eyes with large, hairy, stubby fingers. That was when the young fighter rushed in, slashing the inside of its thigh. The thick artery gashed open, letting free the minotaur's life blood. The brutish bull-man fell to the ground, dying, but far from gone.

As its last act, the minotaur pulled itself to its knees and lunged at Rishkiin, intending to gore the man with its dangerously pointed horn. It failed horribly. Rishkiin dodged, smoothly slashed the minotaur across the chest, and then plunged his blade into its side. Glimmer delved past the ribs and deeply into the vile thing's heart.

A blood-curdling screech caused Rishkiin to turn in fear. He watched as Sedarus passed out. The minotaur in front of the monk was raising its massive axe.

A leap of rage brought Rishkiin right next to the massive, woolly monster. The young fighter slashed even as he landed on his feet. Blood spurted from the new gash slightly above the minotaur's left hip.

It roared in pain and anger as it turned around, throwing a powerful punch. The massive fist crashed into Rishkiin's face, shattering his nose.

Blood shot forth, instantly flooding his lips and spilling into his mouth. The iron-tasting fluid overpowered his senses.

The forceful blow also rocked him back, staggering. He tumbled over a corpse and crashed to the ground. Rishkiin was helpless for a split second, momentarily stunned and defenseless. He saw Aunddara rush over to the downed Sedarus and begin healing.

Hooves stomped over to the fighter; the minotaur once more had its enormous axe poised for a kill. Then suddenly it exploded, sending chunks of gore soaring everywhere.

Sedarus sat up groggily, Aunddara over him, praying to Tinen. The monk watched as the blood flow stemmed, slowing to a stop. Then his eyes popped open wide as he observed with amazement his tendons beginning to re-cord.

The flash of a glinting reflection from the day's ending light caught his attention; he pulled his gaze away from his mending shoulder. He saw the raised axe above Rishkiin, and he instinctively pushed as much blue energy as he could into its wielder.

The minotaur grunted in confused defiance, but it, like everything else, could not resist the exploding energy. Gore and blood flung upon everyone within a ten-foot radius. Of course, everyone in a thirty-foot radius was knocked to their backs, including the charging trolls and owlbears.

Sedarus had not thought of the full consequences of his action. Aunddara was one of the many who were knocked back. Her spell was disrupted, causing Sedarus to grunt in pain as his ripped skin seared together, leaving a garish scar. His bone had not been properly healed.

He did not care, though; he had saved his friend. *Any pain is worth saving the ones you love,* Sedarus thought.

Haet and Rhamor were too impatient to wait for their two charging minotaurs to reach and blow apart the wagons. Instead, they charged themselves, meeting the bull-men head on as the Black Demon had.

Haet cast the Rod of the Python to the dirt, initiating the magic. The wooden rod elongated into a giant constrictor snake. Instantly on the defensive, protecting its master, the snake placed itself between Haet and the closest minotaur. As the lumbering minotaur closed in, ignoring the massive snake, the magical beast under Haet's control snapped forward and clenched its powerful jaws around the monster's right hip.

The minotaur roared in pain as the snake started to wrap its colossal body around its muscular torso. Haet rushed in, intending to help his pet. He launched a series of kicks and punches but was knocked off his feet by the exploding blast from Sedarus's power.

The snake only tightened its deadly grip as it and the minotaur collapsed to the ground. Enraged and fearful, the bull-man lashed out at the snake, punching and biting at it.

The snake took it all nonchalantly. It bit the side of the minotaur's neck, its massive fangs puncturing large arteries. Blood gushed from between the crevasses of the snake's mouth. Shortly the bull-man lay still, dead for long moments before Haet telepathically told the snake to release the corpse. It did so, but reluctantly.

Rhamor was born and bred for battle. He was made for the adrenaline rushes and the battle wounds and the scars. His armor and shield were a gift from his former grandmaster before he left on the journey with Sedarus. They were perfectly made and magically enchanted, yet they had dents and scrapes from many skirmishes.

He rushed at his assigned minotaur with a war cry on his lips. His blade was leading, his shield was ready. The minotaur had its gigantic sword raised also. As they met, Rhamor, who was the quicker, slashed twice. His first blow severed the sword arm of the bull-man. The second hamstrung the monster, rendering its right leg useless.

Rhamor felt the approval of his battle prowess flowing from his sentient sword. But he had no time to converse with the sword, as a troll was upon him.

The ten-foot monster with gangly arms, which came down past its knees, swung faster than Rhamor could raise his shield. The monster's razor-sharp claws shredded his armor, tearing into his shoulder.

The pain battered Rhamor's mind, threatening to make him heave. The paladin pushed through it, just in time to see Haet's snake snap at the troll, sharp teeth sinking into the enemy's rubber-like flesh. The bite was deep, and the snake's jaw clamped down, unrelenting, forcing the troll to hop around wildly trying to break free. Rhamor swung in a high arc, cleaving the troll's shoulder, chopping off the arm. His backswing missed its mark due to the troll's rearing of its head, its mop of grass-like hair whipping everywhere.

Haet suddenly came from the side and ran at the troll with a torch, knowing that fire was a troll's only fear and greatest weakness, for only fire could prevent a troll's regenerating ability. The monk squarely hit the monster's chest with the fire. Its putrid, green-colored skin crackled, its dry skin soon roasting with yellow and red flames.

Haet's constrictor retreated quickly before it could be set aflame, slithering to its master while simultaneously shrinking back into a wooden rod.

Haet, with his Rod of the Python back in his hands, and Rhamor could not watch as the troll withered in scorching pain, for an owlbear was right on them.

The owlbear's whole body was covered with yellow-brown feathers, its wing-like arms poised ready to attack. It held no weapon, its bear-like claws and hooked beak more than formidable. The thing stood on its thick legs, extending eight feet tall.

The beast pecked at the charging Haet, but the monk was too fast. He jumped, kicking the thing in the kneecap and deftly smacking at its head with the rod. The owlbear's knee caved in and its beak snapped off. It screeched atrociously as it stumbled forward, right onto Rhamor's glorious blade. It did not die instantly, but Rhamor was not feeling very generous. He pushed the thing to the ground to drown in its blood.

Rishkiin was assaulted by an owlbear and a troll at the same time. He and the two monsters traded blows. Claws and beaks were halted by his shield, while his sword nicked and slashed, barely catching his enemies. *I'm getting nowhere with these hack-and-block tactics. Let's get fancy,* Rishkiin thought, then he hurtled backward in order to draw in one of the creatures.

The owlbear stupidly jumped after him. Rishkiin's blade slit the monster's soft, exposed throat. It fell over in front of the charging troll, tripping the second attacker.

Rishkiin took the well-crafted opportunity to slash with his blade, severing both of the troll's legs. It roared gutturally; it could not move, giving the young fighter time to fumble into his pack for a torch. Rishkiin found it, lit it, and set the still-regenerating troll aflame. It was the only way to make certain that the beasts stayed incapacitated and then died.

Sedarus and Aunddara had new friends of their own. Still wincing at his improperly healed shoulder, Sedarus danced around the troll and owlbear, punching and kicking them with unnatural strength borrowed from his deadly powers. Aunddara helped when she could, smacking the owlbear with her mace and bashing the troll with her shield. Yet the two creatures never once turned from the furious monk and his dangerous barrage of attacks. Sedarus viciously kicked the owlbear's knee, hyper-extending the joint. It collapsed in a screech of pain. Aunddara was instantly striking the beast.

Finally, with the owlbear knocked down and out of the fight, the monk ran straight at the troll with a massive push. Sedarus forced blue energy into the troll—too much. The amount of power Sedarus poured forth could not be contained by just the troll. The excess energy leaked from the troll, looking for a host. Seeing the energy racing towards her, Aunddara turned tail and ran with fear-stricken eyes, but the monk's energy found a home in the owlbear. With a huge explosion, both creatures disintegrated, leaving naught but soaring chunks of remains and a fountain of blood.

Sedarus sank to the ground, rubbing his scarred shoulder in exhaustion. His mind wavered in fatigue.

The Black Demon left the five companions to battle the monstrous contingent only to appear right behind the leader of the enemy band, the girallon—a fierce, intelligent, bloodthirsty, and chaotic cousin of the gorilla. White fur covered its whole, very muscular body. The beast had four massive arms and two stout legs with nothing but its claws and a muzzle full of razor-sharp teeth for weapons.

The Black Demon looked around attentively, searching for any other monsters. There were none that his eagle eyes could discern. By the sounds of the ferocious battling less than a mile away, the Black Demon guessed that the companions were struggling against the girallon's minions. The two were alone.

"Tehehe!" the Black Demon laughed from behind the oblivious girallon.

The feral, four-armed beast turned just in time to take a bolt to the face from the man's magically enchanted crossbow, filling it with a burning sensation. Then electricity coursed through its veins. The Black Demon laughed again, this time with more pleasure, as he watched the ten-foot creature fall to its knees, completely helpless.

"I kill you, I will!" the girallon yelled in the giant tongue.

A mad laugh. "Tehehe! You can't even move!" the Black Demon spat at the girallon.

The beast started to get up, the electricity from the bolt fading. For his efforts he only got shot again, this time in the chest. The fiery pain was fiercer than before, and the Black Demon could tell. He laughed once more as the creature convulsed in withering pain.

The dark figure replaced his crossbow in its holster and drew his blades. Long moments were filled with only the monster's grunting. The Black Demon allowed the girallon to stand up. "You pained me, now I do pain to you!" the creature yelled.

"Call off your men ... monsters!" the Black Demon demanded with a cackle.

The four-armed beast responded by rushing, swiping first with its top two claws, then its bottom two. Both sets struck the Black Demon as he jumped into the attack, getting close to the girallon. The sharp claws barely caught his back, tearing deeply. He scowled in pain, but he'd had worse. Letting a growl go he replied with a stab of his finely made and powerfully enchanted sword. The frost blade entered the girallon's furry chest. A chilling blue flame erupted, catching on the fur and hide quickly.

The beast immediately dropped to the dirt and began rolling around manically. Another laugh burst from the lithe figure as he watched the girallon, its fur mostly burned away, try standing once more.

The Black Demon decided to end it, though, and viciously stabbed the monster in the chest with his green-glowing dagger. The dark figure silently commanded his fiendish weapon to feed upon the body, but to leave the head unaffected. Instantly the girallon's muscles and skin began to wither and decay. It was being eaten slowly and painfully. The monster screamed, but the laughing man only cackled harder. Within seconds, the hundreds of pounds of flesh and muscle were nothing but a pile of gray-blue dust, leaving only the very large girallon head.

The Black Demon sheathed his blade and hurriedly began to sing. The song brought wisps of blue healing force to the figure's torn flesh and clothes. Both were repaired, restoring the man to full strength. He then picked up the head, holding it almost lovingly—for it was, after all, his trophy.

Then, with a picture in his mind, the Black Demon was standing at the bottom of the hill, in close proximity to the wagons. He silently watched as the companions valiantly fought the trolls and owlbears. A hysterical snicker escaped him as Sedarus utterly destroyed the last owlbear and troll, blowing their body parts in every direction. The companions rallied once more, readying themselves for another wave of enemies. They truly looked battle worn and haggard. The Black Demon walked from the trees. He burst into a fit of giggles at the companions' confused faces.

"Where have you been?" Rishkiin growled. The lithe figure ignored the young fighter as he joined the friends at the wagons.

"What happened to you?" the Black Demon asked Sedarus, who was peculiarly pale. His skin itself was much whiter than before.

"I do not know," Sedarus said faintly. Using his power and extending that energy into two beings at once had cost him, leaving him severely fatigued.

The figure took out a spherical diamond attached to a string. He lightly blew on it, making it spin violently.

"Hmm," he said, his brow scrunching in thought, as if trying to complete a puzzle.

"What?"

"You used your energy when magic was being cast around you."

"So?" Sedarus asked, not seeing the point being made.

"Well," the Black Demon chuckled, smiling, "it disrupted the spell. When that occurs, devastating effects are produced."

"What happened to him, Black Demon?" Rishkiin asked, angrily gripping Glimmer.

"Black Demon? *The* Black Demon?" Aunddara asked, taken aback. Everyone ignored her.

"I cannot tell for sure, but it is safe to say that Sedarus will stay as pale as he is right now. Forever," the man added with a particularly inappropriate giggle.

"All right, enough with that bloody laugh!" Rishkiin yelled.

"*Tehehe*!"

Rishkiin started toward him, but the Black Demon was unperturbed.

"Enough, Rish," Sedarus said calmly. Rishkiin started to stomp off, calming down. "What do you have behind your back?" the monk asked the stranger.

"This?" The figure produced the head of the girallon. "It is what remains of the recently deceased leader of that band." He dropped it on the ground, letting it roll in the dirt.

"Who in the Abyss *are* you?" Aunddara asked, her breath stolen.

"I am Balatorensial Es'Vensual," the man said with a grandiose bow toward Sedarus the monk. "I am your guide and protector. I am the guardian."

Chapter Fifteen

Aunddara stood in the dark, her jet-black armor magically concealing her better than she could ever hope to be concealed without it. She was surrounded by trees, each pine needle swaying in the chilly night breeze. The cleric recalled her day, the battle with the raiding monsters. She acutely remembered staying out of the actual fighting, reserving her physical energy for the tiresome duty of calling for magical healing. She remembered the terrible feeling that burst inside her chest every time she looked upon Sedarus and his unnaturally pale skin. Aunddara shivered, and not from the wind. She could not help but blame herself for his condition.

The cleric of Tinen walked in the dark, shuffling in and out of the trees, snapping fallen twigs. She made her way to the top of a hill. It was large enough that she could see all around her. She found, in the distance, her friends setting up camp at the scene of the battle. The merchants had given up on the caravan and their wares, most of which had been destroyed during the battle, and any that were still intact Rishkiin had already scavenged for the group. None of the caravan travelers returned, even after the Black Demon had chased after them and told of the monstrous band's demise. A fire soon was raging, and Aunddara faintly heard voices.

Tears overwhelmed her as she mentally pictured Sedarus. The way he used to be. His skin had been olive, tan, smooth, and his chiseled form was one that many women had gotten pleasure from looking upon. Now he was ashen white, his skin coarse and uninviting. She knew that he couldn't care less, but that did not help the guilt weighing heavily upon her delicate shoulders.

"I am so sorry, Sed," Aunddara said quietly to the wind. A single tear ran unchallenged down her soft cheek. "I love you."

"Whoa!" a voice shot through the dark.

Aunddara's shield was instantly shining bright, her mace in her hand as she twisted to meet the newcomer.

"We just met. Give us a little time to get to know one another! Tehehe!"

"Bela … Balatur …" Aunddara stumbled over the odd name.

"Balatore, please!" The shadowed man walked forward, unconcerned that the cleric had yet to lower her mace. "And like I said, we've only been properly introduced this very day!"

"I wasn't talking to you!" Aunddara snapped, replacing her mace at her right hip.

"Oh, of course not! You spoke to Sedarus the Pale One." He gave another of his now-familiar laughs.

"Do *not* call him that!" Aunddara snarled through gritted teeth.

Balatore replied only with another spate of laughter. He walked over and stood next to Aunddara, but he faced toward the roaring fire. Silence encompassed the two for minutes that seemed like hours to Aunddara. She finally turned to face Balatore and asked a burning question. "What do you see with those eagle eyes?"

"I see colors that you cannot dream of. I see the lies woven from each mouth, see farther than you can run in five minutes."

"How did you get them?" the cleric asked, her voice steeped with awe.

Balatore did not immediately reply. He turned from her and reached up with one hand and rested his fingers right below his eye. He was silent for so long, deep in reliving a vivid memory. Aunddara thought that he would refuse to answer.

"They were a gift from a god."

"Which one?" Curiosity bulged from every vein inside of Aunddara. "You don't strike me as someone who would like to owe a debt to anyone, especially a god. I mean no offense, but you don't act like one who follows the Goodly God."

Another long moment of silence slid between the two. Balatore then turned to face Aunddara. "May I call you Aun?"

"No!"

"Aunddara, then. It was indeed Tinen, the only god of good." Balatore paused then added, "And I owe him nothing. He still owes me, even after he gave me these eyes."

Astonishment rocked Aunddara's very core. Her mouth gaped at Balatore. She barely remembered that Balatore was looking at her. His face was racked with humor.

"Tinen owes *you*?" she finally muttered.

Balatore nodded solemnly.

"What did you do that could possibly put a god in your debt?"

This time Balatore chose not to answer. He returned his gaze to the camp. Minutes slipped away, unhindered by either. Aunddara finally began to fidget, shifting her feet side to side.

She ended the quiet. "How is your hair that color of gold? I've seen some exotic people in my lifetime and have *never* seen hair so brightly gold!"

A smile broke onto Balatore's features. His toothy grin grew wider as Aunddara started to smile without completely knowing why. The cleric watched as the man brought his hand up to his left ear. Earrings littered the lower half of each of his ears, but only the left had a ring that pierced the cartilage near the pointy tip. He fiddled with that one, smiling even wider, his eyes going wide, as if recalling a fond memory.

"What?" Aunddara asked, still smiling. She was irritated because she honestly did not know why she was grinning stupidly.

"Nothing. Let's just say that I have a bag of tricks on my belt." Balatore laughed loudly, startling the nearby animals.

Another long and quiet moment passed. Then it was broken by Balatore. "You know that Sedarus can never love you more than he can as of now, don't you? You will never be anything but a friend to him."

Pain filled Aunddara's gorgeous green eyes. "He could. Maybe someday."

"You are mistaken, my dear. And you know it, like I do." Balatore's eyes actually looked as if they were sorrowful for the tearing-up cleric.

With a yell of pure rage, Aunddara raised her mace as if to attack. She pulled up short, due to an ocean-green-glowing dagger tip prodding at her throat threateningly.

"Now, my dear! Is that the wisest course presented to you?" Balatore asked, all hint of sorrow replaced with cold ice.

Aunddara suddenly walked away, annoyed, and as if Balatore had read her mind, another giggle came forth. The cleric shook with anger all the way down the long, winding game trail. Soon she entered the camp, lit by the crackling fire.

The flames licked the night sky with yellow tendrils. Red coals encompassed the bottom of the fire pit. The warm waves that swept over her were welcoming, comforting. Yet she hated the thought of walking over and sitting, only to be taunted by Rishkiin and his snide comments.

Then without warning, without a wisp of sound, Sedarus was next to her, his pallor almost luminescent in the dark night sky. "How are you?" he asked in a whispering voice.

"Fine," Aunddara lied.

Sedarus nodded, his lips a tight line. He knew that she was lying. He also knew that she blamed herself, carrying guilt that was his, only, to carry.

"It was not your fault, Aunddara," Sedarus said, looking straight into her breathtaking, green eyes.

She could not hold his gaze; she looked to the dirt she was kicking with her leather boots. "I know."

"Yet you stand there, slumped over in agony!" It was the first time in his life that he had ever raised his voice in anger toward Aunddara.

She looked up, shocked beyond belief. She sputtered, trying to find words. Sedarus was quicker.

"I am sorry, Aun. It's just ... by the Abyss! This is not your burden to bear! This pale skin bothers me not! And if that is the extent of the damage, then I consider myself lucky!"

A moment passed between the monk and cleric. Aunddara was acutely aware of the stares from her three other friends. She started to blush and was thankful that it was dark, with the fire beginning to burn low.

"Come," Sedarus said, slinging his arm over her shoulder. "Come sit with your friends."

She wasn't going to protest.

Chapter Sixteen

Balatore was late for a meeting with his master, but he did not care. He stood still, watching Aunddara stomp away with an inner fire deep within her soul. Pangs of sorrow shot from every corner of his body. The anguish was not from the saddened Aunddara, but because of a memory of someone lost to him.

With a grief-stricken sigh, Balatore turned and quickly walked to his rendezvous point. His master was already there, pacing impatiently. When the figure saw Balatore, he ceased to walk.

"Balatore."

"Tinen." Balatore bowed slightly.

"Where have you been?" Tinen growled irately.

"I was shedding light upon a rather dark subject." Balatore bowed again, with indifference.

"Do you wish my ire upon you?" Tinen asked, walking so close to Balatore that they were nose-to-nose.

With a thought and the aid of his magical ring, Balatore was behind the god. He held out his hands to his sides and smiled.

"Ire from a Goodly God? The *only* Goodly God? You give me too much." He laughed a laugh only he was capable of.

"I have not the time to play your games, Balatorensial! Do not test me," Tinen seethed. He continued through gritted teeth, "I may still owe you my life, but *all* debts are discontinued in regard to my son!"

"Are we not all sons and daughters to the great Tinen?" Balatore asked, his grin childish.

"You know what I mean. No harm is to come to him."

"Have you seen him lately? He is a bit pallid. Tehehe!"

"I know!" Tinen growled, turning away. "I was there, using his female friend as a conduit for my healing. Then he used his power, disrupting everything!" The god sighed, concern wrapped about him.

"I've used my Diamond of Revealing, the very same one you gave to me. His pallor is the extent of the damage."

Tinen relaxed visibly, a smile taking over his scowl. "Thank you, old friend."

Balatore bowed once more.

"No harm is to come to him, Balatore. I mean that," the god warned.

"None shall. Sedarus is safe with me, as you once were. Never forget that!"

"Never shall I, my friend." Tinen placed his open palmed hand on Balatore's shoulder. "Make certain Sedarus reaches the library first. You will have plenty of tomes to decipher; even with your skill, it will take many days."

Tinen turned and began to fade.

"Talk to him. Tell him to trust me!"

If the god of valor and courage heard, he made no indication. He faded all the way and was gone.

With a chuckle, Balatore pulled out his lute and began to strum on the strings. With a grin plastered to his face, he began his short journey back to the camp.

Sedarus awoke with a start, his honed muscle reacting to a presence, one with immense power. He lurched to his feet, sending his destructive power forth into the being. No explosion came, confusing the monk for a split second. Then he realized who he had put his energy into.

"Forgive me, my lord!" Sedarus begged Tinen, falling to the ground in a bow. The fall soiled his robed knees.

"Look at me, my son," Tinen said.

Sedarus slowly raised his gaze, ashamed beyond belief.

"There is naught to forgive," the deity continued. He was perfectly intact, no injuries, withstanding the full force of Sedarus's power.

Of course I cannot harm him! Sedarus thought. The monk looked around the camp. The red coals still smoldered bright enough so that he could make out objects. None of the shadowy shapes were those of his friends.

"Where are my companions? Are they debilitated?"

"No, no. They are completely healthy and are sleeping."

"I cannot see them, Mast—" Sedarus saw the glint of irritation in Tinen's eyes and quickly changed his sentence. "I cannot see them, Father."

"That is because you are in the Realm of the Gods," Tinen spoke, a smile once more present on his handsome face. "Control your thoughts; bring pictures of your companions to mind."

Sedarus closed his eyes and thought intensely of his companions. Then he opened his eyes. His face displayed surprise. There, lying next to him, was Aunddara, and on his other side was Haet. He heard Rishkiin snoring audibly. The monk also saw Rhamor, with his blade in hand, on watch.

"Can they see us?" Sedarus asked Tinen.

The god shook his head. He looked at Sedarus intently and snapped his fingers. The fire roared up suddenly, lighting the camp brilliantly. Tinen walked slowly around Sedarus, inspecting his pale skin.

"It is as if fire ash is stuck to your body," the god said to himself. "Hmm. I'm going to try and remove this curse that has beset you."

"It does not bother me, Father," Sedarus humbly stated.

Tinen either did not hear or ignored the monk. He placed his right hand over Sedarus's heart. A soothing feeling encompassed the man, giving relief to his scarred shoulder. But his skin stayed ashen.

"Lord, it is not a burden for me, honestly."

"I know. I can feel it when someone lies to me. As can you."

"Me? I can do that?"

"Yes, and many other miraculous things." Tinen paused. "Trust in Balatore; he knows what you need to do. He knows what you are."

"What I am?" Sedarus asked, bewildered. "What does that mean?"

"Trust in the elf."

"Balatore is an elf?"

Tinen nodded.

"And he knows what I am?"

Again the god nodded.

"What am I?" Sedarus asked, walking up to Tinen.

"Good-bye, my son." Tinen started to fade away.

"What am I?" Sedarus roared at the dissipating god.

Sedarus woke up surrounded by his friends. All had scared looks in their eyes.

"Sed, you okay?" Aunddara asked.

"Ahh!" Sedarus growled with frustration.

"Sed?"

"Where is that bloody elf?" Sedarus bellowed.

"Elf?" Aunddara asked. "They don't exist anymore, Sed. They were wiped out in the Great War thousands of years ago. You know that."

"Someone rang?" a melodic voice sang from the darkness of the trees.

Sedarus raced to Balatore, his eyes wild. "What am I?"

"Ah, Tinen spoke with you. Good."

"What am I, elf?" Sedarus spat in Balatore's face, grabbing onto his shoulders as if he was going to shake them.

Then the elf wasn't there. Instead he was behind Sedarus, laughing.

The monk turned, angry. "By the gods! If you do not tell me, I will send energy into your little finger and make it explode! What am I?"

Everyone was startled, including Balatore. Rishkiin recovered quickly and whispered, smiling, "Do it, Sed!"

There was a pause; silence surrounded them all.

"I will ask one last time, elf. What am I?"

"A very angry monk. Tehehe!"

Rishkiin started to laugh as well, drawing a curious glance from Balatore. The young fighter said, "You're in for it now!"

Yet instead of exploding Balatore's little finger, Sedarus slumped to the ground. "Please, what am I?" he implored.

"Desperation is not what will answer this very interesting question, my monk friend," Balatore replied.

"What will?" Sedarus asked, defeated.

"The Great Library of Anzzow, of course," the elf stated with a now-familiar cackle.

Chapter Seventeen

Sedarus had calmed down and was now sitting with his friends and Balatore around the fire. They had been questioning the elf on the Great Library of Anzzow. Currently, silence enveloped them, besides the crackling flames on the logs. The flooding light was beginning to dissipate, and each was barely able to discern the features of the next.

"Are you a real elf?" Sedarus asked.

"Yes," Balatore replied.

"Can you prove it?" Haet calmly inquired. He sat defensively on the ground, as if he expected Balatore to attack.

The elf moved his long, gold hair, which glittered in the fire's light, and exposed his lengthy, pointy ears.

"Okay. I'm sorry," Haet replied, but he still did not relax.

"See! I told you he was a fairy!" Rishkiin laughed.

"*Not* a fairy," Balatore argued.

"Sings a lot, has long ears, dresses queerly ... yup, fairy!"

"Oh, swallow your tongue, Rish," Aunddara snapped. "You don't know what you are saying."

That put a surprised look on all their faces. Why would Aunddara come to Balatore's defense? Sedarus looked carefully at his friend. He did not know if it was his growing power, or if he simply instinctively knew that there was something underneath Aunddara's glittering eyes. What was it? The monk asked himself. Adoration for the exotic elf?

Sedarus looked at Balatore, sure that he would kill the elf if he was grinning wickedly. Instead he was looking at the cleric just as confused as everyone else.

Sedarus was silent the rest of the night, subtly switching his gaze between Balatore and Aunddara. The cleric's eyes never left the majestic elf, ogling his lithe figure. She did not try to hide that she was completely enthralled with the elf.

It was growing late, and it was Balatore's turn for watch. Sedarus lay on his bedroll, closing his eyes and pretending to sleep. After a long time, sure that he and Balatore were the only ones awake, he stood up. He walked quite silently but was not surprised when Balatore calmly turned to face him.

"Sedarus," Balatore tranquilly spoke, bowing slightly to the monk.

Sedarus never stopped walking, but grabbed the elf's arm and pulled him along.

"What is this about?" Balatore asked, his voice not cold, yet not warm either.

Sedarus did not reply. Irritation gripped the elf; he disappeared, reappearing right behind Sedarus. The monk felt the elf behind him and instantly turned, making a slight chop to his throat. The force was just enough to cause the elf to cough and gag for air, startling him. Once again he disappeared.

Sedarus turned, halting the glowing dagger by gripping Balatore's wrist. He deftly twisted, at the same time kicking the legs out from underneath the elf. Down went Balatore, his dagger falling to the ground with Sedarus's other hand clasped over his throat. The monk did not squeeze, which was the only reason why Balatore did not blink himself away again and shoot Sedarus with his crossbow.

"What do you want, Sedarus?" the musical voice questioned acidly.

"You saw the way Aun looked at you this night," Sedarus said.

"Yeah, so?"

"I know that you have a few magic tricks up your sleeves—"

"In my pouch, really," Balatore interrupted. Sedarus glared at him. "But continue your ranting."

"I can *feel* that you have magic within you! Are you dazzling Aun with your tricks?" Sedarus asked tartly.

"No. It is just my naturally good looks, tehehe!"

"Then you will not pursue her. Her virtue will not be taken by someone who would just throw her away when he's done with his wiles!" The monk's face was contorted with rage, his brow scrunched together, his mouth in a snarl. Sedarus was truly frightening, even to the usually imprudent Balatore.

There was a silent pause, then Balatore laughed uproariously. "Is that what this is about?" Instead of waiting for the answer, Balatore blinked himself a few feet away from Sedarus, still in front of him. He held out his hands to the sides, signifying his submission. "You will have no problem with me, Sedarus. At least not where Aunddara's virtue is concerned!" He concluded with a milder giggle.

"I know ... now."

"You do?"

"I can tell when you're lying," Sedarus said. "But of course, you know that. *You* know what I am," the monk replied, seething.

"Ah! But of course." Balatore bowed indifferently.

"Sorry for our misunderstanding," Sedarus spoke whisperingly as he turned to walk away.

"Oh, I understand!" Another tinkling laugh. "You had to protect your woman."

That stopped the monk cold. He swiftly turned and rushed at Balatore but quickly halted his charge; it was impulsive and unwise—not in the least due to the hand crossbow pointing at his head.

"That is unnecessary," Sedarus breathed deeply, fighting the strong urge to explode Balatore's crossbow hand. "I am under control now."

"I see." Balatore lowered the crossbow but did not replace it in its holster.

"Aunddara is not my woman."

"She wants to be."

"Preposterous!" Sedarus growled.

He was met with a chortle. "Come now, Sedarus. Do you expect me to believe that you of all people cannot see the truth behind her caring and worrying?" The elf put his crossbow away and walked forward.

Sedarus paused, looking down in the dark. *The dark!* he thought. *I can see in the dark!* He pushed it from his mind.

"You can feel the truth in my words, milord." Balatore bowed once more.

"I am no one's lord," Sedarus limply stated. He was hardly thinking of that. His mind could not stray from the truth that Aunddara was in love with him.

"Ah, but you are mine!"

"No, Tinen is your lord. As he is mine," Sedarus said, looking up into Balatore's eagle eyes.

"I am afraid not, to both of those statements. *You* are mine, and no one, not even the Goodly God, is yours." Balatore walked up to Sedarus, who stiffened as he heard the scraping of the elf's blade as he slid it from its sheath.

"Do I have to kill you? I do not want to, but if you attack me, Balatore, I will."

"No, no. Tehehe! I offer my fealty." He kneeled, the dirt not clinging to his clothes, and he bowed his head, offering Sedarus his frost-encrusted blade.

"I deny it," Sedarus stated simply.

"Why?" Balatore was more curious than angry.

"I will not accept fealty from anyone."

"That will change, milord."

"Do not call me that!"

"You have no hold over me, as you will not accept my fealty. I can call you what I want … milord." Balatore grinned, ending with a mischievous chuckle. "Take my fealty and you can order me to stop calling you so. Of course, I may or may not obey. I am usually insubordinate. Tehehe!"

"You will do as I ask?" Sedarus's curiosity was piqued.

"Err … usually … depends on what you ask."

"What am I?" Sedarus asked, lowering his body so that they were face-to-face.

"I am sworn not to reveal that."

"By whom?"

"Tinen."

"You said you were usually insubordinate. And plus, *I* am your lord," Sedarus stated, his voice drowning in cynicism.

"So you accept?"

"Accept what?"

"My fealty, of course!"

"Yes, yes. Just tell me what you were sworn not to," Sedarus said, impatience rising into his chest.

Balatore heaved a dramatic sigh. "I cannot, milord; Tinen would destroy me." There was a pause, then a laugh. "At least he would try!"

"I give your fealty back," Sedarus said dryly. "You are free."

"Tehehe! Too late, milord; I am now yours to command."

Sedarus rolled his eyes and heaved a sigh at the words.

Balatore quickly rose to his feet, sliding his sword back into its sheath and picking up the magical dagger. It flared its ocean-green color as he did so.

"Why are you sworn not to tell me?"

"Like I know the reasoning behind a god," Balatore scoffed with another small laugh. "Well actually I do, but—"

"You cannot speak of it. Yes, yes," Sedarus droned. "Can you tell me why you are dressed, as Rishkiin puts it, like a fairy?"

"You … are … so …" Balatore fought for the right words, his body actually shaking with disbelief.

Sedarus tossed his head back, his mouth wide, and issued forth a barking, erratic noise of laughter. The tone and volume both rose to a peak and then fell once more as the monk's breath ran low and he ended the effort.

"Ugh! Was that like the second time you've ever laughed? You really need to work on that," critiqued the master of a thousand laughs.

"I am sorry, Balatore." Sedarus turned to leave, but he found his path blocked by the elf, his blades in his hands.

"Move out of my way," Sedarus said, pushing the flat of Balatore's sword aside.

Curiosity grasped the elf. He touched Sedarus with the flat of the blade again as he passed by. The monk whirled around, ready to fend off any attack. None came. Balatore just stood there, looking utterly confused.

"This does not hurt? Does not freeze?"

"No. Why? Should it?" Sedarus was cautious.

"Well … yeah." Balatore replaced his blades and brought his Diamond of Revealing from his magic pouch. The spherical diamond started to spin uncontrollably once the elf blew on it.

"Ah! That's why."

"What?" Sedarus was now curious as well.

"You have a cube on you, correct?"

"Yes," Sedarus replied, warily. "Why?"

"It is a Cube of Frost Resistance. Self-explanatory, really."

Sedarus fished out the small obsidian cube and asked, "This item I found is the reason your sword cannot freeze my skin?"

"Yes."

"How strong is this?" Sedarus asked inquisitively.

"Fairly strong," Balatore stated.

"Strong enough to resist the horrible frost breath of a white dragon?"

"I could hardly know!" Balatore declared. "But I know one particularly nasty white dragon. I could arrange a meeting. Tehehe!"

Sedarus eyed Balatore closely. He then turned and stalked off.

"Maybe you should start recruiting soldiers."

Sedarus turned around, his eyes popped open. "Why in the world would *I* do that?"

"An army might be helpful," the enigmatic follower explained, "since you are the one who must bring the world from darkness."

Sedarus rushed to the elf, drawing so close that Sedarus could feel Balatore's hot breath. "What do you know?" he demanded.

"Many things, I assure you, milord." Sedarus felt the bursts of breath from Balatore's fierce giggle.

"I mean about what is to come."

"I could not tell you."

"Why not? I order you to!"

"It is not that I will not. It is that I cannot." Balatore smiled. "I cannot see the future. No one can, not even the gods."

"Are my friends in danger?" Sedarus asked, his pale skin luminescent in the moon's glow.

"More than you can imagine, milord." Balatore halted the monk, as he was about to rush to the aid of his companions. "Not in immediate danger. Yet they walk with you."

"Of course they do … what do you mean?"

"That you are targeted," Balatore informed.

"By whom?"

"I know not."

"Then how do you know at all?"

"Because that is how it always is." Balatore's voice was soft, sorrow filled. He let a long, defeated sigh draw out.

"Are you all right?" Sedarus said, even as he was surprised that he was concerned for the annoying elf.

"Yes, milord. Thank you for your concern. But tonight you need your rest. I'll keep vigilant watch over you and your friends this night—and always."

Chapter Eighteen

"You insolent fool!" Tinen snapped as soon as Sedarus was out of hearing range. "You told him—"

"Nothing! I suggested an army of faithful soldiers would be needed. Just giving him the advice you never got. I tired of Trathcot winning, always with the upper hand."

"Trathcot does *not* have the upper hand," Tinen sputtered, referring to the evil god of murder and deceit.

"Please, Tinen, do not lie to me," Balatore stated, irritated. "Trathcot is winning this war. He has been for thousands of years. But maybe soon he'll be put in his rightful place."

Once again Tinen was reminded why he so trusted Balatore. The elf was never afraid to tell the terrible truth, if it so helped his purpose, no matter to whom—even a god.

"I will not live through another eon of hell!" Balatore spat, irritation turning to outright anger.

"How was it my fault that you were living in hell, Balatore?" Tinen asked.

"Because of your stubbornness, your thick skull would not let in the truth!" Balatore raged, turning to face the deity.

Tinen took Balatore's ranting nonchalantly. The elf finally bowed in respect and silently asked forgiveness.

"So you are going to build him an army?"

"Yes," Balatore replied. "As soon as I can. I will be the general if I must."

Tinen chuckled. "You? A general of an army?"

Balatore joined in laughing with his former master.

Then Tinen was suddenly serious. "You face the penalty of oblivion for giving aid to Sedarus. You know we cannot interfere, only counsel. If Trathcot finds out, you will be destroyed, body and soul, and doomed to oblivion. Forever."

"Then do not tell him I've done so," Balatore said.

"I shall not, but if he were to find out—"

"How would he?" Balatore interrupted. "I do not have daily meetings with the god of murder and deceit."

Tinen nodded, accepting the retort. "Why do you think that Sedarus will have trouble accepting the truth?" he asked, moving on.

"Because he is like you."

"True, but I believe he is stronger than I ever was."

"Meh," Balatore said, shrugging as if Tinen's opinion did not matter, which it did not. "Whether he accepts the truth or not is neither my concern nor in my control. What is my concern is the creation of his army. I will not be on the losing side … for a second time."

"Losing side?" Tinen asked. "We lost a few battles; you earned a few scars … so what?"

"A few scars?" Balatore nearly screamed. He was hysterical for the first time in his life.

He touched the gold earring at the top of his left ear. Suddenly his features reverted back to his natural form. He once had been beautiful, but the multitude of flaming scars now covering his face made that impossible to believe. His right ear was missing entirely, as were chunks of his lips and cheeks. Tinen could see cracked teeth from within the holes in the scarred cheeks. The hideousness of Balatore's true features filled the deity with pity, which only enraged the elf even more.

Balatore spoke, his torn lips not even touching each other. "You know nothing of what I've given for you and your father!"

Tinen lowered his head in shame, knowing that what the elf said was true. He knew that he had asked and asked and asked of Balatore, and the elf had never disappointed him. Not once. "Forgive us, Balatore," the deity said.

Balatore sighed, reaching up and touching his earring, bringing back the magically altered, beautiful face.

"So you will be ready for what is to come?" Tinen asked after a moment's pause.

"Depends. What is to come?"

"You know that I cannot tell you, as my father before me could not."

"Then we will be as ready as can be." Balatore turned from Tinen, obviously finished with the chat. "Speak with Rishkiin if you want Sedarus to construct an army," the elf called as he walked away.

"The young fighter? Why?"

"He is the one who will lead the soldiers effectively."

"I shall," Tinen said. "And then I will call upon some of my devoted followers to aid you and Sedarus."

"Good."

Balatore sat on a limb of a tree overhanging the campsite. He gazed at the red coals yet did not see them, instead looking far back into his memory, replaying a horrid moment in his life. He unconsciously caressed the scars on his face that were hidden by his magical earring. Balatore kept on witnessing the troll shredding his face into nothing but garish gore. Over and over he heard the beast's roars of glee, the bloodlust-filled grunts and barks, reliving the terror he had experienced back when he was young. The elf remembered his whole family disowning him because of his hideousness, all except his wonderful wife. She was the person who had brought him from his self-imposed prison, the only one who had even cared.

Memories of her beautiful, gold hair, violet eyes, and perfect figure led his memory back to the horror of her demise. He saw her rapist and murderer fleeing from her broken body.

Balatore's breathing quickened, rage filling his lungs. He vividly recalled his sword cutting into the mongrel's flesh. The elf could recollect every puncture, every slash he had inflicted in his lover's killer. He remembered the distasteful emotions that had swelled within him as he'd returned to his wife's lifeless form.

Tears rolled down his deceptively alluring face as he recollected her funeral. He was the only one to attend, due to his wife's own family having cast her out for not leaving Balatore. Anger at the world expanded inside his chest; his blood boiled with wrath.

A perfect picture of her face, unscathed and whole, popped into his mind. He knew instinctively that Tinen was giving him peace from his sordid past. He quietly thanked the deity, sighing with relief as the picture not only stayed with him, but started to expand. It lovingly embraced his mind, leaving room for naught but itself.

"Oh, Alesmi," Balatore sighed, smiling at the sound of his wife's name. Just saying it, Alesmi, brought light into what seemed dark and dreary.

"Who's Alesmi?"

Balatore leapt to his feet on the branch, pulling free his blades. Luckily, his glowing dagger lit up the speaker's face, below. It was Aunddara. That he had not heard her walk beneath the tree instantly sent anger coursing through him.

"What do you want?" Balatore snapped as he placed his sword and dagger back in their sheaths.

"I want to know who Alesmi is. That is why I asked," Aunddara barked back, beginning to climb the tree.

"No, you came over here because you are attracted to me," Balatore replied angrily, wanting nothing more than the memory of his lovely wife to surround him with loving caress.

"I am not attracted to you!" Aunddara scoffed, looking at the shining moon. It was large and unobstructed by clouds, its rays flooding everything.

"Then why have you climbed up this bloody tree?"

"Err ..." Aunddara fumbled for words, unsuccessfully.

"You are attracted to me," Balatore stated. Then a sudden inspiration came to him. He gave a tinkling laugh. "Or you are just pretending to be fascinated by me! To what end? To make Sedarus jealous?"

Aunddara's silence spoke volumes.

"Ooh, we're getting somewhere!" Balatore laughed quietly again, his old self seeming to come back to him.

"I don't know what you are talking about, elf." Aunddara was nearly invisible with her magical armor, yet with his eagle eyes Balatore could easily make out her features. He could tell that she was flustered, his comments making her blush.

"Oh, but that path will end badly for you," Balatore said solemnly.

"What path?" Aunddara raged, though quietly so as not to wake anyone up.

"Pursuing the Pale One."

"I told you not to call him that!" Aunddara snarled, punching his arm.

"You are neither my master nor someone I would care to listen to." He chuckled. "My master would say the same as I, though."

"And who is your bloody master? I will have to kill him, too!"

"*Tehehe*! The Pale One holds my fealty!" Balatore grinned. "Will you kill him?"

Aunddara paused in shock. She did not know what to say other than, "He has your allegiance? Why?"

"It is really none of your business." Balatore grinned mischievously.

"He is my companion and friend!" Aunddara nearly shouted into the night sky.

"He is milord! I would not betray him to some woman who fancies me!" Balatore said dramatically, smiling wider with every second.

"Fancies you?" Aunddara jumped from the branch.

"So it was but a facade, my dear?" Balatore feigned hurt.

"You are completely impossible!" Aunddara growled as she stalked back to her bedroll.

She was followed by the elf's gently rolling laughter.

Chapter Nineteen

Balatore was awake, not having been able to rest, when dawn came rolling around. He greeted Sedarus as the monk arose, first among his friends to do so. Silence then engulfed the two for many moments.

"What you said last night … about me leading this world from darkness. Was it true?" Sedarus eventually whispered, almost to himself, yet Balatore heard.

"Of course!"

"You could have been lying," Sedarus argued.

"Yes, I could have. Though if I'd lied, I would have made up a much more fantastic story. But alas, I did not. You are an essential figure for the future. I spoke nothing but the truth," Balatore stated.

"How could that be?" Sedarus asked.

Balatore grinned. "Well, I told you what actually is, not something that I made up." He laughed. "That's how the mechanics of telling the truth works, milord."

Sedarus snapped his gaze up, not appreciating the elf's jibe.

Balatore sighed dramatically. "You were destined to bring this dark world into the light the moment you were conceived by your miserable father and whatever whore that could tolerate his—"

"That's enough! If you ever speak about my mother that way again, Balatore, I will be forced to slay you where you stand!" Sedarus would not tolerate any ridicule about his mother—a mother he had never known, who had died in child birth.

Balatore saw that he had made a mistake, a serious and potentially dangerous one. He bowed. "Please forgive me, milord."

Another long and quiet pause passed between the two, and then Sedarus said, "I know you are not lying, but it is impossible!"

"As is disintegrating giants, knowing when magic items are activated, knowing when lies are spread before you. Shall I go on?"

"I get your point!" Sedarus sighed, defeated. "You were saying that I should recruit soldiers … why?"

"You'll need them." The elf's eyes went hazy, as if going through a memory.

Sedarus asked, "How do you know?"

He chuckled gently, mirthlessly. "I've been through this a few times." Balatore's eyes returned to focus as he looked at Sedarus.

"Been through what?" Sedarus questioned, his brow scrunched in confusion.

"The brink of destruction," Balatore replied.

"All your half-truths and cryptic words are getting irksome, elf." Sedarus was trying hard to control his anger. "I am not some savior; I'm not some vital being!"

"Yes, Sed, you are!" a different voice called from behind him.

Sedarus turned to face Rishkiin standing alone in the morning's haze. His body seemed to be engulfed by glaring rays of gold.

"Why would you say that, Rish?"

"As much as I hate to agree with that fairy, I do. Plus, Tinen visited my slumber." Rishkiin walked forward, unsheathing Glimmer. Balatore moved to place his body in between the two, protectively.

"Move out of my way, fairy!" Rishkiin snarled.

"I cannot allow you near milord with a weapon."

"Move, Balatore," Sedarus said, placing a hand on the elf's shoulder. "He means me no harm."

Balatore was not convinced, or he wanted to not be convinced, yet he moved all the same.

"I offer you my life and my soul, my lord." Rishkiin bowed, offering the hilt of his magic sword.

The young fighter remained there for long moments as Sedarus thought. Before he reached out for the sword, he looked at Balatore. "An army?"

Balatore grinned, nodding.

The monk clasped the hilt with his hand. His skin was bone white. Glimmer shivered, it seemed to Sedarus. He mentally asked the blade why.

Your power! the blade replied. *It stings us!*

Sedarus quickly returned the sword to his friend, who rose to his feet.

"Do you not feel like you're betraying Tinen's trust?" Sedarus asked.

"If he had not suggested that I pledge myself to you last night, then … it still would not have mattered," the young fighter said, shrugging.

Balatore laughed.

Rishkiin continued as if he had not heard the elf. "As far as I understand, Tinen needs you for some reason. And you need your friends. I am with you, Sed."

"Well, Commander," Sedarus said, fully facing toward Rishkiin, "will you fill all our water skins? I found a creek beyond those trees. The water looks relatively clean."

"Commander?" Rishkiin asked, surprised. A commander in an army was the second highest rank, just below a general.

"Commander?" Balatore asked, his voice revealing his displeasure. He then continued, catching Sedarus's glare. "What say you, Commander of the Pale One's army?"

"Don't call Sed that!" Aunddara roared, interjecting as she rose from her bed. Haet and Rhamor simultaneously rose as well.

"No, Aun," Sedarus said, smiling, looking at his skin. "I like it."

Balatore cackled and looked at Rishkiin. "Well, Commander … your lord asked you to perform a duty. Now if you are incapable, I would be happy to comply."

Rishkiin snorted with rage as he picked up the six identical leather water skins. He disappeared through the trees.

While he was gone, Balatore started a fire and began cooking breakfast, while Haet and Rhamor pledged themselves to Sedarus. Tinen had come to each of them, also, suggesting that they give their fealty to their leader and companion.

Aunddara began to kneel, but Balatore halted her. " You cannot pledge yourself to Sedarus. Your divine magic comes from the one who holds your fealty, Tinen. Sedarus will not be able lend you healing magic, as he does not reign in the heavens." He paused and pointed at Rhamor. "He will have enough trouble with the paladin's healing miracle, having sworn himself to Sedarus."

Aunddara glared at the elf, knowing a lie when she heard one. Sedarus looked at Balatore knowingly, inquiringly, yet the elf gave nothing away.

At that moment, Rishkiin returned. He placed his water skin on his log and began dispensing the others. As he sat down, he locked gazes with Balatore, never moving his. Balatore took a sip of water.

"Ha!" Rishkiin shouted, standing up, gaining everyone's attention. "I pissed in yours! You just drank my pee!" The young fighter then drank from his water skin. It took him a moment to realize that the liquid was warm. His eyes popped wide, and he spewed the liquid everywhere.

"That is why I switched water skins." Balatore let out a wild cackle, laughing even more as Rishkiin gagged himself, trying to vomit the rest of his urine. He did so ... directly onto the fire and the food that was cooking.

"You imbecile!" Balatore yelled. "Well, that ruins breakfast."

"Ugh!" Aunddara covered her mouth. "I need to wash up now."

"Would you like an escort, milady?" Balatore asked kindly. Too kindly, Sedarus thought.

"Yes, thank you." Aunddara and Balatore disappeared into the forest.

"What was that all about?" Haet asked as he walked to Sedarus.

"I do not know." Sedarus was curious, but then his head started to tingle. Subtly, then more steadily he began to hear a voice. It was deep, somber. It was Rhamor's! Sedarus could not make out the words; he looked at his friend. Rhamor had his eyes closed, his head bowed.

"What is it?" Haet asked, worried.

"I can hear Rhamor praying ... to Tinen," Sedarus gasped. He was surprised just as much as Haet.

You can hear his thoughts? What about mine? Haet asked silently. A wide-eyed Sedarus turned to face his monk brother.

"Rhamor!" Haet called. The paladin got to his feet, his sentient sword in his hand. With a thought from Rhamor, his sword burned with an angry white light.

"What is wrong?" the man asked, slightly confused.

"Sedarus can hear you praying. Could you hold off until he can control his powers more?"

"Oh." Rhamor grinned sheepishly. "Sorry, my lord."

"I am not your lord," Sedarus objected.

"With all respect, you are, sir," Rishkiin said wiping vomit from his goatee.

"Fine, but I am still your friend. Sed will do. Please!"

"Thanks!" Rishkiin said, smiling. "*Milord* was going to take a long time to get used to!"

Sedarus smiled, glad to have at least Rishkiin think of him of a friend still—if not a normal person. "Sure thing, Rish," he replied.

"Where'd Aun and Balatore go?" Rhamor asked.

"Into the forest," Haet answered.

"To do what?"

"Aunddara's washing up," Sedarus said.

Rhamor frowned deeply. "I don't like it."

"I think we might have to castrate the fairy," Rishkiin growled.

"No," Sedarus said, calming the two. He was listening to Balatore's thoughts. Sedarus was befuddled as to how he could hear his friends' thoughts … all but Aunddara's. Sedarus could only surmise that he heard the thoughts of his subjects. "They are talking right now, nothing more."

"Why don't you want me to pledge myself to Sedarus?" Aunddara queried.

"You mean, give yourself to him."

"Bite your tongue! What is wrong with giving my fealty to the lord of my choice?"

Balatore did not answer. The silence lasted long, agonizing moments.

"Answer!" Aunddara raged.

"You told me to bite my tongue." He giggled madly. "You contradict yourself."

Aunddara took in large breaths, her chest puffing out in rage.

"Because if you do so, you will be connected to Sedarus!" Balatore yelled. "Intimately so."

"That is what I want!" Aunddara yelled back.

"I know. But he is not just some lord you can give your fealty. You'd be giving him your complete soul. He would see your deepest, darkest thoughts," Balatore said, whispering. "That is not what the Pale One wants. It would be torture for him! It is my job to protect him! Even from lovesick friends," Balatore said softly. "Find someone else to dote on."

He left Aunddara crying by the creek.

Chapter Twenty

The warm sunlight did not last. Black storm clouds rolled in around mid morning. Pouring rain pelted the companions as they ran as fast as the muddy ground would allow, having let the fleeing merchants take their horses. The companions skirted the road, remaining under the thick cluster of pine trees, hoping that the trees would deter the rain. They didn't. Rhamor and Rishkiin cursed the horrid weather soaking their armor.

Everyone shivered in the cold rain—except for Balatore. The elf's clothes remained completely dry, wholly unaffected by the precipitation.

Only one of them was grateful for the stormy morning. Aunddara was shivering, but not from the cold dampness. Her vision was not blurry from running water but from weepy eyes. None of her friends could decipher the truth, thankfully.

Balatore kept watch over the heartbroken cleric. She was constantly falling behind, grabbing the sides of her chest in a self-encompassing hug. One time he slowed his pace to walk beside her, but she stiffly looked the other way and stomped rapidly away.

"You may have been too stern with her, my friend."

Balatore slowly turned and then bowed to Sedarus. He was completely taken off guard by the monk's presence suddenly behind him. The last he had known, Sedarus was near the front of the single-file line.

"Milord, I spoke words that needed to be said, nothing less and nothing more." Balatore bowed once more, solemnly. He was regretting having halted the cleric's pursuit of love.

"Do not feel regret, Balatore."

Sedarus just kept on surprising the elf.

"You are growing dramatically stronger, milord," Balatore stated.

Sedarus ignored the comment and continued on with the subject of Aunddara. "Aun loves me, but I cannot return that love. Not the way she wants."

"That is exactly what I told her," Balatore replied. "Yet I feel rotten for doing so."

"That is because you know what she feels," Sedarus calmly stated, walking beside the elf.

Rain ran like tears from Balatore's eyes.

Sedarus continued, "Alesmi is proud of you."

Balatore whipped around, grabbing Sedarus's soaking-wet robes. "How did you know that name?" the elf yelled.

The others looked back at the outburst, curious. Rishkiin made a grab for his sword, a smile on his face. Haet halted the young fighter.

"I was the one who sent you the unblemished picture of her last night, not Tinen. I am not sure how I did so, but I knew the moment your heart was lifted, I felt her presence. She is proud of you," Sedarus stated again.

Balatore let go, arched his back, and screamed with anger. He quickly curled into a ball and began to weep. Sedarus motioned for the others to go on without them. His friends, all wide-eyed, obeyed nonetheless.

"She came to me last night," Sedarus said, laying his hand on Balatore's sobbing shoulder. "Alesmi told me her story and yours. She has never left your side throughout your journeys. She loves you very much.

"Cast aside your anger at the gods—past, present, and … future," Sedarus pled. "It is wasting you away. I see your true form; I know what happened. I can see the past; I watch as Tinen leaps full on into a den of trolls, foolhardily. You saved him, even while suffering many horrible wounds, many of them mortal. Yet you survived. Why?"

Balatore panted with suffocating rage. He looked up, his magical mask broken to Sedarus. His scarred, contorted face moved in disgusting unison to say one word. "Hate!"

"Your hate is not directed at me or Tinen. Who, then, Balatore?" Sedarus knew the answer, but he wanted to hear it from Balatore. He wanted the elf to admit his anger so he could clasp a hold of it and rid himself of it.

"I hate him! I hate him so much!" the elf screamed in Sedarus's face.

"Who?" Sedarus coaxed.

"The one who ra … raped and murdered my Alesmi," the elf stuttered through body-jerking sobs. Genuine tears ran down Balatore.

"Who, Balatore?" Sedarus softly asked again.

"My brother! I *hate* him!"

"I know, Balatore, I know. But you need to forgive, to let go of your anger." Sedarus wrapped the elf in hug, lending his own strength to his friend.

Balatore wept in Sedarus's arms for only moments before he could support himself again. He stood, staring at Sedarus, unashamed of his tears.

"When did you become so wise?" he asked.

"As soon as I decided to listen," Sedarus said, his ice-blue eyes never leaving the elf's eagle orbs. "Quickly now!" he stated. "Let us catch up to our friends."

The two made up the distance fairly quickly and easily, even through the rain and mud. All of them were in dour moods as they stalked through the forest, each secluded from the rest. The day rambled on, thunder coughing and lighting striking.

By midday, Ashten Vale had entered their sights. The forty-foot stone walls and the iron-bound gates made the group feel at home. The temple in which they had grown up was surrounded by a massive city, thrice as large as Ashten Vale. Even so, their worries seemed to lessen as they entered a city once more, passing by the greeting guards.

The city was square, with four surrounding walls. Just on the inside of the walls were residences. Then closer to the center of the city was the market district. Shops of all sorts lined the streets, as did several different inns. Finally, at the center of the city was the keep, its spires rising high into the sky.

"We should make for an inn—"

"Help me! *Help!*" a feminine voice roared above the wild wind.

Blades were instantly in the companions' hands. They raced toward the screaming woman, Rishkiin leading the group down the alley. It was dark and stank of spirits and vomit.

At the back of the alleyway, five men were tearing at the woman's clothing. She thrashed and hit and kicked at them, keeping them at bay, yet she clearly could not hold out much longer. Rishkiin roared, rushing forward.

As soon as the five men turned to face the newcomer, the young fighter activated the magic in his ring. Silently he disappeared. His loud movements were covered by the thundering disapproval of the rainstorm.

The men were surprised beyond all measure, but they had not the time to ponder, for there was Rhamor, closely followed by Sedarus and Haet. Before even the paladin and the two monks could reach the thugs, a flaming bolt shot past them, plunging into the closest man. He was flung backward, and then he convulsed as electricity shot through his veins. He never got up again.

Then another man was down, his severed head touching the wet cobblestones before his body could react and collapse to the ground. Rishkiin appeared, standing above the beheaded man, growling in rage at the last three. He lunged forward, running a man through with Glimmer. He retracted the sword just as the last two street-rats ran away in fear. Sedarus and Haet ran after the two, but the two men had escaped through the sewers.

The two monks returned to the group as Rishkiin quickly sheathed his blade and rushed to the damsel. She could not have been more than twenty-five years of age, and her beauty halted the young fighter. Her sapphire-blue eyes glinted in the storming sky, her long, blond hair whipping in the strong wind. She sported such a figure that even Haet could not avert his gaze.

"Err … milady … are you all right?" Rishkiin had the mind to ask, still staring at her beautiful form.

"Yes, but my eyes are up here, sir knight."

Her voice was liquid gold! Rishkiin could hardly breathe, her beauty swiping away his breath.

Rishkiin coughed, slightly embarrassed. He took the lady's outstretched hand and helped her to her feet. He coughed once more as he realized his gaze was still upon her figure.

"My apologies, dear lady," Rishkiin stated as he forced his eyes to the gray cobblestone. His gut turned as he felt her delicate hand slide down to his.

"All is forgiven, sir knight." Her pearly white teeth nearly shone in the dark as she smiled widely.

"He is unquestionably *not* a knight, milady," Balatore interjected with a spurt of laughter.

Rishkiin's goatee quivered in rage, and then he whispered so just the lady could hear, "*He* is unquestionably a fairy!"

The blond-haired woman giggled, her un-held hand covering her cherry-colored lips. She momentarily locked her gaze with Rishkiin.

For one so versed in reading humans, Balatore grinned as he discerned what was to come. He couldn't suppress a titter—not that he would ever quell a laugh!

"What is it?" Sedarus whispered, standing next to the elf, rain droplets running down his white face.

"Well, with the gratitude that is emanating from this young female, I would say that our friend will find himself having a pleasurable night, if you get my meaning." Balatore gave an exaggerated wink and nudged the monk.

"May I ask your name?" Rishkiin questioned.

"Elzera Ashten," the lady replied.

"Ashten? As is Ashten Vale?" Rhamor asked.

"Yes. I am the daughter of the city's baron."

"Well it was lucky that we happened to come this way when we did, Milady Ashten. Are you wounded? I am a cleric and would be pleased to assist if needed," Aunddara stated as she walked to the woman.

"None that would require the healer's touch, Madame Cleric," Elzera said. Her intelligent eyes ran up and down Aunddara, sizing her up. The baron's daughter was apparently pleased, for she smiled at the cleric of Tinen.

"Come with me," Elzera suddenly pled, turning to Rishkiin and pulling on his arm. "My father will want to thank you personally for saving me."

The companions followed, some more enthusiastic than others. Rishkiin was smiling at the court lady the whole way to the keep, leading the others. Rhamor and Aunddara came next, then Haet. Sedarus purposefully stayed back with Balatore, who took his lute out of his magical pouch.

"Do you think that Rishkiin and Elzera will get us into trouble?" Sedarus asked the elf.

"Undoubtedly, Milord. Tehehe!"

"What should we do?"

"I care not what *you* do. But as for me … I shall write a song!"

Chapter Twenty-One

Baron Irel Ashten had insisted that the companions dine with him and his daughter that evening. They sat at the darkly polished oak table. Each felt refreshed, having just taken a bath and cleaned up. As blood-stained attire was ill-suitable for court dinner, Baron Irel had gathered fitting clothes for them.

Sedarus gazed around the table. Baron Irel sat at the head of the table, of course. To his right was his daughter and to his left was Rishkiin. The young fighter looked rather handsome; he had trimmed his goatee which had started to become wild, and he was dressed in a black velvet doublet, which was lined in silver and had jeweled buttons.

Oddly enough, Rishkiin's frock matched Lady Elzera's perfectly. Her fantastic dress seemed to have been woven around her stunning features. The dark satin gown, like Rishkiin's doublet, was lined with silver.

Next to Rishkiin was Rhamor. The holy knight had settled for something less ostentatious than Rishkiin. The burly man wore a simple white cotton, laced-up gambeson. Across from Rhamor was Aunddara, who looked gorgeous in her dress. It was a two-piece rayon gown with golden champagne floral designs, its sleeves lined in a deep burgundy. Tightly around Aunddara's throat was a jewel-encrusted neckband.

Next to the beautiful cleric was the humble Haet who, like Sedarus, was dressed in brand new sky-blue robes. Balatore sat in front of Haet, sandwiched between Rhamor and Sedarus. The elf wore his own tight-fitting clothes. He was also the only person who refused to leave his weapons in his room.

Servants entered the large dining room bearing platters of food. Roasted boar and cooked vegetables covered the entire table. Grins spread across the companions' faces as they stared in awe at the amazing food before them.

Baron Irel stood up from his high-back chair. His face was wrinkled with age and his mane-like hair and mustache were grayed from age, though his voice was strong.

"Thank you all for saving my beautiful daughter. She is all I have left in his world. Now," a smile crossed the baron's face, "let us eat."

As if on cue, music began to softly play. The friends looked around the room. By the roaring fire were three minstrels playing the lute, harp, and recorder. The music was soothing as the companions began to eat. Several different conversations took place at once throughout dinner. Sedarus refrained from speaking. He just watched his friends as they pleasantly bickered and laughed. The monk was relaxed for the first time in several months.

Soon everyone was pushing their empty plates away, their stomachs enjoyably full. Baron Irel quickly excused himself muttering something about "official business." Lady Elzera grinned mischievously at Rishkiin as her father exited the dining hall. The woman grabbed the young fighter's hand and pulled him to a cleared area and began dancing with him. Rishkiin's face reddened as Rhamor and Aunddara scoffed at him. Everyone laughed.

Then, surprisingly, Balatore sauntered to Aunddara and with an extravagant bow, he asked the cleric to dance. The woman's eyes widened. Then with a hint of a smile touching her lips, she agreed. The two rushed to the dance floor.

The three minstrels livened up their tunes, as they now had an attentive and dancing audience. Rhamor, Haet, and Sedarus laughed as their friends danced with enthusiasm. As a new song began to play, Rhamor and Haet stepped in, dancing with the lovely ladies. Sedarus excused himself from dancing, having plenty of fun watching.

As the hour got late, the minstrels needed to take a short break from playing. This seemed like the perfect time for the companions to retire to their separate chambers. Each thanked Lady Elzera for the wonderful evening, as she in turn thanked them. Her eyes lingered on Rishkiin as they disappeared.

The young fighter could not keep Lady Elzera from his mind as he entered his chambers. Long minutes passed as Rishkiin remembered the night's events. The man shivered with delight as he recalled the woman's soft touch. He smiled, picturing her, as he undressed himself, placing his doublet at the foot of his bed.

At that moment he heard a slight shuffle just outside of his door. He glanced outside his window. It was still dark, the middle of the night. Rishkiin quickly and mutely unsheathed Glimmer and snuffed out the single candle in his room. The young fighter placed himself to the hinge side of the door, readying himself for a fight, should there be one.

The door latch lifted haltingly, and into the dark shuffled a heavily cloaked figure of slight build and shorter than the man.

An assassin! Rishkiin thought. With naught but his brown leather breeches and boots on, he started forward. He deftly placed the tip of Glimmer to the figure's kidney. A startled gasp reached Rishkiin's ears.

"Make a sudden movement and I'll run you through." His voice was dark, relaying death. "Now, slowly turn around and remove your cowl."

The figure complied. Rishkiin gasped and lowered Glimmer. There stood Lady Elzera, clad in a beautiful, rather revealing nightgown. Rishkiin had to bring forth all of his willpower to look directly into her eyes.

Yet Elzera had still more difficulty looking away from Rishkiin's well-corded arms and chest. Her gaze lingered on his body for long moments before she looked to his brown eyes.

"Why have you come, Lady Elzera?" Rishkiin sheathed Glimmer and walked toward her.

"To thank you for saving my life," she replied. Her sapphire eyes could not cease to roam over his muscular abdomen; the orbs clearly foretold her intent.

"Yet you could have done that with more appropriate clothes," Rishkiin teased.

"They would only get in the way," she said, grinning.

Walking forward, she placed her hand on the young fighter's bare chest. She drew so close that the young fighter could feel her hot breath, her touch igniting his inner fire. Pulling her closer, he could feel the warmth emanating from her body. Kissing passionately, they made their way to the bed.

"Balatore," Sedarus called to the elf.

"Milord?"

Balatore was in his room playing his lute. He continued to do so as Sedarus stalked in.

"I am sorry I brought up your wife earlier."

Balatore gulped, stopped playing, and forced his gaze to meet his lord's.

"It's ... all right, milord." The elf began to play once more.

Sedarus nodded and awkwardly turned about, leaving Balatore. The monk returned to his room, which was no more than a servant's abode, the likes of a cell. He had refused anything more, as had Haet. His straw mattress was wet, making a horrid smell. Cobblestone surrounded him, and only a candle lit the windowless room. But the monk did not care, instead focusing on the voices he heard in his mind.

Haet was kneeling, saying his nightly prayer. It felt strange, majestic, to Sedarus. He heard every word with perfection. The monk also heard Rhamor muttering under his breath about needing to see the smithy about his shredded armor. Sedarus heard Rishkiin ... pulling away from that scene, he listened for Balatore.

He felt a strange pull to the elf that he couldn't explain to anyone. But suddenly Balatore was his closest friend, his most trustworthy advisor. He hardly believed it himself. Yet he could not deny what was.

He sighed and laid his head back, searching for sleep that did not come. Instead Sedarus kept a close watch on Balatore's mind, experiencing his raw emotion.

Horrible memories of his brother standing over his wife's body flooded him. Feelings of pleasure ensued, as he remembered cutting his brother, piece by piece. Then the regret, the drowning feeling of being alone, swarmed the elf's chest.

Sedarus closed his eyes, conveying a clear picture of Alesmi into Balatore's mind. To his surprise, the elf's mood switched from regret and despair to full outrage.

Stay out of my head, milord! Balatore's voice rang through Sedarus's mind. He sat up, looking around his room. He was alone.

"I cannot," Sedarus said aloud, still searching his room.

Why not?

"Because you are in *mine*," Sedarus shot back. "Where are you?"

There was a pause.

The elf issued an un-vocalized laugh that Sedarus heard anyway. *I am in my chambers. Please tell me you are not looking around your room for me!*

Silence.

You are? There was another uncontrolled bit of laughter. Balatore's mood changes gave Sedarus a headache. He knew of no one who could switch from depressed to rage to amusement in a matter of seconds.

Milord, you are a ... well you can speak with any of your subjects as if they were right in the room with you ... if you so choose. Tehehe!

Right, well ... as you were, commander, Sedarus thought. He wanted to see if Balatore would still be able to hear him if he used thoughts instead of words.

Commander? That is an outrage! I am your army's general! I am after all your most faithful servant. Not to mention longest.

Sedarus started to laugh, and laughed hard.

Very well, then, he thought. *Good night, Balatore.*

Good night, milord.

Sedarus settled down once more, but again he found he could not sleep. Minutes slipped into hours. Sleep did not come to the man, even after all of his human friends had been silent for many hours.

He noticed that Balatore never slept. Sedarus felt the elf's mind racing throughout the night. At the crack of dawn, Sedarus decided to go speak with the elf.

Balatore, Sedarus thought, *I wish to speak.*

Go on, milord.

In person, Balatore. With that, Sedarus focused on Balatore's heartbeat, which he could feel, and he started to fade out. The monk appeared right in front of Balatore, who was momentarily surprised.

The elf bowed deeply, his circlet-adorned head nearly touching his knees. He stood, grinned, and asked, "What can I do for you?"

"You do not sleep?"

Confusion racked Balatore's brain. "That is undeniably *not* what I expected! Tehehe!" Balatore paced the length of the room for moments and then spoke. "Elves do not sleep, milord. We obtain rest through other activities."

"Like what?"

"Why do you want to know?" Balatore returned.

"Just curious, since you are the only elf I have ever met."

Balatore eyed Sedarus with a keen stare. "We sing, dance, play music, tell tales, and so on. We are the bards of this world."

"And the rest of your kind are truly gone?" Sedarus queried.

"Yes. As Aunddara said the night you revealed my secret, they are deceased."

"I am sorry, Balatore." Sedarus bowed his head.

The elf laughed. "I care not for my kind, my wife being the exception."

"Why not? Do you not care that you are alone in this world? The last of your kind?"

"Well, truth be told, I am not the very last. There are a handful of us left in this world. Four, including me, milord," Balatore said.

Yet Sedarus was not listening. His mind had drifted far away. The monk's eyes popped wide suddenly.

"What is it?"

"Send for everyone!" Sedarus said even as he started to fade out.

But he was stopped by the elf's laughter. "Everyone?" Balatore said mischievously.

Sedarus sighed. "Our friends!"

"*Our* friends?"

Another sigh escaped Sedarus. "*My* friends, then. Just get to the south wall!" Then he was gone.

"Tehehe!"

"Marry me," Elzera stated as she woke up to Rishkiin's brown eyes.

The imprudent fighter was rarely flustered, but this was one of those moments. "What? Why?"

"Well …" Elzera giggled. "We …"

"Yeah, so?" Rishkiin said. "Why would we get married?"

"You are so thick!"

"I know!" Rishkiin agreed, exasperated.

"Why are you afraid of marrying me? You obviously have no problem bedding me!"

"Well …"

There came a sudden, telltale cackle, followed by the words, "Trouble in paradise?"

Elzera shrieked deafeningly and covered herself with the bedding. That brought forth another cackle from the elf.

"What in the Abyss are you doing in my room, fairy?" Rishkiin roared. He got up and reached for his sword.

"I would not advise raising a blade against your commanding officer!" Balatore drew his hand crossbow and aimed at Rishkiin's heart. "I am, after all, the general. Tehehe!"

"Get out!" Rishkiin growled, yet he did not draw Glimmer.

"Sedarus needs us," Balatore stated in a suddenly serious voice. Rishkiin halted for a moment before bustling into movement, starting to don his armor. It was difficult to do quickly, for it was rather heavy.

Help suddenly came; his armor was on before he knew it. He turned to face Balatore, the one who had helped.

"Err … thanks," Rishkiin said awkwardly.

Balatore nodded. "Kiss your maiden, and let us be gone!"

Rishkiin did so and then rushed out, pretending not to hear Elzera's protests.

"What has happened?" the young fighter asked Balatore.

"I know not, Rishkiin, but you need to get Rhamor and Haet and head for the south wall. Sedarus is waiting for you. Go now, with all haste!"

Rishkiin rushed off without another question. Balatore wound his way through the maze of rooms and chambers in the baron's keep. He turned down the corridor leading to Aunddara's room. There a man was kneeling, his eye pushed to a door's keyhole.

Balatore unsheathed his ice-coated rapier and stalked behind the man silently. He touched the flat of the blade to the man's neck and covered his mouth with his free hand. The man grunted in surprise and pain as the blade gave him instant frostbite, then he broke free and ran away, his feet slapping on the cobblestone floor.

Balatore kneeled and looked through the keyhole. There was Aunddara, dressing in her armor. The elf sighed, shook his head, and stood up. He knocked on the door. The cleric answered quietly.

"Who is it?"

"It's Balatore, my dear."

The door swung open, Aunddara's face inches from Balatore's. He felt her hot breath on his face. "Don't call me that."

The elf answered only with a tinkling chuckle.

"What do you want?"

"To be free, but that's not likely to happen."

Aunddara quirked her eyebrows in confusion. "Why are you here?" she asked more clearly.

"Sedarus needs us at the south wall."

At that, Aunddara started straight off in a rush, but she was halted by Balatore's outstretched hand. "I have a faster way."

Without warning his hand hooked her around the hip and pulled her near him. They disappeared, instantly reappearing at the south wall.

"Sed! What is it?" Aunddara asked upon seeing him.

Sedarus did not even look at her. He just kept on staring south, over the wall. Aunddara looked over as well and gasped with horror.

There, at the edge of the forest, stood monsters of all sorts, thousands of them, each and every one drooling in bloodthirsty anticipation.

Chapter Twenty-Two

"Baron Irel!" Rishkiin roared as he joined Sedarus on the south wall. He turned from the oppressing force. "Get the baron!"

"I am here."

Rishkiin swiveled to face the portly man. Baron Irel was alone on the wall a few paces away, no guards besides the few wall sentries. He was dressed in intricate armor, a broadsword on his left hip. The strong wind whipped his long, gray hair wildly and rustled his mustache.

"Baron, lord, you must send couriers to the surrounding cities asking for aid." Rishkiin walked to stand before the baron.

"I cannot," stated Baron Irel testily, disliking being told what to do.

"Why not?" Rishkiin asked annoyed.

"I will not spare preciously needed men. And seeing that force before us, we will need everyone."

"Then you will die, and your city will burn!"

"Commander! Hold your tongue." Balatore walked up, placing a calming hand on Rishkiin's shoulder. The young fighter looked up at Balatore and nodded curtly.

"Commander? He's no commander of my city. Who are you people?" Baron Irel barked.

"We are a secret society, and we can help," Balatore replied. "Our army is to the west. We need you to send a courier to the west!"

"Your army?" the baron questioned.

"Our *army*?" Sedarus whispered.

"Yes, our army, but they will need word of our quandary. So please spare one man and send him to the west."

Baron Irel thought for a moment and nodded disdainfully in consent. He called for the man with the fastest horse. The baron began to give him instructions. Right before he sent the men, Balatore interrupted.

"Come here, courier."

The man hustled over, eager to do his duty.

"You will find the general of his army," Balatore nodded at Sedarus, "in a city call Goe. Do you know where that is?"

"Yessir."

"Good. Give him this scroll." Balatore extended forth a scroll, which seemed to appear out of thin air. Then he quickly retracted it. "But first milord needs to sign." The elf held out the scroll for Sedarus, who took it and looked blankly at Balatore.

"Well, milord, sign it already."

"I cannot. I have no pen or ink."

Balatore came close, whispering, "Tehehe! You do not need any of that."

Sedarus concentrated for a moment. Then with a small flash of blue energy, the parchment was scarred with his name. At the bottom it read: Sedarus, the Pale One.

Balatore took the scroll, rolled it up, and handed it to the courier, who rushed off. Baron Irel just stared at Sedarus with his mouth open and his eyes wide.

"Your lord?" he questioned Balatore, who laughed a mild laugh. "All of yours?"

"Yes," Rishkiin replied. "You would be wise to show respect and to listen to all that Sedarus commands."

"Be still, Commander," Sedarus said after a pause, everyone waiting for him to speak. He faced Rhamor. "Commander Rhamor, you and Aunddara are to gather the women and children and prepare them for a hasty retreat, if necessary, through the north gate." Sedarus looked to Baron Irel to see if he was in accord. He was, reluctantly so.

"Commander Rishkiin, prepare the battlements. Gather the militia and town's guard. Prepare every man that can hold a sword. We will need them all.

"Haet," Sedarus said, facing his fellow monk, "I need you to contact the thieves' guild in this city. Promise gold for their services."

"The thieves' guild? Why?" Baron Irel asked snappishly.

"The thieves have something that could come in handy, something that we do not have."

"What could they possibly have that we do not?" Baron Irel asked, using a voice that clearly stated that he thought the notion preposterous.

"First off, they want to live and are extremely greedy. Second, they are masters of the shadows. Third, their fighting techniques are exceptional. Their strike-and-run tactics could be an asset to our cause. Will my claim have your support?"

The baron thought for a moment, then growled in anger. "Yes, gold will be offered to the thieves that help our cause ... *after* these monsters are gone."

"Good." Sedarus nodded to Haet, who rushed off.

Baron Irel left, shouting orders to the guards that came rushing.

"Do you think we have a chance?" Sedarus asked Balatore.

"Not without your army."

"Which I do not have," Sedarus growled at the elf.

He laughed heartily. "I'm surprised that you haven't asked about last night," he said, switching topics.

"What do you mean?"

"Tinen came to me," Balatore replied. "You did not know?" he asked, suddenly curious.

"No, I did not. What did he say?"

"That he has a contingent of faithful warriors ready to come to the aid of the Pale One. Tehehe!"

"What?" Sedarus was beyond shocked. "So we might actually have a chance?"

"Depends on what you mean ... surviving, yes. Winning, no." Balatore laughed madly again. "Between your power and General Aberoth's army, if he gets here in time, we may survive."

"Aberoth? That name sounds familiar," Sedarus said, racking his brain to find the answer.

"It probably is to you," Balatore replied. "He is infamous for what he was in the past. He was an assassin, a close follower of Trathcot. Then he was betrayed, and he switched sides to Tinen and raised an army."

"Can he be trusted?" Sedarus asked.

"Yes, I know him," Balatore returned.

"How do you know him?"

"Because I am the one who betrayed him," Balatore said, his face suddenly in a pained expression.

A long silent pause ensued. Then Sedarus broke it. "What is the enemy waiting for, out there?"

"There could be numerous reasons. They could be letting fear grip the defenders'—our—hearts. They could be waiting for more reinforcements, or they could be waiting for us to surrender."

The elf started to whistle, continuing after a short while. "I highly doubt that it is the second or third. They already outnumber us by ten to one, and they know we're too stubborn to surrender. They are waiting for fear to settle into our hearts, which of course will not happen while I'm here, tehehe!"

Sedarus went silent, keeping tabs on his friends. He had sent Aunddara with Rhamor because he could not read her mind like the rest of his friends. The monk kept an especially close watch on Haet. His fellow monk treaded, silently, through the sewers, searching for signs of the thieves' guild.

As the day rolled on, more and more men manned the wall. Their numbers ranked into the hundreds, but they were still outnumbered many times over. Nerves started to fry as the day was coming to an end, and the monsters had still not attacked.

Balatore brought out his lute and began to play and sing. His song was one of heroes of old, emboldening the soldiers. It gave them peace of mind.

As dusk came, Rishkiin returned with Aunddara and Rhamor. They were grim and somber.

"We've gathered the women and children near the north gate, my lord," Rhamor said, taking the part of commander seriously. Sedarus knew that his friend was calling him *lord* for show in front of the town's guard and militia.

"Commander Rishkiin? Your report," Sedarus said.

"I've gathered all that could hold a sword. They are on the wall, in the courtyard, or in the armory gathering weapons," Rishkiin stated, his face stone-cold.

"Very good. And the numbers?" Sedarus asked.

"We are numbering in the three to four hundred range, sire," Rishkiin replied.

Sedarus sighed. He looked down the wall line. Men were shoulder to shoulder on the forty-foot-high wall. The fortification was made out of stone, strong and well-worn, allowing the defenders the advantage of owning the stronger and higher ground.

"Where is Baron Irel?" Sedarus asked.

"He was in the armory when I left," Rishkiin informed.

"Fetch him for me."

"Certainly," Rishkiin said. He pointed at a soldier on the wall, "You there, find the baron and tell him the Pale One wishes to speak with him. Go now!"

"Yessir!" The guard left.

The soldier returned with Baron Irel soon, shortly after the sunset. The baron had a scowl on his face; it was clear to all that he detested being summoned by a … monk. "Yes, O Pale One?" he sneered, sarcasm dripping from his words

Rishkiin would not allow that. He snapped out Glimmer so quickly that the baron's guards had no time to react. Rishkiin settled Glimmer on the baron's quivering neck. "Speak to my lord disrespectfully one more time and I shall grant you the gift of silence, for your tongue will be on the ground."

"Commander! Lower your weapon!" Sedarus barked. "You will be disciplined, or you will be dismissed!"

Rishkiin snarled at Baron Irel but lowered his weapon.

"Baron, we need torches," Sedarus said calmly.

"Whatever for?" Baron Irel snapped. Rishkiin started forward, his knuckles white from gripping Glimmer so tightly. Balatore stopped him.

"We need the torches because we cannot see at night," Sedarus stated as if explaining something to a child.

"Fine," Baron Irel said. The man turned and walked away.

Men bustled about, lighting torches, making the fortifications ready for battle. The preparations, however, caused their nerves to begin to split once more. Balatore saw this and again began to sing his songs, ones of valor and courage.

Sedarus's commanders formed up watch shifts, and those who were not on watch slept in the courtyard just below the south gate. Once again this night, Sedarus could not sleep, so he and Balatore stood on the wall together all night. Nothing happened; no attack came. Haet did return from his mission, though.

"Good news, my liege," Haet spoke quietly.

"Yes?"

"The thieves' guild master agreed. He seems honorable enough, sire. For a thief."

"This is good news. Get some sleep, Haet; you will need it come morn. I can feel it."

The brisk morning wind woke most of the town's soldiers. The coldness of the breeze chilled them to the bone. Winter was on its way.

"Sedarus, you'll want the baron up here," Balatore whispered into the monk's ear.

"Why?" But Sedarus got the answer from the elf's mind a moment later. He urgently called to a soldier, "Wake Baron Irel!"

"I'm here, Pale One. What is it?"

"The enemy calls for a summit. There's a white flag." Sedarus pointed. Stalking out of the forest was an isolated group just out of archer range. There stood ten monsters, one waving the flag. They were too far away to be identified by anyone except Balatore.

"The flag bearer is an orc, milord. The leader is an ettin. It is a two-headed giant with orc-like features. The rest are one girallon, five bugbears, and two minotaur," Balatore said, adding his usual laugh as the excitement of battle overcame him.

"I request that Haet, Balatore, Rishkiin, and I come with you, Baron."

Baron Irel nodded grudgingly. He also picked four of his men, and the ten made their way to the gate. It opened just enough to let them out single-file. The guards swiftly closed it behind them.

The ten men made their way to the monsters' delegation. When they were ten feet away, they halted in unison. Silence engulfed them all. Then Sedarus finally spoke.

"What do you want?"

"You, Pale One. We want you!" the girallon growled, its four huge arms rising and falling with each breath. "Baron, spare your city. Give us the Pale One and we will leave you in peace."

"Done," Baron Irel immediately said.

"Not an option," Rishkiin said at the same time. He faced the baron, his hand on the hilt of his sword. "Are you truly that naïve? Do you believe that they will just let you live? Well, they won't!"

"Not your city, not your choice," Baron Irel responded. "Take the Pale One and leave."

All ten of the monsters started forward, intending to take Sedarus. The monk stood still and said quietly, "I'm not going anywhere."

Then he pushed energy into all ten of the monsters. The explosion was massive, sending everyone within thirty feet to their backsides, bathed in blood and gore.

Rishkiin, Haet, and Balatore had expected the blast, so they were the first to their feet. Rishkiin rushed to Baron Irel, putting his blade to the man's throat.

"Give me one reason why I should not slit your throat right now."

The baron could not answer; his eyes were wide, locked on Sedarus, full of fear. It did not even register that his life was in imminent threat.

"Rishkiin, let him up," Sedarus panted. His mind was clouded with exhaustion. Leaning heavily upon Balatore's supporting shoulder, he made his way back into the city.

The horde of monsters was stunned at the explosion. Only the order to charge, which rang from their leader's throat, had them acting once more. Yet they were too late to catch the group of men before they entered the city.

Chapter Twenty-Three

A wave of monsters came even as the group of men returned to the wall. It consisted of orcs, goblins, gnolls, and bugbears. They were all outfitted with finely made weapons and armor, ready for battle.

Rishkiin rushed to the wall and looked over, unsurprised that the assault would finally commence now. He pulled forth Glimmer, letting it shine with all its brilliance.

"Archers, ready yourselves!" he roared, taking the post of commander. None argued, not even Baron Irel, who was still staring blankly at Sedarus.

The beasts came on, carrying ladders and a battering ram. The monsters formed three columns of ten by ten. The creatures marched unusually, like human soldiers rather than ravaging monsters. It unnerved the defenders.

"Steady! Steady!" Rishkiin called out. Then as the front lines came into range, the young fighter shouted, "Fire!"

Hundreds of arrows soared through the air, whistling, promising death. Yet the exceedingly well-trained monsters simply dropped the ladders, holding their shields appropriately to block most of the arrows. Some got by, however, mostly killing weak goblins. The holes in the lines were quickly filled.

"Ready yourselves!" Rishkiin commanded.

The monsters picked up the ladders and began to rush forward again, trying to get in close enough to avoid the onslaught of arrows.

"Archers, loose!"

The previous scene was repeated. Few monsters were injured or killed. Once more the archers fired, and the monsters numbered about two hundred and fifty. They were now too close to the walls for arrows to strike.

"Swords!" Rishkiin roared over the whoops of the bloodthirsty monsters.

The monsters propped their ladders up along the south wall and began climbing them. Rishkiin settled himself right in between two ladders, eager for the battle. He heard the telltale cackle of Balatore and growled with anger.

The first orc popped its head up … its head fell off, lopped off by Glimmer. The second to appear was a gnoll, and it came up swinging its battle-axe. The axe clanged against Rishkiin's shield, rocking the creature back on the ladder. It fought to keep its balance. Yet Rishkiin could not finish it off, for a seven-foot-tall bugbear leapt onto the wall from the adjacent ladder, its massive club flinging a man off the ledge.

Rishkiin jabbed the bugbear in the gut, but the monster did not die. The young fighter pushed with all his strength, forcing the monster back. It fell off of the wall, taking the next four monsters on one ladder with it.

The gnoll had regained its balance and swung again as it jumped onto the wall. The axe caught Rishkiin on the shoulder, but his armor was unrelenting. Even though it did not cut the fighter, the blow stung mightily.

Rishkiin was undeterred. He jumped forward, head butting the hyena-like monster, his helmet protecting his head. The beast flung its head back, its dog face shattered. It fell from the wall, plummeting to the ground.

Rishkiin sliced the gut of the next monster in line, a mortal blow. Rushing up, he pushed against the ladder, grunting with strain. The ladder fell backward, sending the climbing monsters falling.

Meanwhile, a bugbear came up on the young fighter, its deadly, spiked club descending upon him.

Sedarus and Haet caused no end of trouble for their foes. Chaos ensued as they punched and kicked bodies, broke and snapped bones. Orcs and goblins fell left and right.

An orc rushed at Sedarus, sure that he would skewer the monk with his long sword. Sedarus slapped the flat of the blade, pushing it wide while the orc's momentum brought it close. Sedarus punched the beast in the throat, sending blood spurting from its mouth. It gurgled and died.

The monk roundhouse kicked a goblin, its skull crushing under the force. He planted his knee into another orc's chest, shattering its sternum. An incoming gnoll clipped the monk on the shoulder with its flail. Absorbing the blow, Sedarus used the momentum to elbow another orc in the nose. Then he kicked the gnoll in the gut, sending it backward over the wall. He finished off the orc with a twist of his hands, snapping the beast's neck.

Alongside the Pale One, Haet did battle with enemies of his own. He did a front flip, his right heel thumping a bugbear in the chest, pushing it backward. Its heavy body flung into a goblin climbing a ladder at the wall's edge. The goblin fell to the ground, but the bugbear recovered and rushed back at Haet. It swung its morning star, but Haet ducked. He punched the monster in the groin and elbowed it in the abdomen thrice in quick succession. It fell to the ground, groaning. Haet rushed off to meet another adversary, stomping on the fallen bugbear's throat for good measure.

A goblin shouted and ran at Haet. The monk launched himself at the goblin, taking the thing down. They grappled on the ground, but the goblin was no match for the monk. Its own blade ended up in its gut.

Grasping Haet from behind, another bugbear picked him up and slammed him to the cobblestone wall's floor. The bugbear continuously smashed Haet until the monk fell limp, at which time the bugbear threw him over the wall, down into the midst of the swarming monsters.

Balatore levitated above the wall, his crossbow out and firing. Each of his shots was so accurate that it killed its mark. The mad laughter of battle constantly flowed from the elf's mouth.

Yet after killing twenty or so, Balatore grew bored. He replaced his crossbow with his blades and dropped to the courtyard, seeing it had been breached. He began to slash, stab, and hack, leaving a trail of dead foes in his wake. But there were too many for just him, and the town's defenses were dwindling.

"Aunddara! Rhamor! I need you!" Balatore hated shouting those words, but they were true. He could not hold off two hundred monsters when his forces were so small to begin with—and now so diminished.

All through the melee, Balatore was nicked with swords and clipped by clubs. Yet for every one injury that he sustained, fifteen beasts were slain. Balatore turned to focus his efforts on the larger, more dangerous bugbears.

He rushed at one, only to blink himself behind it. He stabbed with his ocean-green-glowing dagger and slashed with his rapier, twirling it just in time to deflect an incoming slash from an orc. The elf decapitated the beast but was blindsided by a club to the back. Pain racked his spine; he knew he was in danger. Fear started to creep up into his heart.

Suddenly the elf felt a warming sensation as Aunddara cast a healing spell upon him. He looked up to see Rhamor dispatch the gnoll that had dealt the blow.

Rhamor and Balatore now positioned themselves back-to-back alongside some of the city's guards. They slew any monsters that came through the broken gate. Yet the guards were neither as experienced nor as skilled as the elf and holy knight. They began to die off.

Worry caressed Aunddara's face, as she was constantly healing Balatore, Rhamor, and the diminishing force of defenders. She knew that they would not last much longer without additional aid.

Rishkiin saw the descending club out of the corner of his eye and did the only thing he could; he activated his magical ring, turning invisible, and lunged forward. Too slow; the young fighter was smashed in between the massive club and the unyielding stone wall, knocking the breath from him. But the invisibility bought him time to recover. Catching his wind, he slashed his blade at the confused bugbear, becoming visible again. Although he missed, Glimmer flared, momentarily blinding the brute. It was enough time for Rishkiin to turn invisible once more. Now he walked behind the bugbear and stabbed the brute in the back, severing its spine. It fell to the stone floor.

"Push the ladders off the wall!" Rishkiin shouted as he shouldered a goblin in the face and pushed as hard as he could against the nearest ladder. Shooting pain in his ribs halted his efforts. He grunted as he braced himself and pushed once more. He could not send the ladder reeling backward on his own.

Then suddenly the ladder was forced away from the wall, sending all the monsters on it falling. Rishkiin nodded thanks to the three men who had helped him. They did not reply; instead all of them focused on slaying monsters as they went along their way, helping others push more ladders back.

It was then that Rishkiin saw the form of Haet being flung over the wall. Fear gripped his heart and soul. He stormed to the edge, calling to Sedarus. The monk looked over the wall, seeing monsters swarming toward Haet's body.

Rage like none other raced through Sedarus's body. He jumped off of the wall, gracefully covering the forty feet to the ground, landing upon a bugbear that was closing in on his friend. He knew instantly from the sharp pain that he had snapped his ankle, but there was nothing he could do about that.

Instead Sedarus forced himself to roll over and protect his fellow monk. He sent one huge surge of power to all the surrounding monsters. Blue waves of energy entered twenty of the creatures, and the resulting explosion flung the rest of the monsters to the ground.

The enemies were startled, giving Balatore and Rhamor the upper hand as they fought their way out from the courtyard entrance. Leading the remaining defenders into the midst of the nearby creatures, they slaughtered the remaining monsters.

Rhamor picked up Haet's limp form while Balatore hefted the now-unconscious Sedarus, carrying them back inside the courtyard. The town defenders shut the broken gate as much as they could and began repairing it to the best of their ability.

"Aunddara! Aun!" Balatore roared as he laid Sedarus in the courtyard. Aunddara appeared from nearby; she leapt over corpses—friends and foes alike—and began to pray to Tinen to heal Sedarus. Tinen replied, sending healing waves into Sedarus.

The monk weakly opened his eyes but could not keep them open.

"Rest, Sed," Aunddara spoke quietly. "Just rest, Sed."

"Aun! Haet needs you!" Rhamor cried.

Aunddara left Sedarus in Balatore's care and rushed to Haet. She gasped in horror. Haet's body was broken, his arms and legs positioned awkwardly. Some of his teeth were protruding from shredded lips. His eyes were swollen shut, his cheekbones bruised and crushed.

"By the gods!" Rishkiin yelled as he stomped down the stairs. "Can you heal him?"

"I will take care of him, Rish. You need to prepare these men for the next attack. That was not the entire army."

Rishkiin nodded and rushed off, shouting orders to repair the gate and get the wounded to healers. He ordered the guards to pile the dead monsters outside of the gate to be burned.

"Can you heal him?" Rhamor whispered.

"I will try, but he's broken nearly every bone in his body, and I'm so tired."

Aunddara began to pray. Waves of energy entered Haet. Some of his bones re-formed before their eyes, making a disturbing cracking sound. Shortly, though, the waves halted as Aunddara slumped to the ground unconscious. Being the conduit for Tinen's healing magic had physically exhausted her beyond what her body could handle.

"Oh, Aun," Rhamor said, sighing.

He switched his gaze to his unconscious monk friend, fear swallowing him whole. Haet's body was still deformed and broken. He was barely breathing, and his heartbeat was weak, strained.

Rhamor leaned in close and whispered, "I pray that you make it, Haet."

Chapter Twenty-Four

Sedarus awoke with a start, ready to kill his enemies. Yet he was on a bed in a room filled with clerics and patients, surrounded by shouts of pain and cries to Tinen. The makeshift healing quarters looked much like an inn's common room, the beds having been brought down from their respective rooms. Tables were filled with healing bandages and ointments.

The monk stood up, but he was instantly overcome by dizziness. Slumping back to his bed, he quickly recovered.

"Milord, you need to take it slow."

"What happened?" Sedarus asked weakly.

"You saved Haet and the rest of us. At least for the moment," Balatore stated seriously. "The enemy has been sending waves of monsters at us. We've beaten them every time, though we're getting battered."

"Where is Haet?" Sedarus stood up again, slower, forcing away the waves of nausea.

"Milord ... he's ... gravely wounded," Balatore said in a solemn voice.

"Take me to him. Now!"

"Certainly, milord."

Balatore helped Sedarus walk as they weaved in between patients and clerics. They reached a bed that was surrounded by three healers.

"Let me see him."

"Once I've explained something." Balatore put a restraining hand on Sedarus. "His only hope is Aunddara. These clerics are not as strong as she. The problem is that she is unconscious and will not wake. She is fine, just comatose." Balatore paused. "These clerics healed Haet enough for him to regain consciousness and the ability to speak, but they cannot heal his serious wounds."

"Balatore, move, or I'll make you," Sedarus said with a tone that made the elf sigh.

He stepped aside. "I'm sorry, milord."

Sedarus was suddenly hesitant; fear filled his lungs as he tried to breathe. With one large breath, he walked forward. The clerics saw who he was and moved out of his way with respect.

"We tried, Pale One, we did," one of the clerics said.

"Thank you," Sedarus replied, moving forward.

Tears stung his ice-blue orbs as he saw Haet's broken body.

"Sedarus," Haet whispered. One of his eyes was still swollen shut, and his nose and face were horribly bruised.

"Haet." Sedarus put a comforting hand on his companion's shoulder. Haet flinched in pain, and Sedarus retracted, saying, "Forgive me, my friend."

The two stared at each other, brothers in heart and soul, if not blood. Tears stormed down Sedarus's face as he knelt beside Haet, holding his hand.

"I'm so sorry. I tried to get to you! I am so—"

"I know," Haet croaked in a whispering voice. "I know also that I do not have much time. I can see Tinen waiting for me."

Sedarus looked around, and sure enough, Tinen was there, sorrow sown into his face. He nodded at Sedarus, and the monk knew that his god was only giving him time to say what he wanted to say.

"Haet, please forgive me—"

"There is nothing to forgive." Haet stopped, gasped for breath. "I finally see what you truly are, Sed." He tried smiling, but that only caused more pain. "I see what your power is ... and it is so beautiful, Sed!"

Sedarus tightened his grip on his dying friend's hand, tears flowing freely.

"I only wish I could have done more for you," Haet whispered, his lungs failing him.

Sobs rocked Sedarus.

"Take ... care ... of ..."

Haet ceased to speak, his lungs slowly emptying, his eyes cold. Then Tinen walked up and rested a hand on Haet's still form.

"No! *No!*" Sedarus roared.

"My child, it was meant to be," Tinen said.

"No! You could have stopped it!"

"I couldn't, my son." Tinen was somber, his voice gentle. "All you can do now is remember him. Remember his love."

Sedarus shook on his knees, tears blocking his vision. He felt the comforting hand of Tinen on his head. Then he felt Tinen's presence disappear. He did not care. He wept for what seemed like hours before Balatore helped him to his feet. The elf walked him to his bed. Sedarus did not notice, nor did he care. His memories ran through his whole life, the joys he'd had with his brother. More tears streamed down his face.

He lost consciousness soon after. His body was beaten, and now his soul also beaten—by memories of Haet's broken body, of the monsters attacking his friend, of the last moments of Haet's life.

Sedarus started to stir, hearing voices. They were talking about him, but he ignored them.

Milord, we need you. Balatore's voice rang through his mind.

Sedarus opened his eyes to see that his bed was surrounded by Rishkiin, Rhamor, Balatore, and Aunddara. Aunddara clasped his hand and helped him to sit up.

"How long have I been out?" Sedarus asked.

"Two days," Aunddara replied.

"Milord ..." Balatore started.

"What is it?"

"You need to rest," Aunddara snapped, glaring at Balatore.

Balatore altogether ignored Aunddara. "The monsters are gathering once again. They have brought giants to bombard the city wall with rocks, and then they will charge through the rubble."

"He is going to rest!" the cleric demanded.

"Let us be gone." Sedarus sat bolt upright, his brows snapping into a scowl. "I look forward to killing them all."

Aunddara looked at him, surprised. He stood up and started to walk, yet he still required help. His ankle ached, but he knew that the pain was all in his head; he had been healed.

As they made their way to the wall, they saw that the town's defenders were all battle worn. Most of them sported bandages on their assorted wounds. Each of them looked at Sedarus with respect, all of them bowing or offering salutes.

Sedarus forced himself to walk without help. He was flanked by Rishkiin and Balatore, who were followed by Rhamor and Aunddara. The group approached the wall's edge; Sedarus looked over the wall to see another barrage coming.

"Archers! Ready yourselves!" Rishkiin's voice rang through the air.

"This will be the big one," Balatore stated. "Their goal will be to wipe out the city, now that we've been fighting for three days and have sustained substantial losses."

"We cannot allow that!" Rhamor growled.

Sedarus looked at Balatore and spoke.

"Giant hunting? You and me?"

The elf predictably replied with cackles of glee at the thought of slaying enemies.

"Sedarus, you cannot go!" Aunddara argued. "You just woke from unconsciousness!" Tears trickled down her cheeks. "And … and we just lost Haet."

Sedarus growled with rage and shouted, "Woe be unto them!"

With that he started to fade out.

The first boulders were thrown just as Sedarus and Balatore appeared behind a giant. This giant bore a resemblance to a hairless human, only about twelve feet tall. Lean muscles formed its entire body. The giant's skin looked strikingly like smoothed stone. Thick leather garments adorned the creature, which Sedarus knew to be a stone giant. In attacking, he did not even confer with the elf; he just silently charged.

Sedarus did not reach the monster; Balatore blinked himself to its eye level and slashed its eyes with his blades. A thunderous roar split the air as the monster crashed unceremoniously to the ground. The giant swatted around for its attacker, but the elf was not within reach, having enacted his levitation. Now he softly floated down and slit the giant's throat several times. It gurgled, drowning in its blood.

Balatore looked around; they were surrounded by trees on all sides except north, where the city lay. The woods were a perfect spot for boulder throwing. In fact, huge rocks were piled to the right of the dead giant, waiting to be hurled.

"We are here to incapacitate these giants as quickly as possible, not exact revenge," Balatore reminded Sedarus as he wiped his dagger clean of the giant's blood.

"I know," Sedarus said.

"Do you? Or are you numb and couldn't care less about anything in the world?"

"Silence!"

A sardonic laugh erupted from the elf. "Milord, the whole city is counting on you to put these giants under. Your friends are counting on you. The time for revenge will come, but it is not right now."

"You talk too much," Sedarus snapped.

"Tehehe! So I've been told. Now! Let's kill us some giants."

They both silently ran to the west, searching for other giants to defeat.

Chapter Twenty-Five

This wave was to be the last. The monsters threw everything they had at Ashten Vale's walls. Ogres, trolls, and several of the two-headed ettins led the barrage. The ettins each had a massive tree stump for a club. The two-headed brutes ranged from twelve to fourteen feet tall, and each of their grimy gray hides were covered with brown fur-like hair. Yellow, rotting teeth protruded from both of the ettins' mouths.

Boulders thrown by the giants outside the wild charge were meant to soften the defenses, both the wall itself and the men who stood upon the wall.

"Fire!"

Rishkiin's voice wafted above death screams, the whistling of arrows, and the snarls of monsters. The onrushing creatures were chaotic, caring for nothing but the blood of the enemy. They charged without caution, without order. Scores of them were slaughtered, and still those that remained leapt over the corpses and continued to charge.

Drool ran down their snouts, their eyes looking for one thing: death. They did not even bother to bring ladders. The two-headed giants known as ettins slammed their tree-size clubs against the wavering gate.

"Abandon the wall! To the courtyard!" Rishkiin ordered as he gripped his sword.

The soldiers followed his lead without question, meeting up with Aunddara, Rhamor, and the rest of the defenders. To their pleasant surprise, they were shortly joined by two hundred more men, all from the thieves' guild. These reinforcements were all thugs, but no one seemed to care.

"On my order, we will fall back to the keep!" Rishkiin yelled as the gate shuddered.

Rishkiin hoped the defenses had allowed time for enough of a gap between the monsters and the women and children. The baron had sent them on their way north two days ago, after the first onslaught.

"Keep the ranks and we're impenetrable! Break them and we fall!"

Rishkiin took a deep breath. These men had no drilling in military ways, so the young fighter did not have too much hope.

The gate shattered.

In rushed ogres and trolls. Rishkiin and Rhamor ordered their swords to light with the most brilliant light they could. The monsters reared back, blinded, covering their eyes in anguish.

Men hidden on the wall poured oil onto the trolls and threw torches upon them. The creatures ignited, their dry skin crackling instantly. The trolls roared in horrified fear and pain.

The ogres ignored their burning companions as they rushed onward. Some threw giant spears, skewering three men to a shaft. The man on Rishkiin's right was the first to taste blood—his own blood. A spear went through his chest. His dying act was to throw his sword at the ogre responsible.

That gave Rishkiin enough time to sever the beast's head from its neck. The young fighter did not stop; he slashed at another ogre, Glimmer's tip cutting its eyes out. The brute rambled around blindly until one of the defenders slew it.

One troll untouched by the flames jumped over its fiery kin. Rishkiin ran and bashed it with his shield, pushing it into the fire. It roared as its skin sizzled. The stench was rotten, horrific.

Rishkiin was caught by surprise as an ogre smashed its club against his back. He roared in sincere pain as the pure force of the blow sent him flying sideways and into a stone wall.

"By the Abyss!" Rishkiin gasped as he fought for air. He struggled to his feet, his full plate armor encumbering him. The young fighter was still on his rump when the ogre swung downward with both hands. It was all Rishkiin could do to roll to the side of the blow.

The ogre rushed at Rishkiin, who still lay on the ground. The young fighter thrust Glimmer upward suddenly, plunging the magic blade deeply into the ugly brute's thick hide. The ogre slid down, impaling itself further.

Rishkiin used the corpse as an aid to stand. He gritted his teeth in pain; he knew most of his ribs were broken, yet he knew that he was still needed. With the force of his will, Rishkiin charged a new group of ogres.

Aunddara stuck close to Rhamor, healing him and others near him. Fear gripped her, yet she fought through it. She rarely took out her mace, so focused she was on healing. The cleric watched Rhamor wield his blade with expertise.

An ettin rushed Aunddara, its hulking, thirteen-foot-tall body covered in grime. The beast had facial similarities to an orc and an unfathomable stench. The lower canines on each of its two heads protruded from its lips, resembling a wild boar. The club the massive brute carried was larger than Aunddara's whole body, yet the ettin wielded it with one arm.

That club came down in slow motion, giving the cleric time to relive her every memory. She saw her deceased parents, her schoolteacher, and the grandmaster of the Temple of Valor. Her friends flashed before her eyes: Sedarus, Rhamor, Rishkiin, and Haet. In an instant Aunddara knew that she would be with Haet. She closed her eyes, ready for the end to come.

It never did.

With a roar of protest, Rhamor pushed Aunddara out from beneath the swinging club, putting himself in harm's way. His body was flung halfway across the courtyard, where he landed with a thump.

"Rhamor!" Aunddara yelped, running to his fallen body.

He was limp, not moving. His helmet had broken from the blow. Aunddara slowly, carefully removed it, revealing a garish wound. His skull was fractured, his face covered in still-flowing blood.

Aunddara, with tears threatening her, prayed for the healing of her friend, thankful that she was near her full strength. The divine magic sapped her into fatigue, but it only partially mended Rhamor's head.

The warrior sat up, feeling the full brunt of a roaring headache. Nonetheless, instantly he had his blade in his hand. The sentient blade spoke words of warning, guiding the paladin and lending him some energy, which caused the glowing blade to dim ever so slightly.

Rhamor stood up, putting himself in between Aunddara and the charging ettin, who had just finished ripping the head off of a brave soldier.

Careful, Rhamor, the paladin's blade warned telepathically.

"I know!" Rhamor growled aloud as he jumped back, avoiding another devastating blow.

Go for the tendons! Take them out, and even dragons would fall!

Rhamor did as his blade instructed. Just as the ettin's backswing came, the holy knight lashed out. A slash appeared on the two-headed monster's right arm, cutting the tendon cleanly. The huge club fell to the courtyard's cobblestone floor.

Another swipe from Rhamor's brilliantly glowing sword slashed the tendons behind the ettin's left knee. It collapsed to the stone ground, and after quick jabs, the creature was dead, new holes in each of its skulls.

Rhamor grabbed his head with his left hand. Only then did he realize that he had lost his shield. He could not search for it then, as he spotted a small group of ogres swarming a fellow soldier. The paladin rushed into the midst of them, hacking and slashing.

The ogres were dead before Rhamor saw the soldier in question. It was Rishkiin.

"Rish! You must call a retreat to the keep! We're losing men faster than an assassin's blade moves!"

Rishkiin looked around; he knew that Rhamor was right, even though he hated to admit that monsters had routed them. "Fall back to the keep! Get the doors!" the young fighter shouted above the tumult.

The retreat was neat and clean. They fell back, going from street to street, fighting tooth and nail. Dead men and monsters littered the cobblestone roads, blood running in streams.

Finally after what felt like an eternity, they caught sight of the large castle, its tall spires a symbol of hope. The men bounded for the front doors, and the soldiers who made it inside first turned and sent a quick volley of arrows into the rushing monsters. The heavy, iron doors clamored shut and were bolted just as the last of the defenders entered.

Rishkiin instructed a barricade to be built. They gathered the castle's heavy oak tables, chairs, and large shelves and placed them in front of the door.

"Clerics, tend to the wounded!" Rishkiin shouted. "Where is Baron Irel?"

Silence enveloped the entire force of defenders. Some looked around, searching for the answer, while others stared at Rishkiin with the answer on their tongues, yet unable to speak.

"He fell," a young, wounded soldier finally said quietly.

The silence continued until Rishkiin spoke again, his voice filled with reverence. "Tinen guide his soul to the next life."

Rishkiin bowed his head and paid tribute to the dead—all the dead.

Chapter Twenty-Six

Sedarus and Balatore stood behind an oblivious stone giant. Its massive arms were at work throwing a gigantic boulder, which soared through the air, landing with colossal damage.

Sedarus started forward, silent as always. But luck was with the giant; it turned around just in time to see the monk and the elf. Balatore instantly disappeared, and unbeknownst to the stone giant, he reappeared on its other side.

The twelve-foot-tall giant paid no mind, instead swinging its club-like arms at Sedarus. The monk ran straight at them, but at the last second he skidded to his right, ducking under one arm. The giant's second swing came from behind Sedarus. Knowing it was coming, the monk performed an early backflip, landing perfectly on the moving arm.

Sedarus screamed with wrath and poked the giant's arm with his right forefinger. The attack had more impact than the giant could have ever imagined, for blue energy rushed into the arm. Instead of exploding, though, the limb cracked as if it were glass, each crack a glowing an angry blue.

Now utterly useless, the arm dropped limply to the giant's side—but not before Sedarus swiftly stepped to the creature's shoulder. He punched, kicked, and jabbed, attacking the giant's eyes, blinding the massive brute. The monk kept his cool in his attacks, not letting rage take control.

He heard a slight click and leapt off of the giant just in time for one of Balatore's magically enhanced bolts to sting the monster in the temple.

The humongous beast fell to its back, dead, causing the ground around it to tremble.

"What did you do to him?" Balatore asked as he levitated up onto the creature's chest. He was staring at the shattered arm, now dark; the blue energy had drained out with the giant's life.

"As I slept, I dreamt of a way to deal a devastating attack yet conserve my energy. I call it the Crippling Touch," Sedarus informed, already on his way to hunt for more giants. He looked toward Ashten Vale; the gates were still holding, but he knew that they would give soon enough.

"Tehehe!" the elf giggled, applauding quietly. "Good name."

He followed the monk, keeping pace easily. They encountered another giant—this one a smaller hill giant. Balatore, wanting some fun, blinked himself onto the stupid oaf's shoulder. With a slash from his rapier and a stab from his glowing dagger, the giant was grievously wounded. The brute collapsed to its hands and knees, whereupon Sedarus jumped in, performing his Crippling Touch right on the giant's heart. It died, horrific pain coursing through its chest.

"I need to learn that! Tehehe!"

Sedarus said nothing, but he could imagine the havoc the elf would cause should he ever gain the power to perform the Crippling Touch.

The bashing on the keep's door was endless. Aunddara imagined how many ettin were swinging away with their clubs. Fear spread among the few defenders as they waited in the large throne room. Rishkiin and his two friends stood in the front ranks. As the door's shivers grew stronger, the gate closer to being blown asunder, Rishkiin turned to face the defenders.

"When the story of the Battle at Ashten Vale is told, it will be a tale of courage and valor and glory! We will become the heroes of the land! We are outnumbered, which is why we are that of legends! Tinen is with us! We *will* be delivered … or we will die with glory! Soldiers of Ashten Vale, ready your blades!" he yelled with conviction.

Cheers erupted throughout the hall. The sounds of swords being pulled from sheaths rang loud. Rishkiin looked at his two friends and smiled.

Then, in a voice so quiet that they had to strain to hear, he said, "For Haet!"

Just then the doors blasted open. Rishkiin turned and charged, roaring with the courage of a thousand men. Glimmer led the final, desperate charge of the men of Ashten Vale.

⤫

Sedarus and Balatore entered another clearing and were surprised to see not one, but three creatures waiting for them.

"Pale One, I've been waiting for you," an ogre said. His warty face was twisted into a grotesque smile, his massive arms folded across his chest and a massive sword strapped diagonally across his back.

"And you are?" Balatore asked, a devilish smile on his face.

"I am Oram," the ogre stated roughly.

Oram the ogre was flanked by two very large stone giants. Though the two giants were much larger, it was clear to Sedarus and Balatore that the ogre was in command.

"I did not think it would take you this long to seek me out, Pale One," Oram spoke nearly perfectly in the common language.

"So you are the leader of this army? I would ask why you are here, but that seems obvious. You want me. ... Why?" Sedarus said as he and Balatore began to circle the three like preying cats.

Oram's muscular chest trembled in a throaty laugh. "My master wants you dead." He waved the two giants on, indicating that they were to attack.

They were much to slow for Sedarus and Balatore. Sedarus rushed the stone giant on the left, while the elf rushed the one on the right.

The Pale One ran and jumped, using the giant's knee as a stepping stone. Sedarus's fist connected with the giant's gullet. He sent energy through that punch, making the stone-like throat shatter like glass. The monk and the corpse tumbled to the ground, Sedarus moving quickly so as not to get smashed.

Balatore made just as quick work of his giant. The two looked back to Oram, who was still guffawing.

"Tehehe! Your guards seemed to have passed," Balatore said, smiling. "I think it is time to call your army back."

All the ogre said was, "My master will be so pleased once I have killed you."

"Who is your master?" Sedarus asked.

Oram ignored him, pulling his great sword from his back. He licked the flat of the blade, igniting it into blood-red flame. Sedarus and Balatore glanced at each other in surprise while Oram admired his flame-covered weapon.

"My master imbued power into my blade," the ogre snarled. "Enough power to kill even you, Pale One!"

Then he charged. A quick slash forced Balatore to backpedal, and a surprising punch caught Sedarus in the chin, sending him backward on his heels. He rolled into a backward summersault, regaining his footing just in time. Oram swiped his red, flaming sword, intending to hit Sedarus's head.

Sedarus ducked, striking the ogre in the groin in the same motion. Oram doubled over, lashing out with a head butt. His thick skull connected firmly with Sedarus's, throwing the monk back with a bloodied nose.

Balatore leapt over the bent ogre, swiping and slashing his blades. Deep cuts appeared on the thick, brown skin, and black blood crept from the wounds. Oram growled in pain, standing straight. He stabbed and slashed at Sedarus, but the monk performed more acrobatics to evade the onslaught. All the while, the elf continued to stab the ogre in the back. Oram ignored the horrific pain, his sole and singular purpose being to kill Sedarus.

Finally a slash of the monster's sword nicked Sedarus in the forearm. The blood-red flames enlarged from the point of injury, engulfing Sedarus. He staggered back to crash unceremoniously into a pine tree. The monk slumped to the ground, not moving, the blood-red flames dying away.

Oram spun around, catching Balatore flat-footed. The ogre's blade clashed against the elf's frosted rapier. Again and again the blades rang together, the two combatants fighting desperately.

Oram was losing too much blood; he began to slow. Then, just as Balatore was about to finish him off, the great ogre absorbed wafting, blue energy and exploded into thousands of bloody chunks.

Balatore was covered in blood and gore. He looked dourly at Sedarus, who was supporting his weight by leaning against a tree. "You couldn't have let me kill him? Now I'm all sticky!"

Sedarus shrugged and smiled, but only for a moment. "This isn't over, Balatore," he said somberly. "He has a master."

"Had, milord. He *had* a master. Tehehe! Now he's nothing but bloody flesh." The elf grinned wickedly.

"But yes, milord, we will have to deal with his master eventually," Balatore then added. He laughed a hearty laugh before finishing, "If we survive, that is! We still must defeat the horde—and by the looks of it, the city is falling."

The first victim of the barrage that Rishkiin brought single-handedly was an ogre. It fell with a slash across its throat. The second was an ettin. Its club had been coming straight at Rishkiin, or so the stupid brute had thought until the fighter ducked low and thrust high, slicing two necks.

The young fighter had returned with such a fury that the monsters feared him, even the twelve-foot-tall, two-headed ettin. He drilled through the ranks of the monster army, supplying mortal wounds, receiving just as many. Rishkiin was constantly feeling the healing touch of Aunddara and the few other clerics.

Then he heard blaring trumps, which seemed to rally the creatures. The paralyzing grasp of fear assailed Rishkiin, but to no avail. He knew that the end was near, yet he did not fear death. The young fighter had lived his life doing what he loved: slaying evil beings.

He regretted only that his friends would probably share his fate. That was the only reason he kept his sword slashing and stabbing … love. Love for his friends gave him unending courage and strength.

Rishkiin ferociously barreled through two ettin giants, hamstringing one. He quickly turned about, slashing the inside of the leg of the other, cutting an artery. Both of the ettin fell to the ground, where Rishkiin quickly poked holes in their chests.

He raised his shield just in time to deflect an ogre's onslaught. It hit him again, and again. His shield arm began to give way, its strength waning. Between blows Rishkiin acted quickly; as the ogre retracted its massive club, the young fighter roared forward, bashing the thing in the head with his shield. With a feral growl, the fighter then hewed the arm from the beast and finally beheaded the ogre, letting its gore flow onto him, making him look like a blood demon.

Ogres and ettin swarmed around. They began to encircle him. He was not afraid, nor was he concerned for his life.

The young fighter charged the closest brute. With a leaping slash, he took its head with him, kicking it at an ettin. The ogre's head smacked into one of the giant's faces. Rishkiin charged the monster, but its club intercepted the leaping fighter, sending him back into the throne hall.

Rishkiin knew that he was finished, but he was too stubborn not to at least take the brute with him. As the ettin raised its colossal club again, Rishkiin readied Glimmer.

Aunddara was afraid, absolutely terrified. Not of death—she would almost welcome it. She was scared of never seeing her friends again.

The battle raged on around her; she even blocked a few blows with her light-emanating shield. She never once had to deliver a hit. Aunddara's enemies were slain by self-appointed protectors who knew that should the clerics fall, all was lost.

Trumpets blew deeply into the air, and like Rishkiin, Aunddara knew that a second army had approached, sealing their fate. The screams around her made tears well in her charming, green eyes. She hated battle, yet she knew that it was necessary.

At once she and her protectors were charged by four ettin. The battle was gruesome and gory. Bones shattered, and gashes spewed blood everywhere. Aunddara was so entranced with her casting of healing spells that she did not see the club coming straight for her. One of her charges pushed her out of the way, accepting the blow without question.

Broken from her trance, the cleric saw body parts fly from the ettin's club. Bile rose into her throat, and she could not resist spewing the contents of her stomach onto the floor.

She watched as the ettin raised its club again, making ready to break her body upon it. As one last act of desperation, Aunddara called to Tinen, asking for aid. Instantly the ettin's course changed—from wreaking total destruction, to cowering in blind fear.

Immediately Aunddara knew that her god had saved her once again! Her relief was short-lived, though. One of the ettin's companions rushed in to finish her off.

Her strength was sapped, used up from continuously casting healing spells. All she could do was dive in between the legs of the ettin. It saved her—for the moment.

A trumpet blared loudly, close to her this time. Then a whistling sound erupted from above her. She watched the ettin rear back in pain as a throwing axe planted itself into one of its heads. A pain-filled scream pierced the air, like countless others.

Aunddara looked around to see her savior. She found many—many new human soldiers rushing through the gates, slaying the terror-stricken beasts. The soldiers counted into the thousands, and they to a man played a part in the destruction of the evil monsters.

Freeing the throne hall was a blood fest. Many men died in that room, yet many, many more creatures of evil were slain.

The streets ran red with blood after the fighting was over. A man wielding spectacular axes stalked into the throne room, and Sedarus and Balatore came in close behind him. The man held himself straight; everyone in the room instantly knew that he was a man of power. He looked around the throne hall, staring into the eyes of the few survivors.

"Defenders of Ashten Vale! You are liberated!"

Chapter Twenty-Seven

"Sedarus!" Aunddara exclaimed as she rushed tiredly from the hall and into the city streets to embrace him. She halted when Balatore intercepted her.

"He's wounded," the elf informed.

"Let the lady attend to the Pale One!" the man with axes said, his hands going to the hilts of the magnificent weapons.

The axes seemed to be made out of some crystalline material. If that wasn't enough to make anyone stare, one was engulfed in a black flame, the other covered in a miniature ice storm that revolved around the axe head. They looked formidable indeed.

Balatore refused to move, his golden eagle eyes meeting the man's remarkable gray eyes. The man was adorned in the finest leather armor. He wore no helmet over his jet-black, short-cropped hair. With solid muscles, he was extremely intimidating, yet Balatore's feet were stationary. The man's eyes clenched into a scowl, and he drew his axes walking forward. None of the defenders were surprised that the weapons looked as if they were at home in his hands.

"Balatore, move."

Sedarus's voice halted the man with the axes. Balatore glared at the man one last time, and then with a bow to Sedarus, he moved.

Aunddara rushed forward, intending to heal the monk, but Sedarus halted her. "I need no healing, Aun."

"But there is so much blood on your robes!"

"Mostly from my enemies," Sedarus supplied.

"*Mostly*, but not all!" Aunddara argued.

Sedarus was suddenly aware that everyone who could see them was watching him. His ice-blue eyes swept over them all, taking everything in. Men huddled in the blood-covered streets waiting for something. It seemed to Sedarus that they were waiting for him. He was immediately embarrassed for a reason he could not specify.

"I need no healing, and that's that, Aun!" Sedarus spat out.

The silence was deafening. No one spoke, and all were still gazing at Sedarus. The monk was instantly grateful for Rishkiin, who limped up to him.

"Who in the Abyss is this?" the young fighter asked, pointing Glimmer at the man with the axes.

"General Aberoth," Sedarus whispered.

"An assassin," Balatore added quietly.

Rishkiin stiffened, positioning himself to protect Sedarus.

"I'm not here to kill the Pale One, Balatore," Aberoth spat. "But I would kill you without a second's thought!"

Confusion racked Rishkiin, Aunddara, and Rhamor. Rishkiin looked to Sedarus, who nodded.

"This is his army," Sedarus said, sweeping his arm in a gesture indicating the hundreds of men in the streets.

"Then well met, General Aberoth!" Rishkiin said, walking forward and offering the brothers-at-arms shake. Aberoth took the offered arm. "You saved a lot of men this day, General," Rishkiin said solemnly. "My only wish is that you could have reached us sooner."

"As is mine, soldier," Aberoth said, his voice detached. He wore a cloak that covered most of his body. It was gray, like his eyes.

"Commander, actually!" the elf chimed in with a cackling laugh.

"Go to the Abyss, Balatore!" Rishkiin and General Aberoth shouted at the same time.

"Tehehe!"

Rishkiin and Aberoth threateningly approached the elf.

"Rishkiin, stop," Sedarus said. "General, I have no hold over you, but if you attack my friend, you will regret it. I thank you for helping this city and us, but I will not let you harm him."

Then as an afterthought Sedarus addressed the smirking Balatore. "Elf … silence …"

To Aberoth's side Sedarus noticed a man whose eyes glinted like emeralds. He had a slender build and hair black as ravens. Sedarus thought back, remembering how this man had shown tremendous prowess in the battle into the city.

"I want no confrontation with the Pale One," Aberoth said, putting away his axes, though seemingly painfully.

"How do you know me as that?" Sedarus asked.

"You are a follower of Tinen, correct?"

"Actually," Balatore piped in, "Sedarus is a man of his own power. He doesn't need a god." The elf chuckled knowingly.

Murmurs erupted from the crowd of soldiers. Some were angry; others were men testifying that they would follow Sedarus to the ends of the earth.

Sedarus sighed and faced the elf. "I said, be quiet."

"What blasphemy is this?" Aberoth raged, taking a threatening step toward Sedarus.

All of the monk's friends, as well as the remaining city's defenders, put hands on their weapons protectively.

"I would advise you to restrain yourself, Aberoth," the man beside him said, putting a cautioning hand on the general's shoulder.

Aberoth heaved angrily but nodded. "Thank you, Solius. Forgive me, Pale One. All I know is that Tinen came to me in a dream. He told me to find the Pale One and give him my allegiance."

Balatore laughed again, madly.

Aberoth snarled at Balatore and then decided to ignore him. He walked up to Sedarus and took out his axes—a gesture that stirred a commotion.

"He means me no harm," Sedarus informed. "And if he does, I shall grant him the gift of the Crippling Touch."

Balatore snickered. Everyone else was lost on Sedarus's promise, but the monk couldn't care less.

"I wish to offer you my fealty," Aberoth said, growling with each word. "Only because Tinen wishes it so."

"I do not want your fealty, General," Sedarus replied.

That caused a pause.

"Why not?" Aberoth finally replied.

"You obviously do not trust me or my men." As the monk spoke, he looked pointedly at Balatore.

"The elf and I have a history that you cannot know! I trust *you*, Pale One, but not *him*!"

Sedarus sighed. He hated this whole scene.

"Pale One, I offer you my services and those of my army. Will you take these or deny these?"

Sedarus looked at Balatore, who grimaced but nodded a yes.

"I do," the monk said. "On one condition."

"What is that?"

"Rishkiin and Rhamor are appointed commanders in this army." There were several commanders in a single army, each with their own contingency of men to command, but each commander had to report to the general.

"That is two conditions, but I agree, so long as they perform with the skills to lead."

"Rishkiin led the defenses of this city. I imagine that many of its defenders will follow him."

A cheer of approval rang out. The defenders started to clap their swords on their shields.

"Fine," Aberoth growled. The group made their way to the courtyard, where Aberoth looked around, viewing all the corpses. He ordered, "Sort out the dead!"

Chapter Twenty-Eight

Sedarus left the courtyard and his friends to fetch the body of Haet. He noticed that General Aberoth kept pace with him, never letting him out of his sight. They were also accompanied by Solius, General Aberoth's friend. Solius was dressed in a simple dirt-stained gambeson and leather breeches.

"What do you want, General?" Sedarus asked as he turned to face the man.

"You must not go anywhere alone," Aberoth said, dipping into a slight bow. It was obvious that he rarely bowed to anyone and that he was uncomfortable doing so.

"I will be all right; we are in the keep, and your men decimated the remaining of the creatures."

"We cannot be certain of that," Aberoth argued.

"Then send out a team to make certain," Sedarus countered.

Aberoth thought for a moment. He looked at Solius and nodded. Solius left silently.

Sedarus started on his way, Aberoth on his heels. The monk was certain that if he stopped suddenly, the man would run into him.

Sedarus slowed as he entered the hospital hall where Haet's body lay. The monk swallowed with difficulty. He stepped forward, going straight for the bed that held the deceased monk.

"Your friend?" Aberoth asked quietly, reverently.

Sedarus nodded, tears welling in his ice-blue orbs, his lips quivering slightly.

"I am sorry, Pale One," Aberoth said. His voice was distant, unattached, and cold.

Sedarus knew that Aberoth was not truly sorry. *How could he be?* Sedarus thought. *He doesn't even know me.*

"Let me assist you in carrying him," Aberoth offered.

"No. I shall do it."

Sedarus picked up Haet as if he was a mere child. Sedarus's strength amazed the general. The monk ignored the gaping man as he started his way back to the courtyard.

The monsters' corpses were piled outside of the city's wall and burnt. The bodies of the men were compressed into one massive grave. Wives, children, brothers, sisters, mothers, and fathers wept.

Sedarus did not place Haet into the mass grave. He, followed by Rishkiin, Aunddara, Rhamor, Balatore, and General Aberoth, went into the field. There he laid Haet's body down.

Sedarus prayed to Tinen, prayed that the deity would watch over Haet's soul as the monk passed into the next world. Sedarus then removed Haet's material items, as was the custom of the monks of Tinen. Keeping Haet's magical ring, Sedarus discarded his friend's clothing then motioned for Rishkiin, who poured oil onto the naked corpse. Rhamor struck the flint and steel to light the body on fire.

The six stood around the pyre until late into the night. All except Balatore and Aberoth shed tears. Eventually, Rishkiin and Rhamor left.

Aunddara continued her vigil next to Sedarus, though her gaze seldom left Aberoth. He had saved her, she knew it; he had thrown that axe into the attacking ettin's face. She was much appreciative.

Aberoth and Balatore were both aware of Aunddara's gazing. Balatore ignored it. Aberoth subtly glanced back at interval. He could not help but feel a pull toward her. Sedarus was completely oblivious to the situation.

As the night wore on still further, Aunddara grew tired, a yawn escaping her mouth.

"Get some rest, Aun," Sedarus said, not looking away from the ashes, which seemed immovable by the wind.

"No, I'm not leaving until you do."

"I do not need rest," Sedarus said quietly.

"Yes, you—"

"No I don't, Aun! Now go; you will need sleep."

Sedarus sighed. Aunddara placed a hand on his shoulder to let the monk know that she understood. She always understood. "Okay, Sed."

"Accompany her, Aberoth," Sedarus commanded.

"Certainly. Would you like me to send more guards out here? With torches?" Aberoth turned and asked as they were departing.

"No, I can see in the dark. And Balatore will be my guard should I need one," Sedarus said, guessing Aberoth's concern. "I shall be fine, General."

"Of course."

Aunddara and Aberoth left. When they were out of hearing range, Sedarus faced Balatore.

"What is it with you two?"

"Aberoth and me?"

Sedarus nodded impatiently.

"He's an assassin. I don't trust him."

"You can stop lying; I know when you do."

The elf laughed knowingly. "Of course!"

"I know that he *used* to be an assassin. He has clearly gotten over that. Now tell me what happened."

"We've run into each other before. On a less civil level, I bested him and his friend in battle. He clearly *hasn't* gotten over *that*! Tehehe!"

Sedarus thought for a moment. Balatore had not lied to him, but that did not mean that the elf had told him all the truth.

"Well, whatever happened needs to be put behind you. Now."

This drew another tinkling chuckle from Balatore. "Already has been … for me. You must speak with your new general, milord, if you want this dilemma entirely solved."

Aunddara and Aberoth walked for a little bit in silence.

"Thank you for saving me," the cleric opened.

Aberoth paused.

"You threw an axe into the face of my oppressor. Thank you," Aunddara repeated.

"Of course, my lady." Aberoth smiled. "Might I ask you a question?"

Aunddara nodded.

"How long have you known the Pale One?"

"Most of our lives." Aunddara's voice turned cold. "He wasn't always 'the Pale One.' He was normal once." She sighed with guilt.

"Ah! It was an accident, I'm sure," Aberoth offered.

"It was, but that does not make me feel any better about it."

Silence ensued once more; nothing was said until they were outside the door to Aunddara's room.

"Thank you again, General, for saving my life," Aunddara said. She smiled sheepishly when the handsome man smiled back, bowed, and kissed her hand.

She shut her door behind her, undressed from her bloody armor, and washed up. She was about to climb into bed when there was a knock on her door. She leapt from her covers and cracked the door open, peeking out.

Her smile dissipated instantly. "What do you want, Balatore?"

The elf giggled. "I wanted to make certain that you found your way back into the right bed. I would hate to have you mistakenly be in Aberoth's."

"Who's to say that he is not in here? That you didn't interrupt something important?"

"Please, my dear! Do not even *try* to insult me. Tehehe! We both know that your virtue is still intact."

Aunddara blushed, averting her eyes from Balatore. "Why do you even care?"

"Umm ..." Balatore fought for an answer. He came up blank.

"Is it because *you* are infatuated with *me*? I think so!" It was Aunddara's turn to giggle.

"Only in your dreams, my dear," Balatore said in a serious tone, a genuine smile spreading on his majestic face.

"But here you are ... in reality ... at my doorstep." Aunddara laughed again.

Balatore returned the laugh. He said simply, "Goodnight," waved good-bye, and then blinked himself away.

Aunddara stood there, smiling and shaking her head. She then shut the door and crawled into her comfortable bed. But instead of falling asleep quickly, she rolled around restlessly. For the life of her she couldn't get Balatore's majestic face and features out of her mind.

As soon as Balatore left Sedarus's side, the monk looked back to the ashes of his deceased friend.

"You may come out … Solius," Sedarus said, not even looking the man's way.

"You saw me?" Solius asked, walking out from the nearby bushes.

He was now wearing some type of armor, and it was unlike any that Sedarus had ever seen before. It was a forest-green color, yet even as Sedarus watched, it turned a different color, to a midnight blue-black. The armor covered Solius head to foot, like a full body suit, with only slits for his eyes and his mouth. It looked as if it were almost liquid rubber. Then, surprisingly, it started to recede; it was as if his belt were vacuuming up the liquid-looking armor. Soon Solius stood before Sedarus, his armor gone, leaving him in naught but peasant's traveling clothes: a loose-fitting dirt-stained gambeson and leather breeches. He didn't even have shoes on. The only thing a fellow traveler would note about the man was the spectacular belt, which was constantly changing colors.

"You are very powerful, Solius," Sedarus said.

Solius bowed, accepting the compliment. "As are you, Pale One."

"What have you found?"

"I report to General Aberoth."

"And he reports to me. Tell me." Sedarus's voice was calm, devoid of emotion.

Solius hesitated for a split second, but he did not want to raise the ire of one he knew to be so powerful. "There is a second group of monsters heading this way."

"How many?"

"Barely a hundred."

"Well then," Sedarus said feeling fully rested and powerful once again, "let us go hunting."

"Two against one hundred?" Solius said, slightly taken aback. "I'm nothing if not wise. We will get more men."

"We need not kill all of them, just frighten the majority of them," Sedarus reasoned.

"There are giants and ogres."

"The bigger the target, the greater the fall," Sedarus grinned.

A smile matching that of the Pale One's erupted onto Solius's face. He nodded and turned about, heading in the direction of the monsters.

Sedarus followed suit. Anger still swelled within him. He was ready to put it to use.

Chapter Twenty-Nine

Sedarus followed Solius through the forest. The night was moonless. The trees swayed in the strong wind. Sedarus's robes and cloak fluttered in the gusts of air. Rain sprinkled the two as they silently ran south. Sedarus could not see or hear Solius, who had gone too far ahead, but he could sense him. That was the only reason the monk knew where they were going. Half an hour passed, silence shrouding them like a coat.

Finally Solius halted a bit ahead, motioning for Sedarus to come near him. Sedarus closed in on Solius and saw a grove of wildflowers filled with five scores of monsters. They were arguing over some unknown subject.

"They know their fore-army was destroyed," Solius reported, listening intently. "They are debating whether to attack or not."

"We shall not let them," Sedarus said, stepping forward.

The monsters ceased to bicker once they were aware of Sedarus's presence. The monk risked a look back to find Solius's strange armor once more covering his body, yet now it was a glowing, pulsing red. Turning back to the regiment, Sedarus saw that the sight of the men clearly struck fear into the monsters' hearts.

"Leave this place; leave Ashten Vale in peace … or die," Sedarus said in near perfect giant tongue.

Laughter erupted, and the biggest giant waved his arm, saying, "Slay the puny human!"

Sedarus smiled. "Wrong answer."

The monk then pushed with open palms, allowing blue waves of energy to enter two score of the creatures. The explosion knocked everyone else onto their backs. Bloody chunks of flesh and muscle rained from the sky, covering all with gore. Some of the lesser monsters retched at the sight.

Solius was the first to his feet. His quick movements were precise and skilled. Four claws sprouted from his armor on each hand, one per finger. He slashed throats, sheared skin from bone, and decapitated fallen monsters. Screams flooded the air as the cowardly creatures fled from the red-glowing devil.

When the fleeing enemies got too far ahead of Solius, he started to launch the claws at them. Like throwing daggers, these claws were deadly, killing many of the monsters. Sedarus was surprised when the claws disappeared from the corpses and started to regrow on his ally's hands.

He was very interested in Solius. He knew that the man was using magic; he could *feel* it. Yet he did not know what kind. It wasn't divine, like Aunddara's, nor was it like Sedarus's own magical powers. The type of magic Solius used was rare indeed—rare, yet extremely powerful.

Solius did not chase the last score; he let those monsters run, fear hounding their every step. The curious man ran back to support Sedarus, who was using all his strength just to stay standing. Dizziness struck him from every direction.

"That was incredible!" Solius raved. "I've never seen anything like that in my life! And I have seen things you cannot even imagine."

"It is just one of the many strange powers I have developed as I have matured into ... something." Sedarus heaved deeply, catching his breath as if he had just finished sprinting several miles.

"I should like to learn what those powers are," Solius stated.

"In time, friend. In time." Sedarus leaned heavily upon the man. "But for now, let us return. Ashten Vale is safe."

Solius walked the wall, knowing that he would find Aberoth up there. He was correct. The general was alone with a torch. Solius approached the man from behind, silently.

"Careful, my friend," Solius stated.

"Of what?" Aberoth did not even turn to see who had spoken; he knew that it was his long-time friend.

"That cleric is no Isabelle," Solius said, referring to Aberoth's murdered wife. "Do not get involved with that one."

Aberoth twisted and shot his friend a warning scowl. "Do not presume to give me orders!"

Solius stared into his companion's gray eyes. "I mean not to, Aberoth. But you cannot deny the similarities in Isabelle and the cleric."

"Her name is Aunddara," Aberoth stated.

"And you are attracted to her!" Solius shot back.

"I never denied that," Aberoth said quietly.

"You cannot bring back your wife! No matter how bad you want her … need her."

"I understand that, Solius. It has been two years; am I not entitled to move on?"

"You are, my friend. But you have not, and you're looking for your Isabelle, even in another woman." Solius sighed. "I don't want you to fool yourself into some fantasy, Aberoth."

"Nor do I!" Aberoth yelled, facing the younger man.

"Then use caution if you choose to romantically pursue this Aunddara," Solius advised.

Minutes passed in silence. The rain picked up, beginning to pelt the two. Shivers ran down both their spines, yet they did not move for shelter.

"What have you found out about the Pale One?" Aberoth finally asked.

"What they say about him is true," Solius said. His voice was one tone, emotionless. "He wields a power that can kill two score of giants and ogres. I have just witnessed it myself."

"That is what I found out, too … how is it possible?"

"I know not," Solius stated. "But the mere fact that Tinen came to you, ordering you to serve under the Pale One is enough evidence that he is something … inhuman."

"What do we do?"

"You are the general of his army ... lead his men, Aberoth, as you were made to."

Once more silence encased them, though this pause was far shorter than the last.

"And what of Balatore?" Aberoth asked.

"I do not know yet," Solius replied. "For now I shall keep my eye on him."

"And should he make a move against us?"

"We destroy him. We should have long ago, but ..."

"But he was stronger than us then," Aberoth spat.

"The elf is strong, but he is not a match to us anymore." Solius hoped that what he said was true. He then continued, "Yet if we kill the Pale One's advisor, Sedarus will slay us all."

Aberoth had pause. "Is he capable?"

"Without a doubt!"

The general's eyes widened. His friend was the most powerful being he had ever known. *How could this simple monk kill Solius and me?* Aberoth thought.

"I am anything but simple, Aberoth," Sedarus's voice rang out.

The two startled men looked around, terror touching them. Sedarus began to fade into existence nearby. He faced the general and his companion, and they both bowed.

"You read my thoughts?" Aberoth asked bluntly.

"Yes. I can read all who promise me fealty. And since there are many men that I do not know, I must search their minds. I, after all, cannot allow my subjects to plan an assassination unbeknownst to me." Sedarus's ice-blue eyes were hard.

"We were not planning anything," Solius stated calmly. His thoughts strayed to how he knew he had magic that could at least injure the monk.

"That would be inadvisable, Solius." Sedarus turned his gaze to the man, whose enchanted armor was once more gone, concealed in his belt.

"Forgive me." Solius bowed.

"Certainly." Sedarus faced Aberoth. "You need not fear retribution from Balatore."

Aberoth's eyebrows rose in question.

"I have ordered him that the past is to remain in the past. I have come to give you the same orders." Sedarus fixed them with stern stares. "I know not what occurred in the past between you three, but I know that Balatore has saved me countless times. I will side with him, and you will die if you choose to ignore this order."

"We will obey, Pale One," Aberoth stated instantly. He did not fear the threat. Yet the look in Solius's eyes told him that Sedarus was no one to infuriate.

"Good." Sedarus turned to walk away, his torn, bloody robes drenched. "I hope that I can trust you. It has been a trying few days, and I have little trust left in this world."

"You will have absolutely no trouble with us, Pale One," Solius stated.

"And Aberoth," the monk added, "Aunddara is like a sister to me. If you hurt her, I'll kill you." He faded away without waiting for a response.

Aberoth stared wide-eyed at Solius.

Chapter Thirty

Sedarus was standing above Aberoth when the general woke up. He was startled, yet he concealed it decently. He stood and stretched. The man looked into Sedarus's ice-blue eyes, which seemed softer than the previous day.

"I wanted to apologize for my inappropriate actions earlier," Sedarus said, his voice sincere, as the two began walking to the city's courtyard.

Aberoth was staggered. He did not fully know what was expected of him; his liege had, after all, just apologized to him.

"I accept ... and I understand what you said," Aberoth said. He continued, "Aunddara is a close friend of yours. As you said, she is like your sister."

"True, she is someone who would be avenged. I do not mean that as a threat, just as the truth," Sedarus declared.

"If anyone understands that, it is I," Aberoth returned softly, his gray eyes going to the bloodstained cobblestone. He took a large breath, letting the cold air touch his lungs. "My wife and son were taken hostage. Solius and I hunted their captors. When we caught up with them after a long, trying journey, they were slaughtered in front of me.

"That is part of the road that led me here. I have done things that I regret, and I have done other things that I would not change."

"I am sorry for your loss," Sedarus said. "Then you understand, even better than I, what it is like to lose a loved one."

"I do, my liege."

"None of that," Sedarus said, waving his arm. "Just Sedarus."

"Certainly, Sedarus," Aberoth said, smiling. He was reminded of himself. Aberoth never liked it when his men called him *lord* or *liege*.

"My friends are preparing for our journey. I came to tell you that our destination is Anzzow. Four days of hard traveling."

"Your journey will be longer than four days, Sedarus," Aberoth stated.

Sedarus raised an eyebrow.

"With this many men," the general began to explain, sweeping his arm around him, indicating to the thousands of men in and around the courtyard, "breaking camp in the morning, marching, then setting up camp at dusk takes time away from the day. It will take us twice, maybe even thrice that time."

"Then I suggest you get your men moving, Aberoth." Sedarus smiled warmly. "Thank you for all your help. I hope you can learn to trust me."

"I do," Aberoth said.

"Partially, but not completely."

"I doubt not you, but Balatore."

With that the general started calling orders to his soldiers. When he finished, he faced Sedarus once more. "On my journey to rescue my wife and child, Solius and I ran into Balatore. We befriended him, but he betrayed us."

"I do not doubt it," Sedarus said. "He does seem the type. Yet I will not have quarreling inside my ranks. He will be punished, as will you, if he goes against my will in this matter. He is not immune to my wrath, I assure you."

"Well we wouldn't want that, would we? Tehehe!" Balatore swaggered over and offered his hand to Aberoth. The man's jaw clenched with rage, yet he slowly took Balatore's hand in his.

The elf gave another chuckle. "How's the family?"

Aberoth charged, roaring, his magnificent axes already in his hands. Balatore's crossbow came to hand. Yet quicker than both was Sedarus. He kicked Aberoth in the chest with enough force to send him reeling backward. Simultaneously, he slapped his hand against the crossbow, making the bolt miss its mark. Then with his other hand he performed the Crippling Touch on Balatore's hand.

Balatore's melodic voice pierced the air with a scream. The elf dropped his crossbow. His hand was glowing blue through cracks in his skin. Balatore knew that his bones were shattered and his tendons were ripped.

Everyone nearby stared wide-eyed at the elf's hand. Balatore began to hum, and wisps of blue healing power entered the limb. He managed to heal the ripped, cracked skin, but he knew that his bones and tendons remained injured.

"I told you to leave Aberoth be!" Sedarus screamed, ignoring the countless pairs of eyes that were locked on him. He was certain that he had just convinced the men that he was as powerful as the rumors said.

"You will be disciplined, Balatore, or you will be nothing! Go see Aunddara," Sedarus told the now-submissive elf. The monk turned and faced the thousands of flabbergasted soldiers.

"Discipline is your new dictum! If we have no discipline, then we are dead. Back to work."

Sedarus faced the gray eyes of Aberoth, who was still on the ground. The monk helped the general up.

"Is that one of the powers you have gained?" Aberoth knew the answer, but he needed to hear it from Sedarus.

"Yes, and I have many others. You have seen some."

"What are you?" Aberoth asked in awe.

Ignoring the man, Sedarus said, "Have your men ready as soon as possible. We leave when you are packed up." He turned and left the stunned general.

"My dear!" Balatore called through Aunddara's door.

She cracked the door open. "What in the Abyss do you want—" She gasped, seeing Balatore's deformed hand. She pushed the door fully open and pulled Balatore inside her room. "What happened?"

The elf giggled, grinning. "Do you need my cloak?"

Aunddara looked down at her slightly revealing nightgown. She scowled at Balatore and grabbed her own cloak, which was lying on her bed, and covered herself, blush coloring her cheeks. Balatore gave another giggle.

"What happened?" Aunddara asked again.

"Sedarus used his Crippling Touch on me," Balatore said truthfully.

Aunddara snorted disbelief. "What *really* happened, Balatore?"

"I slapped the buttocks of a rather gorgeous woman. Her husband hit me with a club."

"Thank you for telling the truth," Aunddara stated, and she began to pray to heal Balatore's hand.

The elf laughed at the beautiful woman, shaking his head, a wide grin covering his face.

"Did you have to pack so much power behind the Crippling Touch?" Balatore asked an hour later, feigning hurt. He was waiting for Sedarus on top the wall.

"I put in the bare minimum, Balatore," Sedarus said.

"Ah! Do you care that much for me? Tehehe!"

"You are my friend; I would never hurt you without reason."

"Believe me, you had reason. But I would not have agreed to accept the Crippling Touch had I known how severe the pain was. I did not even have to fake that yelp of pain." Now his yelps were back to the usual ones of laughter.

"This was *your* plan, Balatore," Sedarus said plainly.

"And it worked! Tehehe! Even General Aberoth believes that you are … well, something other than human."

"What am I?" Sedarus asked, looking down.

Balatore softly chuckled. "You will find that answer soon, milord!"

Sedarus sighed, shaking his head. A short pause ensued. Balatore was listening to the whistling wind and the tapping of a light rain. Sedarus was trying to sift through the thousands of voices that he was hearing. They were like a loud hum, giving him a headache. He closed his eyes in pain, trying to focus on one voice in particular: General Aberoth's. The general was trying to hasten his men.

"You showed your power to Solius?" Balatore asked.

"Yes," Sedarus replied.

"Good. He is sure to tell Aberoth."

"In fact, he has already."

"Good!" Balatore said with a cackle. "You've just earned four thousand loyal subjects. Word will spread of the Pale One and the Battle of Ashten Vale." Balatore faced Sedarus and grinned. "Soon you will be the talk of the land."

"And this is good?"

"Yes … and no," the elf said mysteriously, laughing.

"What do you mean?"

"You will grow in subjects, but your enemy will also know of you."

"That is why we need to get to the Great Library in Anzzow?"

"Yes. You will learn what you are and what you need to do." Balatore sighed.

Moments passed, then Sedarus said, "Thanks."

"Tehehe! For what?"

"For everything you have done for my friends and me. They do not like to admit it, but if it were not for you, we would be dead."

Balatore felt like laughing again, but he held it in. "You're welcome, milord."

The rain intensified, as did the wind, going from whistling to howling. Sedarus focused his gaze on the courtyard; men were bustling about, preparing themselves for the journey.

"Aberoth is coming; I need you to leave, Balatore."

Balatore feigned a frown. "I'm hurt."

"Now, Balatore," Sedarus commanded.

Balatore gave a good-natured smile, bowed, and blinked himself away. A few minutes passed before Aberoth found Sedarus.

"Pale One, we are ready to depart. Also, I sent Rhamor and Rishkiin ahead with the men I have placed under their command."

Sedarus looked at the general, puzzled.

"To ensure we are not met with any surprises along the road," General Aberoth clarified.

Sedarus nodded saying, "Good."

Chapter Thirty-One

Almost ten days had passed since Sedarus's army departed Ashten Vale. They had been making good time until they entered the mountain range surrounding the city Anzzow. The steep terrain of the sharp mountains had slowed the army.

While the men began setting up camp and cooking dinner, Aunddara had slipped away and followed a game trail up the side of a mountain. The sun was descending behind the mountaintops, spraying red, pink, and orange across the sky. The fiery orange orb flared one last time for the day. Aunddara spent thirty minutes watching the magnificent sight.

"Beautiful, isn't it?" Aberoth asked, walking up from behind the woman.

"Absolutely," Aunddara stated, locking stares with Aberoth.

He was fixated with her amazing green eyes. He kept studying the cleric's blushing face, finally realizing that a long moment had passed and he was still staring at her. He coughed slightly and turned back to the pink sky. The two were on a cliff overlooking the army's camp. Smoke from cooking fires began to rise into the sky, blocking the view.

"You love Sedarus," the man said.

"Well, of course I do. He's my friend."

"You look at him like he is more than just a friend," Aberoth said, stating the obvious.

Aunddara blushed scarlet and looked away from the general. "I wanted to be with him, yet we cannot be together. His destiny is far greater than to be with me. I've moved on."

"Ah … of course."

"Why do you and Solius hate Balatore so?" she asked, shifting topics.

Aberoth ignored her. He walked over and sat down at the cliff edge, his legs dangling over. Aunddara took in a sharp breath. She was frightened of heights, yet she mustered the strength and courage to sit next to the man.

"I did not mean to dredge up past memories."

"I-it's okay."

"I'm sorry," Aunddara said, gravely. She placed her hand on his strong shoulder. He looked deep into her eyes. Aunddara stared back into his gray orbs. They were dark … blank.

"I have committed atrocities, Aun," Aberoth stated, looking below, to the camp. "I've murdered men. Killed women. Each and every one deserved it, but it makes no difference." Aberoth's voice was coated with sorrow. He was deep in his dark memories. Pain filtered into his eyes. "You bring these horrible memories to me!" he admitted.

Aunddara blanched, her eyes wide with surprise. Her gaze never left Aberoth's face. "I am sorry … I'll leave you alone." She started to get up, but a restraining hand clasped around hers.

"Please, don't go."

"You just said that I reminded you of your sins." Aunddara was flabbergasted.

"You are the spitting image of my deceased wife. It was the want to avenge her murder that drove me to become like the monsters that killed her. I tried to hide it, but I was every bit of a monster as they were. But I realized that I couldn't live with such evil, and ever since that day I have devoted myself to Tinen.

"Your presence is also soothing to me, a respite for a weary man," Aberoth told her. "If you are disgusted by me, I will not hold it against you."

"You did what you had to, to bring you to this spot in your life. We can only ask the gods for forgiveness," Aunddara said slowly.

Aberoth leaned forward, intending to kiss the cleric, but he was interrupted by a laugh.

"Tehehe! So beautiful!" The elf sighed dramatically. "Ah! Love … the greatest gift the gods could give to us."

"I beg to differ," Aberoth stated. "I'm certain that my axes in your chest would be the greatest gift the gods could give."

He said it with such a calm, cool voice that Aunddara had no doubt that his past was as shady as he had declared. She became unnerved by the man.

"Meh! One cannot always have what he wants!" Balatore laughed uproariously and winked at Aunddara. He chortled as she blushed.

"What in the Abyss do you want, Balatore?" Aunddara snapped.

"I am afraid that I must take your company away, my dear. Tehehe!"

"You can try," Aberoth barked, standing up to face the elf.

"The Pale One requires your presence, General," Balatore stated, grinning. "Shall I tell him that you are indisposed?" He chuckled still more.

"Go to the Abyss, elf!" Aberoth growled.

"I'll meet you there," Balatore said, suddenly very serious, deadliness in his disposition.

"You may find me more powerful this time around. Last time you had the jump on us … not the next time. No, Solius and I will kill you this time around."

"You remember what happened to my hand?" Balatore asked dryly. "That will happen to you as well, my friend. I've given up my grudge against you and your psychic friend. You would be wise to do so as well. Tehehe!"

Aberoth pushed past Balatore, muttering curses beneath his breath. The elf replied with his usual cackle, looking down at the slightly confused cleric.

"May I join you?" Balatore asked graciously.

"If you answer my questions."

Balatore laughed lightheartedly and sat down, rather close to the cleric, yet she could not find the strength to pull away from him. She could smell lavender on his clothing, the scent drawing her to him.

"Now that we are comfortable," Balatore said, "what is your question?"

"What did you do to Aberoth and Solius?"

Balatore's smirking face tightened into a frown assuming the mask of tasting something sour. He looked down. Instantly Aunddara knew that he was anguished.

"I was roaming the world, as I have done for eons past, when I was presented with a job. I was to capture a rather annoying vigilante. I did not know the man who hired me but did not ask questions, for the price he was paying. I was to meet my contact in a faraway city. On the road I saved two men in battle. They were Aberoth and Solius. They told me their quest to find the kidnappers of Aberoth's wife and son."

Aunddara rocked back slightly at that, but Balatore did not notice and continued with his story.

"We ventured together, our direction the same. We became close friends. They saved me countless of times, as I saved them countless times. We finally entered the city where I was to meet my contact. The contact was not alone; he had a garrison of men. They congratulated me on the capture of the vigilante.

"I was confused until my contact ordered his men to seize Aberoth and Solius. The two attacked me. I was trying to explain, but they would not hear it. They were restrained and taken away.

"After, I killed my contact and began a search for my two friends. But they were long gone, and I never found them."

Aunddara soaked it in. She pieced together what she knew from Aberoth and what she had just gained from Balatore. She believed the elf.

"I'm sorry that your friendship was ruined," Aunddara said quietly.

The elf never heard her; he was still talking, fixated on the subject. "They were the first real friends I'd had since my dear Alesmi died." His voice was racked with pain.

Aunddara shook the elf. He looked at her, his gold eyes not truly seeing her. "Balatore, if you try and explain to Aberoth—"

"No," Balatore replied.

"Why?" Her voice was exasperated. She put a shaking hand on his slender shoulders.

"No," the elf said again, quietly. He looked to the rising moon, blinking away tears. "No, it is better that I stay captive and let loneliness be my warden. The ones I love end up leaving me anyway."

With that he used his magical ring to blink himself away.

"Pale One," Aberoth said, bowing low.

"Aberoth, good," Sedarus said, looking up from his steaming hot stew. "Would you like some stew, General?"

"No thank you," Aberoth politely denied.

"Very well," Sedarus replied, taking a mouthful of the hot substance. He seemed unbothered by its heat.

"You summoned me, my lord?" Aberoth prompted.

"Yes, I did." Sedarus said. "Tomorrow we will come into view of Anzzow. We will camp outside of the south gate. Balatore will enter the city and the Great Library. He said he has many tomes to decipher before we will know what we need."

Aberoth nodded. "I will make the preparations for you, my liege."

Rhamor and Rishkiin had reached Anzzow several days before the bulk of the Pale One's army. The two companions and the four hundred men that they commanded had set up camp just outside the metropolis. Anzzow was one of the largest cities that either of the companions had ever seen. For days the two sat outside the hundred-foot city walls, looking at the spires of the city's castle. They longed to enter the city, but not to visit the city's keep, inns, or marketplace. No, they wanted to visit the esteemed Great Library of Anzzow.

Finally when Sedarus and his army reached them, they were sorely disappointed, for Balatore was the only one to enter the city.

Balatore entered the city of Anzzow without the guards positioned at the gate and the walls seeing him. The streets were deserted, as it was the middle of the night. The elf had a purpose, and he quickly made his way through the massive city, ignoring the many buildings, statues, and homes. Balatore's destination was the Great Library of Anzzow.

With the magical properties of his ring, the elf was soon standing outside the library. He paused, taking a deep breath and slowly letting it go before stalking forward and pushing the golden double doors open.

Instantly he was assailed by the smell of ink and old parchment. Directly inside he saw a desk manned by a monk in blood-red robes. The monk of Feldoor saw Balatore and stood up. Sauntering up to him, Balatore bowed slightly.

"Ah, Balatorensial, it has been a long time," spoke a melodic voice in the ancient elven language from underneath the cowl.

Balatore laughed expressively. "Not nearly long enough, Seydor, my friend." Balatore scanned the room, noting that they were completely alone. It was an unusual thing, yet not enough so to concern Balatore.

"Were we ever friends, Balatorensial?" Seydor asked, pulling back his hood to reveal angular features and pointy elf ears.

"No, we weren't," Balatore said, grinning. "But then, elves like us don't have friends. No offense, but you are a monk who sits in a library all day. And me ... well, I am intolerable. Tehehe!"

"And yet for some reason you are one of the few elves still alive."

"I ask myself every day why that is," Balatore said nonchalantly, the smile on his face widening.

"Feldoor knows why ... and so do I," Seydor said, his voice turning into a whisper.

"Do you now?" Balatore's thin eyebrows arched in interest, his grin slipping away.

Seydor nodded. "The gods won't harm you. Trathcot wouldn't even dare touch you."

"Yes, well, I am under the protection of Tinen." Balatore shrugged, a smile once more on his magically beautiful face.

"That is not why you still live and you know it!" Seydor yelled, and then he sucked in a breath, his purple irises wide with alarm. "Forgive me."

Balatore laughed. "Since when have you ever asked forgiveness from me?"

"Ever since I found this," Seydor said. He rooted inside a secret compartment beneath the desk and lifted out an ancient leather-bound book. The dim light of the torches was enough for Balatore to see what was on its cover. It was an intricately drawn portrait of himself.

"You know what this is, I presume," Seydor said. Balatore didn't answer. "It is the life's journey of Velvenbrox. Of you."

A severe frown encompassed Balatore's face. It quickly became an enraged scowl. "Give me that book!" Balatore's voice sharp with anger. Seydor quickly complied. "You read this?"

"Yes I did," Seydor said meekly, lowering his gaze.

"Have you even whispered the contents of this tome to anyone?" Balatore was visibly shaking with wrath.

The elf in the blood-red robes shook his head quickly. Balatore closed his eagle eyes and shook his head, rubbing his face in despair.

"But Feldoor knows," the librarian added.

"We must destroy this book," Balatore deadpanned.

"No! You can't! I won't allow it!"

Balatore cocked his head and laughed loudly. "How are you going to stop me?" he suddenly asked.

"I will ask Feldoor to speak with you."

"The god of knowledge has no sway over me. Tehehe!"

"Maybe not ... but maybe he can help."

"How?"

"I know not, but if anyone can help you, it is he." Seydor bowed then turned and left the library, leaving Balatore alone.

Balatore sighed deeply, slowly shaking his head, shutting his eyes, and clenching his teeth. Then with a purposeful breath, he said, "Feldoor, please, I need your help."

"I am here, Velvenbrox," a soothing voice said behind him.

"That is not my name anymore," Balatore said, turning to face the god of knowledge.

Feldoor was tall, over six feet, but his features were soft. He was obviously someone who spent more time reading books and studying than out practicing his martial prowess. He was dressed like his followers, in blood-red robes. His head was devoid of hair, and his brown eyes were piercing, all-knowing.

"I have come, my old friend," Feldoor said. "What do you need of me?"

"I need help. The contents of this book must be destroyed."

"You cannot destroy what you have created until you have completed the task which you yourself set upon your soul."

The answer was infuriating to Balatore. "Then you destroy it!" he yelled, spittle flying from his enraged face.

"I cannot … yet there is another way to undo what you have done," Feldoor said, his face shadowed with true concern for Balatore.

The elf's face lit up in hope. He asked, "How?"

"Go back to your old life." Feldoor said nothing more, letting that sink in for a moment.

Then Balatore spoke. "And if I cannot do that?"

"Then you will spend eternity searching for a solution that was right in front of you, and we will spend an eternity waiting for you. You know what you must do, Velvenbrox. But it will take courage that I cannot even imagine."

With that, Feldoor faded away.

A wrath-filled scream escaped Balatore as he crumpled to the ground. Hours passed before he even stood up; when he did, he was in such a dour mood that he didn't even bother to start the tedious task that was before him. He just sat in terror, thinking of what he must do … and how it might kill him and his friends.

Sedarus stood on a small outcropping overlooking the metropolis of Anzzow, the City of Knowledge. He could see the separate districts bustling with busy men and women. The monk looked for the Great Library. It was an easy building to spot, as it was the second largest in the city, only the castle's spires rising higher.

Sedarus then peered at the outskirts of the metropolis, just outside the city, and found his army. It had grown by a thousand men, totaling now between five and six thousand. When they had first arrived, the city's people had thought they were being besieged, which of course was not the case.

Sedarus started to fade out as the sun began to rise. He appeared in front of his army's camp. They had been there for about a week. Balatore had forbidden anyone to come with him while he made preparations at the Great Library. Yet this day was to be different. Everything was ready for Sedarus.

"I want you and Solius to come with us," Sedarus said to Aberoth.

"Of course. Let me speak with one of my commanders, and then we can be on our way." He left, shouting orders to his men. Fifteen minutes passed, and he and Solius walked over to Sedarus and his friends.

"We are to meet Balatore in front of the Great Library," Sedarus informed.

Aberoth's face darkened. Sedarus looked hard at the general, who averted his gray eyes from the monk's stare.

"Let us go." Sedarus said.

He quickly turned and walked away. He heard the questions burning inside of each of his friends' psyche. He ignored them all. His own nerves were almost overwhelming. Excitement ate at his insides. He tried focusing on the metropolis instead.

The walls were one hundred feet tall and twenty wide, with men posted on the wall every ten yards. It was almost exactly like Quwe. Sedarus was taken back to his earliest memories of walking in his home city.

The gates were of spiked iron on the outside. A portcullis and a wooden gate fortified the city's entrance. Guards manned the gate, questioning Sedarus and his group as they entered. They told the guards that they were meeting a friend.

As the group entered the city, they were instantly beset by the smell of cooking bacon and eggs. Cooks and vendors littered the streets, showing off their merchandise. Guards patrolled the roads, making certain that order was maintained.

"The Great Library is in the heart of the city," Sedarus informed.

Wonder and awe filled the minds of all the companions as they swiftly walked through the slowly filling streets. The crowds thickened as they got closer to the Great Library.

"Feels like home," Rishkiin muttered. Rhamor nodded his agreement.

The group rounded a corner and started down a boulevard. There, in the center of the avenue, was the library, stairs leading up to it. Pillars supported the massive three-story building, its marble the purest white.

Sedarus wasted no time in ascending the stairs. He spotted Balatore near the huge, gold double doors. Balatore nodded to the group, his face grim as he lay his gaze on Aberoth and Solius.

"So, what specifically have you been doing to prepare for my coming?" Sedarus asked as Balatore turned and led them through the gold doors.

"I've been looking through tomes, deciphering them, trying to locate the exact volume we need," the elf replied.

"We could not have helped?" Rishkiin asked irritably.

"The tomes were in ancient elven."

"Solius speaks that language, though I know not why." As he said this, Aberoth curled his lips in disgust as if he had received a massive whiff of a horrific stench.

The elf chortled loudly. "No one knows ancient elven anymore. No one except a select few, and I can tell you that Solius knows nothing of that very old language."

"Have you found what we need?" Sedarus inquired, the tone of his voice revealing his anticipation.

"I have, milord."

"Good." Sedarus started inside. "Aberoth, Solius, stay at the door."

The two did as he commanded.

As Sedarus entered the Great Library, he followed by Rishkiin, Rhamor, Aunddara and Balatore. They were stunned. Three floors of massive shelves crammed with books filled the inside. Thousands upon thousands of volumes were there. Sedarus would not have been surprised if every answer to every question that he had could be answered in the library.

Monks in blood red-robes sauntered about. They were silent, their cowls pulled low over their faces. They did not speak to anyone, just walked around, each with some unknown purpose.

"This way; it's on the second floor."

Balatore led them up the stairs. They entered a labyrinth of shelves and books and were lost within minutes. Only Balatore knew where they were going. He weaved them in and out, never losing his direction. The walk soon ended.

Balatore spoke to himself as he searched for a certain tome. He whispered in a musical language, one that none of the group could understand. His fingers ran through intricate signs, symbols that were unknown to all around.

"Found it!" he exclaimed with tinkling laughter.

His excitement was not lost on Sedarus. The monk was visibly shaking as Balatore pulled down a black, leather-bound book. Its pages were stained yellow due to the eons of waiting, unread.

"This tome has the answers to your questions. It will tell you who and what you are, and what you must do." Balatore handed it to Sedarus. The monk's hands shook as he handled the book. To his surprise, the leather cover featured an elaborate picture of him. He gently opened the massive manuscript, its pages old and fragile. He quickly scanned the first page, and then his eyes popped open wide, his breath catching in his throat. Sedarus looked at Balatore, who was smirking knowingly. Then his glazed eyes stared at the rest of his friends.

"What does it say Sed?" Rhamor's deep voice rang.

He started to say something but was interrupted by a feminine voice filled with ice. "I'm sorry to cut your gathering short, but I'm going to need that book!"

Sedarus felt chills run up his spine. The monk twirled around to look upon the speaker who gave him an eerie feeling. It was one of the red-robed monks of Feldoor. The librarian pulled back her hood, revealing a beautiful woman.

"Hand over the book, handsome … or die," the woman snapped.

"Madame, I cannot—" Sedarus started to speak, but it was Balatore's turn to interject.

"Kill her, Sedarus! Now!"

Not hesitating, Sedarus pushed energy forward. His blue waves of power were met with red waves of energy. The explosion was devastating, blowing books and shelves alike apart. Everyone within a thirty-foot radius was flat-backed, including Sedarus—but the woman remained on her feet. She laughed hysterically, unnerving everyone, as she rushed and picked up the black book that had been flung from Sedarus's grip.

Aberoth! Solius! We need you! Sedarus sent telepathically to them. He jumped to his feet, launching himself at the woman, but he was intercepted by twenty red-robed figures. The men using the facade of being monks shed their robes and attacked. Rhamor and Rishkiin drew their swords to fend off the false-monks.

Sedarus jump-kicked one of the pretenders, snapping his neck. Guilt sprang into his gut; he had killed plenty of monsters, but he had never killed a human before on purpose. But he had not the time to ponder over it, for a score more of the pretenders were between him and the fleeing woman. She kept on cackling as she fled to the stairs.

"Aberoth, you need to control your emotions around our new lord. Your thoughts as well," Solius advised.

"I know," Aberoth sighed, pacing in front of the gold doors.

"You feel for her, my friend. I can see that."

Aberoth laughed. "I cannot lie to you, even if I wanted to." He sighed again and looked into his friend's piercing green eyes. "Yes, I feel for her. She does remind me of Isabelle, but that is not the only reason."

"She may not share the same feelings, Aberoth. You must know that."

"I do. What do you want from me? I will not cease to grow my relationship with Aunddara."

"I advise caution. That is all."

Aberoth was about to reply when he heard Sedarus's call for help in his mind. He looked at Solius, slightly confused. The look on his friend's face told him that Solius had heard it too.

The general pulled out his axes faster than a flutter of his eyes. Aberoth looked at Solius and he wasn't surprised that his friend's curious armor was crawling over him, covering him from head to toe. Its color was black, and a haze began to waft from it. Instantly claws grew from each finger on the armor.

Both men charged into the library. Inside, men were shedding their disguises as monks of Feldoor.

Aberoth did not ask questions. He charged a group of the men who were drawing wicked-looking swords and chopped downward with his left axe, the one he called Terror. The black, smoke-like tendrils that surrounded the head of the axe wafted into a nearby man's nostrils. The man suddenly screamed, horror filled, then dropped his sword and fled, fearing for his life.

Aberoth hacked with Deathbringer, the axe in his right hand. Its head, swallowed by its personal ice storm, buried itself into an assailant's chest. The general wrenched free his crystal axe, yet because it was buried deep, the dead man's sternum came with it.

Another man stabbed at him. Terror smacked against the flat of the blade then hacked once across the man's sword arm. The limb fell to the ground, blood dripping and pooling. Screams and the clanking of metal rang throughout the library.

Aberoth tore through three more men, hacking and burying his axes. He gashed and slashed, sending blood flowing freely from the wounds that he inflicted. He sustained a few cuts himself, but nothing serious.

Now town guards rushed into the building, only to explode from a red wave of energy. The explosion knocked Aberoth to his backside. He leapt to his feet again just in time to see a woman rushing down the stairs. Aberoth started to make his way to her but was halted by a yell from Sedarus.

"She's mine! Kill her guards!" Sedarus was still on the second level, but he leapt down the stairs, sending a wave of blue energy into the fleeing woman. She cackled and then grunted in pain.

All the fighters now were knocked to the floor. No one even bothered to get up anymore as Sedarus and the woman sent waves of energy into each other, red and blue flying everywhere—into books, shelves, and the walls as they tried to kill each other.

The battle lasted but mere seconds before the woman launched an exceptionally large energy blast. Redness flared throughout the library. The explosion sent even Sedarus to his back. By the time he leapt to his feet, the woman was fading fast. She waved, grinning wickedly, leaving her remaining guards to be slain quickly, without mercy, by Sedarus's force.

"Who was that?" Sedarus asked, enraged.

Balatore laughed heartily, loudly. "Tehehe! Like I would know." He closed his eyes and sung a melody, invoking wisps of blue healing power to enter his wounds.

"You *would*! Just how you knew that I am a—"

"Silence! Both of you!" Aberoth shouted. "What in the Abyss has happened?"

"You just witnessed the clash of good and evil, Aberoth," Balatore stated.

Sedarus sighed with the utmost defeat. "She stole the book."

"What did it say?" Rishkiin asked out of breath.

"It said I am a god."

Chapter Thirty-Two

More city guards rushed in, their swords drawn. They charged toward Sedarus and his friends. The monk shouted at the guards to cease their attack, but to no avail. Anger rose inside his chest.

"Halt!" the monk roared, his voice raging above the clashing sounds of battle. The guards were startled at the intensity of power that they felt coursing through the air as the monk yelled. They stopped their attack, mostly due to fear, long enough for Sedarus to convince them that they meant no harm.

Sedarus rushed from the pile of corpses inside, heading for the library's golden doors. His friends were close on his tail.

"Where are you going?" Balatore called to the monk, his lithe, agile figure keeping up with relative ease.

"To find that devil woman!" Sedarus shouted back, pushing through the crowd gathered at the Great Library's stairs.

The elf poured forth a long, deep laugh before saying, "That devil woman is your cousin!"

Sedarus looked curiously at the elf.

"How in the Abyss do you plan on finding her?" Aberoth bellowed, just behind. He and Solius were keeping pace with the monk and elf. Aunddara, Rishkiin, and Rhamor were falling behind, though they stayed within eyesight.

"I … do not know!" Sedarus admitted, although he kept on running toward the outer gates. As soon as he passed through the city gates, he stopped running, his breathing not at all labored.

"Let's think about this for a moment," Balatore said seriously.

"What is there to think about, Balatore?" Sedarus raged. "We find this woman and take back the book! It is that simple!"

"Yes, but how do you propose we do so?" Balatore asked, heaving.

Huffing and puffing, Rishkiin, Rhamor, and Aunddara finally caught up to the group.

"I don't know!" Sedarus shouted in the elf's face. "All I know is that the book is in danger!"

"Is not!" The elf chuckled knowingly. "Only a god can harm or alter that book, and it is forbidden for them to do so."

"The book said I was a god," Sedarus spat, getting in Balatore's face. "Is that true?"

"Tehehe! Yes. Well, only a half-god now … but you are getting stronger day by day. Obviously!" Balatore grinned.

"You said that woman was my cousin."

Balatore nodded.

"Therefore, she is also a god, I presume. She has the same powers as I."

"Yes. She is the daughter of Trathcot, while your father is Tinen—your true biological father."

Sedarus turned from Balatore and his friends, completely taken aback. He had to forcefully control his breathing. Everything had just happened so fast that it was difficult for him to take it all in, let alone accept it.

He turned back to face the elf and asked, "She's a god; could she not destroy the book?"

"No, she is not yet powerful enough."

"So the book is safe?" Sedarus sighed with some relief as Balatore nodded. The demigod added, "Yet it is still in her hands."

"Yes, and that is a problem. You see, after you touch that book, you have one year to complete the task given to you. Otherwise, evil will hold the upper hand in the heavens when you two Ascend," Balatore said.

"When we *what*?" the flabbergasted monk asked.

"What task?" Rhamor asked at the same time.

"You two will Ascend," Balatore raised his hands in a visual diagram, "into the heavens, and you'll take your rightful place as the Goodly God. And she will become the god of evil."

"What do you mean?" the monk asked, his voice no more than a strained whisper.

"Well, the simplest way to describe it is … Tinen is stepping down, and you are taking the throne. Tehehe!"

"What should we do then?" Sedarus asked the elf.

"Get the tome back, obviously."

"I understand that, but how?"

"How would I know?" the elf asked, annoyed.

"Tinen!" Sedarus suddenly called, seeing the deity before him.

"Where?" Aunddara asked intently.

"There." Balatore pointed, bowing slightly.

"I cannot see him!" Aberoth growled.

"They cannot see me because I am on the plane of the gods," Tinen said.

"How come Balatore can see you?" Sedarus asked, his curiosity making him momentarily forget his urgency.

Tinen looked at Balatore quite uncomfortably. Balatore shook his head with a look of deadly seriousness on his face, and Tinen said, "That is not what I came to speak about."

"Of course not," Sedarus said, bowing. "The book! It has been stolen."

"I witnessed it," Tinen growled with wrath. "There was naught I could do to stop it, as Trathcot held me at bay." Tinen spat on the ground with utmost rage.

Sedarus asked, "How do I find this woman?"

"Her name is Sithel, daughter of my *dear* brother," Tinen sneered.

"We don't have time, Father!" Sedarus quelled. "How do I find her?"

"South—you will find her in the Sands of Chaos."

"Prepare the army, General!" Sedarus ordered, looking to Aberoth.

"Yes, my liege," Aberoth said, and he immediately began calling out orders. The men around them bustled into furious work, taking down the camp.

"Which city?" Sedarus asked, facing his father.

"Tejhet, the City of Chaos."

Epilogue

Sedarus rode on his gallant steed at the head of his army. Rain bombarded the army as they marched south, to Tejhet, to retrieve the book. To the right of him was Balatore; to the left of him was Rishkiin. Behind them were Rhamor, Aunddara, Solius, and General Aberoth.

Sedarus queried Balatore, "When we first met, you said that you've been through this before. You meant this Ascension?"

"Yes," Balatore stated in all seriousness. "Like I've said, I've been the guardian to another like you, leading their Ascension phase."

"My ... father?"

"Yes, I led Tinen to the gates of heaven themselves, as I shall do with you," Balatore said.

"How old are you?" Sedarus asked with a bewildered expression on his face.

The elf laughed at Sedarus's expression. He quickly halted, remembering that it was his lord he was laughing at and that it was unwise to insult a god. "I am eons old, milord. Eons!"

"So my father was once human? Like me?"

"Tehehe! Yes, and he was much more trouble than you. It will be for the best once you replace Tinen."

That cold reality stung Sedarus. He looked at Balatore. "What will come of my ... father?"

"I do not know." Balatore met Sedarus's gaze. Sedarus knew that the elf was not lying. The elf continued, "Sithel, your dear cousin, is your counterpart to this Ascension."

"Counterpart?"

Balatore laughed gently and said sarcastically, "You catch on fast, milord." Sedarus frowned, prompting his friend to continue. "The Ascension is an ancient rite. It occurs after the gods of good and evil have had thousands of years of ruling. Being a god is exhausting; their power burns out.

"Once their tenure nears its end, they each mate with a mortal, conceiving a divine baby. Once those children mature, they replace the gods of good and evil. But before they do so, each child must complete a task."

"What is my task?" Sedarus asked.

"It is written in the book." Balatore's eyes were dark. "I could not tell you even if I wanted to, for I know not."

"What was my father's task?"

Balatore chuckled, recalling the memory. "He was supposed to steal an unholy artifact of his counterpart's father. Then he had to take it onto consecrated grounds and convert it into a holy artifact. But the worst came. Trathcot found us, and he had an army of monsters at his disposal. We had to battle our way to the holy grounds. We lost so many men in our last desperate battle." Balatore sighed sadly.

"So my father had to steal an unholy object and take it to his father? What did Trathcot need to do?"

"To stop us. And he did."

"What is the point of it all?"

"To see who is stronger," Balatore stated blankly.

"So it is just a game? A rat race?"

"No. These tests are to see who will hold the upper hand in the heavens. Your mission may not be the exact same thing as your father's, but the point is, if you beat your counterpart, you hold the upper hand in heaven."

"Who holds the upper hand now?"

"Trathcot won. He beat Tinen in this test! Isn't it obvious who rules the heavens?" Balatore asked, suddenly angry.

"Trathcot rules." It wasn't a question.

"Yes. The first few centuries after these gods' Ascension were the hardest for Tinen. He was almost swallowed into oblivion because of the evil. He's still not on even grounds with the god of murder and deceit. I'm hoping it will be different for you."

"Why do you care so much about making sure I am on the upper side of the heavenly pantheon?"

"Tehehe! Because you are one of my few friends. Very few. Okay, my only friend." Balatore laughed again.

Sedarus was surprised. "You and my father weren't friends?"

"Hardly! I was more of a servant to your father, but I feel like you accept me as a friend."

Sedarus nodded and was quiet for a very long time.

"So Sithel's task was to steal the tome from Sedarus?" Rishkiin piped in.

"Not necessarily," Balatore said. "I believe that she went rogue. She hasn't been following the holy rules that control this 'rat race,' as Sedarus puts it."

"So what was the purpose?" Aunddara asked.

"If one year passes and Sedarus does not complete his task or kill Sithel, then she wins. Evil will utterly destroy good, and this world as we know it will end."

"What do you mean 'utterly destroy good?'" Rhamor asked the elf. "Would Sithel not just hold the upper hand in the heavens?"

Balatore was shaking his head the entire time the holy knight spoke. "If Sithel succeeds, it'll be the third time in a row that evil has ruled. This world would not be able to handle it. It would be destroyed."

That hit Sedarus hard. He knew above all else he could not allow that to happen. Sedarus would retrieve his book and complete the task at hand.

Or in trying he would kill his cousin ...